TARNISHED CROWN

ROBIN D. MAHLE
ELLE MADISON

WHISKEY WILLOW

For our Beta Team...
Your strong opinions made this book what it is.
We love you.
Even if you did lose all objectivity somewhere around chapter ten.

"I can't see behind your eyes
But I'm sure that there's a storm
Give me thunder, give me rain
I can't take silence anymore"
Just Say - Nine One One

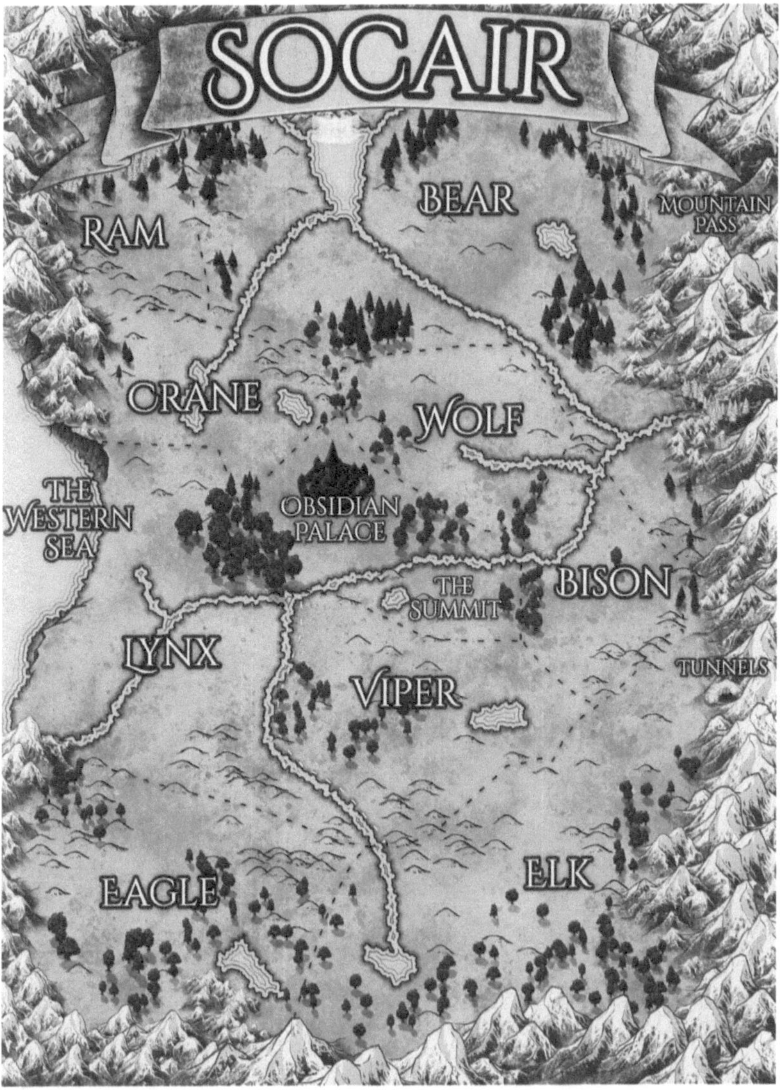

SOCAIR

BEAR

MOUNTAIN PASS

RAM

CRANE

WOLF

THE WESTERN SEA

OBSIDIAN PALACE

BISON

THE SUMMIT

LYNX

TUNNELS

VIPER

EAGLE

ELK

CHAPTER 1

My father always said my big mouth would be the death of me someday.

I had thought he was kidding, but the joke was on me because here I was, a twice-over prisoner in an enemy kingdom, headed toward what was sure to be my untimely demise.

All because I couldn't keep my mouth shut.

Though, I certainly wasn't the only one to blame.

I glared at Lord Evander's profile, the hair that was even darker than his soul falling carelessly onto his brow while the bastard had the nerve to take a catnap after casually ruining my life.

My fingers twitched toward the dagger sheathed on my thigh.

To do what? Could I kill a man while he was sleeping, even if he was a monster?

I didn't know.

And if I could, what would I do then, surrounded by his guard, and beyond that, by a kingdom who would just as soon see me hanged as help me, based solely on the color of my hair?

I couldn't go back to Theo and risk him getting caught up in a war on my behalf. I couldn't get home until the mountain pass opened. I was well and truly stuck here.

Still, I would feel better with my dagger in my hand.

Keeping my gaze fixed on Evander's face, I slid the seafoam colored skirts of my borrowed dress up, inch by inch, careful not to jingle the charm on my bracelet. We hit a bump in the road and I froze, but his eyelids didn't so much as flutter.

When I reached the sheath, I slowly worked my way up to the hilt, wrapping my fingers around the bare-chested siren and tightening my grip as I removed the blade from its casing.

I only took my eyes off of my captor for a fraction of a second to make sure I didn't cut myself, but it was still too long. A hand clamped around my wrist, stopping my arm in its tracks.

"I wouldn't." Evander's lightly accented voice rang out in the enclosed space.

I went still, fear creeping along my spine and stealing my breaths. Had he sensed the movement, or had I made more noise than I meant to? Slowly, deliberately, I met his eyes.

"I would hate to have to put you on a leash, Lemmikki," he purred.

The light shifted in the carriage, the shadows on his face making him appear even more sinister than his voice sounded. Storms churned in his pale gray eyes, a quiet lethality brimming just under the surface, and I scoffed.

"Somehow I doubt that." Especially considering he was still calling me his *pet*.

He leaned forward, one hand still holding my wrist, while the other removed the dagger from my grasp. Fire rose up inside of me, but I loosened my grip and allowed him to take it, shrinking away as soon as he sat back.

He chuckled, a cold, empty sound. "You may as well get some rest, Princess. We won't stop until nightfall."

He didn't break eye contact even long enough to look at the dagger, tucking it inside his partially buttoned coat before leaning his head back against the carriage wall.

Blood pounded in my veins. I still couldn't believe this was happening. That everything, starting with a single ill-fated trek down the tunnels, had led me here, with my life in the hands of the heir to the most savage clan in all of Socair.

CHAPTER 2

The carriage jolted over the bumpy roads, and the jostling craggy landscape only added to my queasy stomach. Though most of that was nerves. Or fury. Or both.

I managed to hold my tongue for a solid ten more minutes before I couldn't stand it anymore. "For someone who claims they didn't want another war with my kingdom, you're doing a damned good job of starting one."

His features twisted with derision. "Don't sell yourself short, Princess. You did that all by yourself."

Arrogant. Arseling.

"Only one of us made the conscious decision to incite a war," I reminded him.

He sat up a little straighter. "While the other was just too asinine to avoid it. Do you think that's better?"

My cheeks flushed with something between shame and fury. "I think anything is better than the sick games you play."

"Which games would those be?" He raised his eyebrows in polite curiosity, and I shook my head bitterly.

"You knew all along about the blood debt, and you were perfectly happy to sit back while the Summit decided to kill me. So what was it? Did you just want to wait until I had the tiniest sliver of hope before you swooped in and crushed it?"

"Contrary to what you've obviously been brought up to believe, not everything is about you." His conversational tone was worse than outright snark would have been. "Storms, is everyone from Lochlann this impossibly self-centered?"

My jaw dropped. "I think it's fair to say that my being ripped away from my fiancé and taken as someone's *pet* very much *is* about me."

"At least you've come to terms with it. Forever is a long time for you to be in denial."

"The hell I have," I spat back. "And we both know forever isn't on the table when my father finds out you took me."

It gave me no pleasure to say that, not when the people I loved would be on the front lines. Not when I suspected Evander would just as soon kill me as hand me back over, if only to spite the people he so clearly disdained.

Instead of looking affected by my bleak prediction, though, he only sighed and leaned his head back against the carriage like he was bored.

"Ah, relying on Papa to bail you out of trouble? You could at least *try* to be original, Princess, or do you enjoy being a walking cliché of a middle royal child?"

His words hit uncomfortably close to home, and I was scrambling for a response when the carriage came to a sudden halt in the middle of nothing but sparse, dead trees and steep hills.

My heartbeat stuttered in my chest.

Why were we taking a break already? Hadn't he just said we weren't stopping until tonight?

Fear tore its way through my shield of anger, long enough for me to realize that it was one thing to bait Lord Evander when we were at the Summit with strict no-bloodshed laws and Theo never more than twenty feet away.

It was another to do it here, now that he *owned* me, surrounded by his men who would never step in on my behalf.

Mila's words came back to me, freezing me in place.

"Since the war, they're...barbarians. No one is safe in their territory, with random raids to slaughter the villagers they deem 'disobedient,' and they attack the other clans at will. They've only managed the alliances they have because everyone is terrified of them.

"And Evander...Don't let that pretty face fool you. He's the worst one." She trailed off, her face losing a shade of color.

For the first time, it truly occurred to me that I was

completely at his mercy. What if I was wrong about what he wanted from me?

Steely resolve flooded my veins. However Lord Evander wanted me to be his *pet*, I sure as hell didn't intend to make it easy on him.

CHAPTER 3

There was a light rap on the carriage door.

Evander calmly buttoned up the top of his coat, adjusting the collar of his pristine black military outfit. Then he rapped back, and the door abruptly opened to reveal a similarly black and white clad guard nodding in Evander's direction.

The lord narrowed his eyes before exiting the carriage and shutting the door behind him.

I peered through the windows, surveying the surroundings. There was no stream to water the horses, nothing else of any note. If this was a break to relieve ourselves, why call Evander out first?

Surely there was no other reason to stop here. At least, not one that boded well for me. Evander returned only a handful of seconds later, abruptly cutting off my macabre line of thought.

When he wrenched the door open, I resisted the urge to press myself farther back into the carriage.

To give them a reaction is to give them power. I repeated Fia's words in my head like a mantra, sure it wouldn't be the only time I needed to rely on them.

The arseling lord blinked impatiently, pulling a bundle of fabric from under the carriage seat and tossing it my way.

"Put this on," he ordered. "We're switching to horses now."

"Why?" I shook the garment out to see it was a large, black cloak, trimmed in fur, just like the ones the men were wearing.

"Because I was desperate to hear you complain about something." His tone was laced with exasperation.

A guard appeared at the opening of the carriage, holding out an arm for me to step down. He shot an exasperated look at Evander, then turned back to me with a calming expression.

"Just for safety, Your Highness. The carriage is slower and a bit too obvious." His accent was thick and guttural. "So we will ride ahead with a group of ten or so, and the rest will stay behind with our things."

Interesting that they cared about my safety when I was no more than a prisoner, but then, Evander had made many comments about using me for leverage at the Summit. I was of little use to him dead.

"We weren't worried about that before?" I asked.

The guard exchanged another look with Evander before answering.

"We've spotted some suspicious activity," he said shortly.

I debated asking more questions, but his firmly closed lips told me that was all he would say on the matter.

"Thank you..." I trailed off, waiting for him to fill in his name. It was hardly his fault he worked for an arseling.

"Kirill, Highness." He had a kind face, deep blue eyes crinkled in earnestness and full lips that smiled easily, reminding me of Mila.

"Thank you, Kirill." I nodded, taking his proffered arm.

Behind the carriage, some of the men were already moving things around from the pack horses to the luggage hold in the back. One of them was rifling through my trunk, pulling out things at random and stuffing them into a saddlebag.

I narrowed my eyes when he got to the lacy undergarments Mila had gifted me. His throat bobbed as he swallowed, pinching the thin chemise between his thumb and forefinger. The guard next to him laughed, startling him into dropping it on the ground.

The clumsy offender looked in horror between my flinty expression and the underthings currently strewn on the road for the entire halted company of guards to see. Finally, he moved forward to pick it up, but I'd had enough.

Gathering all the dignity I could muster, which was, to be

frank, not very much, I marched the few feet to where the soldier was standing, bending to scoop the chemise up.

Chuckles rang out around me.

"Clearly, this is the closest any of you have been to what's under a woman's dress, but do try to control yourselves," I huffed out, stuffing the garment into the new pack.

There was a stunned, tense silence, and I turned to find Evander standing with his arms crossed, a muscle ticking in his jaw.

I had less than a second to wonder if I would ever stop getting myself into trouble before Kirill's laughter rang out, booming across the empty space.

"She's got you there, Igor."

A few of the men seemed to take that as their permission to laugh as well, though the others were still glaring at me. I released the breath I had been holding as the moment passed without incident.

Even if Evander did look like he wanted to murder me.

One of the men brought over a light brown horse, one of the smaller ones of the group—which wasn't saying much, considering they were all massive—and the lord gestured for me to mount up.

I glanced between the horse and the horse's arse...erm...Evander, before shaking my head. "I'm not riding with you."

"Relax, Princess." He sighed. "No one here has any desire to share a mount with your cursed hair."

The tension in my shoulders eased a little. "You aren't worried about me running away?"

"Surrounded by ten trained men in an unfamiliar terrain with no food, water, or supplies?" His expression turned contemplative. "On second thought, it does sound like something you would do. Kirill, tether our horses."

Well, that's what I got for opening my big mouth. Again.

Kirill let out a low chuckle, but brought an impressive looking black warhorse over to bind to the pale brown one. Evander gestured again for me to get on the horse.

He didn't offer a hand to help me up, which was unfortunate because it deprived me of the pleasure of ignoring it.

I moved toward the horse, but my leg was less than halfway to the stirrup when I ran out of room to maneuver in my narrow skirts. I nearly pitched forward, catching myself on the side of the saddle.

A flush crept up my neck and into my cheeks, one of the many perks of my ginger complexion.

"Blasted Socairan skirts," I muttered under my breath.

This was, at least, one of Mila's dresses, but it was still far more restricting than the wide, flowy skirts favored in Lochlann. No wonder the whole kingdom thought women were incompetent, when they dressed us so we could hardly function.

And here I was, proving the bastards right.

To the stars with that. I hiked the dress up scandalously high, nearly halfway to my knees, to try again, but still couldn't make it.

That time, there were a few titters around me, equal parts uncomfortable and amused.

Just as I was preparing to yank the entire thing up to my waist, if only to mount this stars-blasted horse on my own, there was an exasperated sigh behind me.

Before I could react, two hands came on either side of my waist, turning me and lifting me bodily up onto the saddle.

"The goal was actually to get there *faster*, Lemmikki." Evander stood next to me, his smug face level with my elbow and close enough that I contemplated the damage I might be able to do with a well placed jab.

Instead, I took a moment to adjust my skirts in my stupid side saddle position so I didn't actually attack him. "You know, it really is hardly fair that I have such a charming nickname and you don't. Tell me, what *is* the Socairan word for 'arseling?'"

Evander only blinked irritably before mounting his horse, but Kirill helpfully chimed in. "I don't believe there's a direct translation, Highness, but I think *aalio* would suit your purposes nicely."

The *aalio* in question shot him an exasperated look, and I bit back a smile.

"Excellent. Well then, Lord *Aalio*. Off we go."

CHAPTER 4

W e rode for what felt like hours, though the sun had hardly moved at all above us. I was grateful for the little warmth it offered, especially since the air grew colder the farther north we rode.

Whatever residual fae blood I had gave me an awareness of the weather that had been fairly useless until I came to Socair. It was pretty worthless here, too, for that matter, since all it did was tell me I was going to spend the evening freezing my arse off.

Sure enough, only hours later, I was shivering. Gusts of wind whipped through my cloak, chilling me to the bone.

It wasn't just the weather, though. The men were wary, on alert, and their tension permeated the air until I felt like I was breathing it into my lungs.

Kirill let out a low whistle.

One by one, the soldiers shifted ever so slightly in their saddles. Kirill continued casually talking to the man next to him, but his eyes darted back and forth over the hillsides. Several others did the same, yawning and stretching or talking as if they had no cares left in the world.

All the while their eyes roamed our surroundings.

Stars-blasted hells.

I had traveled with soldiers often enough to know when something was wrong. I risked a glance over my shoulder before Evander hissed a warning at me, not taking his eyes off the road.

My heart galloped wildly in my chest, and I took a steady breath through my nose. For all that Kirill had said we weren't an appealing target to the Unclanned this way, we were apparently appealing enough. To someone, at least.

"Have you ever used a saber?" Evander asked in a low tone.

Furrowing my brow, I nodded. *Once.*

He visibly warred with himself before pulling one of the blades criss-crossed at his back and pressing the hilt into my hand.

"Der'mo," he muttered. "Do try to refrain from stabbing me with it, at least until we take care of this."

My lips parted in surprise, but I closed my fingers around the hilt. He held on only a second longer before reluctantly surrendering the weapon to my care, already going for his other blade.

A thrum of energy coursed through me. Whether it was fear of the battle or shock that he was arming me, I wasn't sure.

Regardless, it wasn't a moment too soon.

Because that's when I heard the battle cry ring out.

CHAPTER 5

Every man was now holding a weapon or two and forming a circle with their horses, protecting Evander and me in the center.

It was just in time for an onslaught of men to emerge from the hillside, each of them with the telltale *B* branded on their foreheads. Soon, the sound of clashing steel echoed between the hills along with the cries of our assailants.

Evander's gray eyes were lit up with ire as he untethered our horses before turning to fight with his men.

I wondered again about the rumors.

The man before me now was nothing like the casual, condescending arseling from the Summit or even the carriage. There was an unrestrained quality to him, ruthlessness coupled with cold, brutal efficiency as he tore his way across the battlefield.

He was a blur of furious motion and precise strikes. Each of his blows landed with deadly force, cutting his opponents down, one right after the next.

Kirill was to his right, and it was clear that the two had trained together, likely along with their warhorses. His strikes were just as powerful and his aim just as deadly.

Watching the ten men take on the Unclanned erased any doubt as to why everyone was so afraid of them. If they had a large army and all the men fought like this...there would be no standing against them.

My breaths came quickly as I spun my horse around to get a clearer view of the battle.

Everywhere I looked, the Unclanned seemed to be less interested in fighting the soldiers than getting past them.

Some of them barely paid attention to the guards blocking their paths or the swords that met their axes and pitchforks. Instead, they focused solely on the center of the ring.

On me.

Movement from the corner of my eye had me spinning around. Two of the Unclanned crept between Igor's mount and that of another Bear soldier, while more Unclanned attacked from the sides.

These men had to be desperate to risk an assault on foot against both trained men and trained warhorses.

But desperate for what? Vengeance? Against my people, my family?

Fear raked its way down my spine with jagged claws.

The Unclanned men were closing in on me, and I was never going to be able to defend myself riding side saddle like this.

I scrambled to slice through a seam midway through my dress, careful not to cut myself or the horse with the blade of the saber. Once I had a decent sized split, I tugged at the seam with my free hand until it ripped all the way to my thigh.

If the Socairans were so stars-damned concerned about propriety, they should have had dresses I could move in to begin with. Although, even the Lochlannian soldiers would be scandalized by this.

Nothing for it now.

Shoving my cloak behind my shoulders for easier movement, I flipped my mostly bare leg over to the other side of the horse. It was just in time for the two men to sprint toward me, weapons bared.

Their eyes widened when they took in the sight of me, either my scandalously exposed skin or the horrifying shade of my hair.

Either way, their shock worked in my favor. I took advantage of their stumbling footsteps, lurching my horse forward to meet them head-on. Belatedly, the man on the left threw his pitchfork like a spear.

Ducking against my horse's neck, I veered us to the right to avoid the impact, but it wasn't fast enough.

The pitchfork was halfway to my face when a blur of black

motion shot in front of me, splitting the handle in half. Evander and his destrier flew through the air, trampling the man who threw it.

I cringed at the aftermath, meeting Evander's stormy gaze instead of focusing on the corpse beneath him.

He held my stare for mere seconds before looking past me, fury twisting his features. I spun around in time to see the other Unclanned man hurtling toward me, sword drawn and ready to strike.

Forcing my horse to pivot, I met the man's blow with my saber in one swift movement, using his momentum against him. He stumbled backward as I spun my horse around and charged at him again. The *Besklanovvy* had barely gotten to his feet before I raised my blade high in the air and brought it cleanly down across his collarbone with a sickening crunch.

Warm blood splattered a macabre pattern onto my pale green gown, soaking through until I could feel the wetness against my skin.

He sputtered before falling to his knees and dropping his sword. I braced myself for the next assailant, but there was no one behind him, only a bare stretch of land leading far away from this place.

Away from Evander and his men.

Evander was fighting one of the few remaining men, and the other soldiers were distracted, either fighting or assessing one another for injuries.

The desire to run back to Theo consumed me.

But all too quickly, reality dawned on me.

Mila had said she would come to me, to stay safe until she could, and Theo had promised to fight for me... If I escaped now, they would never even know where to find me or what had happened to me.

Besides all of that, there was nowhere for me to go.

In the unlikely event I found a kindly soul who didn't hate me for my hair or my kingdom, who was willing to hide me...I didn't want to think about what Evander might do to that person.

I swallowed hard, my eyes still locked onto the distance as I convinced myself that leaving would just be another in my long list of bad decisions.

Maybe this wouldn't be as terrible as I thought. Maybe I could even find an ally in the Clan Wife. Theo had said she was from Lochlann, at least.

Evander pulled me from my thoughts when he rode his horse up beside mine, facing me. He used his tunic to wipe the blood from his blade before sheathing it. Then, both hands shot out to gently trail up and down either side of my torso.

"Where are you injured?" His deep voice was strained with exertion.

I was too startled to do anything but stare at him.

"Lemmikki, where is it?" This time, he sounded impatient to the point of urgency.

His fingers were probing down to my hips, my thighs, and it was enough to shake me from my stupor.

"I'm not. It's not mine," I answered quickly.

It just belonged to the man I killed. *Again.*

Is that all this place is? Storms and death?

Evander pulled his arms back to his sides, and his shoulders seemed to relax incrementally. He nodded his head in one rapid motion before grabbing the leather strap on my saddle and connecting it to his once more.

He held out a hand, gesturing toward the sword, but his eyes didn't leave mine.

Instead of loosening, my fingers gripped the hilt tighter. "What if they come back?"

He let out a long-suffering sigh. "Then I'll give you the sword back, but I can't very well have you eviscerating me in the meantime."

Having seen the way Evander moved on the battlefield, having witnessed the calm lethality in his gaze, I knew I didn't pose an actual threat to him. But I also knew that if he wanted this sword, there was nothing to prevent him from taking it.

So, I handed it back, still dripping with the blood of the man I had just slain.

His eyes narrowed slightly, but he didn't say anything. Instead, he cleaned the blade before sheathing it at his back, directing our horses to the rest of the men.

All around us was death. While all ten soldiers on our side were still standing and relatively uninjured, there had to be nearly thirty of the Unclanned on the ground.

The battle had ended quickly, in spite of that, and I wasn't even sure that any of the assailants got away.

Part of me was grateful for the skill of the Bear soldiers because it was the only reason I was still alive. The larger part of me was terrified at knowing these men were my new captors.

More than that, if my family waged a war to bring me home, these were the men my people would be up against. Lochlann might win over time by sheer numbers, but how many casualties would we sustain in the meantime?

And with my father and uncles and cousins on the front line, what were the chances they would all make it through alive?

CHAPTER 6

We rode hard to get to Wolf Estate. Sir Nils, sadly, had not yet returned from the Summit.

Fortunately, there was a man who appeared to be his son available to cast bitter, judgmental looks in my direction.

It never got old, the way the Socairans blamed me for their war with my people two decades ago—a war *they* had been the aggressors in. I sighed.

Just a pointless, endless cycle of hatred and blame and death.

"Kirill, please escort my Lemmikki to the room adjacent to mine. She can't bear to be very far from me." The arseling's voice cut through my haze of exhaustion.

I bristled. Did that mean he was planning to help himself to my rooms? Surely, he would have just put me in the same one, if that was the case. I comforted myself with that thought and the likelihood that there was something I could use as a weapon in that room.

Kirill led me to my room, letting me know a maid would be up soon before he excused himself with a kind nod.

A plush bed waited in the corner, beckoning me like a beacon in the night. All I wanted to do was fall into the covers and sleep for the next six months. But first, I had to find a weapon.

And change my disgusting clothes, which, of course, I couldn't do without assistance.

Rifling through the room took very little time, though all I managed to come up with was a lantern I could smash over someone's head and a comb with a pointy end that might be perfect for stabbing a certain arseling lord's eyeball.

I placed both on the table closest to the bed, then paced the room until the maid came.

I wished Davin were here. The silence never stretched on too long when my favorite cousin was around. He would have made a joke about the accommodations, about the predicament we had landed ourselves in.

Or we would have found the nearest decanter and drank until we didn't care about what the people thought of us.

Landing myself in the Socairan dungeon had been one thing when my best friend was in the next cell, but being here, alone, with no way out, leaving Davin to tell my father I wasn't coming home, just as he had been so worried he would have to do...

Would Iiro uphold his end of the bargain to keep Davin safe now that I was no longer in the equation?

There was no use dwelling on that. Theo promised he would take care of my cousin, and I believed him. Especially now that we were...whatever we were.

I didn't want to think about that either, about the way Mila's father had announced that our engagement was severed, or about the anguish on Theo's face when Evander took me from him.

By the time a knock on the door sounded, I didn't even care about the horrified expression on the maid's face. I was grateful for anything that distracted me from the mess I had landed myself in once again.

CHAPTER 7

I f I hadn't hated Evander before, I certainly had no problem dredging up the emotion this morning.

He looked fresh as a stars-damned spring daisy, cleanly shaven and alert, showing no sign at all that we had ridden hard yesterday and slept a scarce few hours.

Meanwhile, I hobbled out to the stables with dark purple circles under my eyes and my wild curls even more unruly than usual. My back and thighs screamed in protest when Evander lifted me into the uncomfortable side saddle position, but short of cutting my skirts again, I had no other option.

Even I had more propriety than that. Besides, I needed the extra warmth of intact skirts. The light tingling in my spine told me it was going to be another blustery, frigid day.

As soon as we took off, he set a miserable, grueling pace. My stomach sank as we rode mile after mile away from the Summit.

Away from Theo.

The day only got more fun when the telltale pins and needles in my spine proved, once again, that my fictitious weather toe was never wrong. The only benefit to the mild snowstorm we rode through was that it forced Evander to slow down for a while.

Then it was back to our previous breakneck speed until the sun hung low in the horizon, outlining a sizable village.

The buildings were in slightly better shape than the ones in

Elk and Viper had been, but the impoverished state of the people remained the same.

It was the villagers themselves that gave me pause. Since coming to Socair, I had seen people in Elk, Wolf, and Viper, and one thing had remained consistent. The lack of little ones. Theo had explained that a plague had swept through when he was a child, leaving many without the ability to have children.

But in Bear...

Children were everywhere. They were more subdued than the children back home, but running and playing all the same. The sound of their laughter was both a balm to my soul and a sharp, stinging pain, as I missed my younger sisters more than ever.

"How are there so many children here?" I asked Evander.

A few of the soldiers shot startled glances over their shoulders, but of course, didn't deign to respond.

"I thought the plague had..." I trailed off, belatedly realizing that it was probably a sensitive subject for some of them, one that Theo had not broached lightly.

Evander let out a long sigh before speaking, his features hard.

"Yes. The plague destroyed much of Socair and limited its future. But Bear was mostly spared that when my father closed the borders."

Closed the borders? I thought about that for a moment. It made sense, to keep the sick out in order to keep the healthy safe.

"I didn't see any walls along the border," I began, musing. "How did—"

"By killing anyone who tried to enter," Evander cut me off with a clipped tone.

My stomach lurched. *What?*

A small voice in my head told me to stop asking questions that I wasn't prepared to hear the answers to, but of course, I didn't listen to it.

"So, anyone who wanted to visit family or friends, they were...killed?"

Evander nodded his head, still not meeting my gaze. "And any who showed symptoms."

This time, my mouth fell open. It was unfathomable. Between this and the battlefield, Bear's reputation for savagery certainly made sense. The sound of a child's laugh rang out once more, and this time, it was hard to find any joy in it.

They had saved an entire generation, but at what cost? Could the end ever possibly justify those means?

CHAPTER 8

We were stabling our horses at the inn when another contingent of soldiers appeared, dressed identically to the ones with us. Their white bear emblems stood out in sharp contrast on their sleek black sleeves, evidence that they had not been traveling as long as our party had.

"Taras!" Kirill greeted the man in front, a man who looked startlingly similar to Evander.

He was roughly the same height and build, if a little leaner. He had the same midnight hair and swarthy skin, but where Evander's eyes were gray, his were bright blue. A small, relieved smile graced his full mouth when he looked at Evander, though his expression hardened when his eyes met mine.

He was easily one of the most handsome men I had ever seen. It was too bad he was apparently an arseling like his...brother? Cousin?

Taras' eyes narrowed and he directed his attention to Evander. "I see we need to talk."

Evander nodded with a resigned expression, and they walked a short distance away for privacy. I, of course, had no intention of granting that, so I strained my ears for any snippets of their conversation.

Evander spoke so low I couldn't make out a single word, but I caught a few lines from Taras.

"Have you thought about how *she* will react?"

Interesting.

Who was *she*, and why were they concerned about any woman's reaction? Perhaps Evander was in a betrothal of his own, which could be good news for me. Surely no woman would want her future husband to bring home a...*pet*.

Evander's response was lost, but Taras shook his head irritably. "Honestly, Van, what exactly was your plan?"

I started to tiptoe closer because that was something I very much wanted to know as well, but Kirill stepped next to me, giving me a knowing look. I shrugged because, really, what had they expected?

He shook his head, though his features remained congenial. "Glad to see you aren't too shaken by the Unclanned attack."

"There are rebels in Lochlann still, so it isn't the first time I've been attacked on the road."

He widened his eyes, but didn't immediately respond.

I belatedly registered that he said *Unclanned* in the Common Tongue, and not *Besklanovvy*, the Socairan word. "Why do you all speak the Common Tongue?"

Kirill smiled like he was happy I asked. Or maybe he was just a nice person, in general, which seemed odd given that he seemed to enjoy Evander's company.

"Clan Bear is vast, encompassing both the plains and the mountains. The Common Tongue does not vary as much as the Socairan dialects, and it's important to not have misunderstandings when you are giving soldiers orders."

That made sense.

"So the villagers?"

"Those who are not soldiers usually speak their local language," he confirmed.

I nodded my understanding. Then, because I had really nothing to lose at this point, I said, "Why are you being nice to me when I'm your prisoner and your enemy?"

The corner of his mouth tugged upward again. "You may be a prisoner for now, Princess, but I see no reason you have to be the enemy."

The words were oddly comforting. I opened my mouth to respond when the pompous sound of Evander's voice stopped me.

"We'll take the eastern route tomorrow to avoid the Unclanned. Apparently, there are more of these larger bands gathering farther north." His tone was as bored as ever, but there was a tense set to his shoulders. "Be on alert."

"And here I thought Taras just missed us," Kirill commented.

"Like I would cross all of Bear just to see your ugly face," Taras fired back.

Now the dour man was just lying. Kirill had strong features, an aquiline nose and a cleft chin, but he was by no means unattractive, especially with the smooth olive skin most of the Socairans had.

More like a giant mass of raw masculinity. Whatever their faults, the Socairans did not lack for beautiful people. That had been my first thought on seeing Theo, even back when he was just the uptight man who was imprisoning me.

Even before he became so much more than that.

Conversation floated toward me, the men muttering about the odd attack yesterday.

"Are those large bands unusual?" I interjected, grateful for the distraction. "A group like that attacked us on the way to the Summit."

My voice rang out louder in the stables than I was expecting, and several of the soldiers gasped or glared in my direction. Here I had almost let myself forget the delightful Socairan mindset that women were only to be admired from a distance. Silently.

Taras' eyes widened and flitted from me to Evander.

"Iiro said there were easily forty men," Evander explained.

Taras' face paled. "Iiro? She was with Elk before you..." His words trailed off as he ran a hand through his hair in exasperation. *"Der'mo."*

At least someone recognized what a nightmare this entire situation would be.

"Der'mo, indeed," I echoed, trying to roll the R like they did.

Kirill and the boy named Igor barked out a laugh while the others stared.

"Ah, I see you have taken to learning Socairan for the truly important things, just not for when your life was on the line," Evander said, pinching the bridge of his nose.

"Well, I have to keep my cliché middle-royal-child priorities in line, after all."

If I hadn't known any better, I might have thought he was

biting back a smile. But that was impossible. To possess a sense of humor, he would have had to possess an actual soul.

I ignored the niggling part of my brain that reminded me that he hadn't actually hurt me, that he had armed me when I was in danger. It didn't matter because I wouldn't have been in danger to begin with if it weren't for him.

He *stole* me, my life, my future, my relationship, and I refused to give him the benefit of the doubt after that.

Evander ushered us from the stables to the inn next door, and I could swear that the collective hearts within the building stopped beating as soon as he lowered his hood.

All conversation ceased, leaving no sound but the crackling fire in the hearth, beckoning me like a warm and toasty beacon.

But sadly, none of us moved. It was as if everyone in the main room was afraid to speak in his presence. *Or just too captivated...* Several of the women gawked at Evander and his perfectly symmetrical features.

The rest of the patrons stared at him with pure, unadulterated fear. Between the rumors and what I had witnessed of his skills in battle, I could understand why.

"We only have five rooms left for the night, Sir," an elderly man said as he entered the room. His accent reminded me of Kirill's.

"Perfect. We will take them all," Evander said, turning to face his men. "You can draw straws for who sleeps in the rooms and who sleeps with the horses."

The elderly man dipped his head in respect, handing over several keys.

"Rest up men, and even if you're in the stables, know that I most certainly have already drawn the shortest straw," Evander handed one key to Kirill, tilting his head significantly in my direction.

Kirill nodded, and we followed a member of the staff up a set of rickety stairs and into a room with the number four carved unevenly into the door.

I had roughly two seconds to feel relief at finally being away from Evander and able to sink into a bed when my brain and eyes caught up to one another.

There were two beds.

Everyone was sharing rooms and Evander said he had drawn the shortest straw.

Son of an aalio.

CHAPTER 9

I paced the small room, trying to calm my temper. It only seemed to make it worse.

My nightgown wasn't helping. The frilly, high-necked monstrosity practically choked me with every step. Though if it had been Mila's thinner, more comfortable gown, that would have presented a different sort of problem.

At least a servant had come to help me change and deliver food, so I didn't have to rely on Evander for that. Still, that did nothing to quell my aggravation. Everything I did and ate was completely in his control.

My heartbeat was thundering erratically in my chest by the time he strode into the room, cradling a bowl of soup in one hand and using the other to close the door. It looked so *normal* for someone who was such a complete and utter bastard, that it momentarily rendered me speechless.

He gave me—and my outfit—a disdainful once over, and I resisted the urge to flush.

"And here I thought touching me was the furthest thing from your mind." I echoed the words he had used while we were dancing at the Summit.

His fingers went to massage the bridge of his nose, and he took a deep breath. "I'm not here for...that. Storms, even I'm not that much of a monster."

I stiffened at the disgust in his tone, narrowing my eyes at him. "Says the man who stole me and called me his *pet*."

49

"Rightfully claimed, you mean," Evander countered. "And you and I have *wildly* different ideas of the word pet."

"Then why are you sharing my room?" I demanded.

"Technically, you're sharing my room, but I wasn't going to accuse you of ill intentions." The corner of his mouth tilted up.

I scowled at him, and he sighed.

"There are two beds here, for storms' sake," he said, sitting on the corner of the one closest to the door. "Everyone is sharing, and it isn't like anyone else was volunteering to room with the Lochlannian."

Relieved about that in spite of myself, I cast about for another reason he couldn't stay. "So it wasn't enough for you ruining my life and future, now you're going to destroy my...reputation?"

I had always been a mediocre liar at best, but I was hoping he didn't realize how long ago that ship had sailed with my antics in Lochlann.

That hope was dashed quickly when he raised a single, condescending eyebrow.

"From what I hear, you did that pretty well on your own, Lemmikki."

I made a valiant attempt at a disbelieving expression, and he leveled a look at me, holding up a finger.

"The guard you were found in the tunnel with—"

"That was different. Davin is—" I stopped before I could say *my cousin*, but what I replaced it with was infinitely worse. "A eunuch. All of the Lochlann...royal...princess guards are, for...obvious reasons."

He made a thoughtful face that I was fairly certain was mocking, holding up a second finger. "I believe there was also the business with the 'stableboy?'"

I internally cursed the man who had turned out to be a spy for Socair.

"Well...that was...also different. Because we had a deep connection..." From his face to mine. "In our souls."

Was I the only one who realized how ridiculous I sounded? No. He definitely heard it, too.

"Ah. Indeed. But then, of course, there was Lord Theodore in the smuggler's hole. Honestly, I couldn't be less concerned with your prior escapades, Lemmikki, but as you raised the issue of your reputation, I feel compelled to ask, was that also different?"

Mila was right. They really did do nothing but gossip at that stars-forsaken Summit.

"Obviously," I said with more confidence than I felt. "Theo and I were...practically married."

Evander choked back what I was certain was a laugh. "Of course. So *practically married* that you waited until death was the only other option to agree to it."

Though I had been mostly lying, the full force of that statement hit me, how drastically my life had changed in two weeks and then changed again. I should have been safe in Theo's arms right now, headed back to his clan as his wife and ready to start our life together.

Instead, I was here, sharing a room with Lord Arseling and his never-ending condescension.

I gave him a smile that was more a baring of my teeth. "I'm sure your sparkling personality makes you an expert in interpersonal relationships, but you really don't know the first thing about mine."

He snorted. "But your ninety-second engagement gives you a wealth of insight? You know, I think I'll forgo taking criticism from someone who has managed to become a captive two times over in as many weeks."

I saw red. I had never been prone to anger, but Lord Evander had me clenching my fist just to avoid punching his smug face.

"You know, I think *I'll* forgo defending myself to a man who *took me as his slave*," I spat. "I may not have the moral high ground in many situations, but I'm fairly certain I have it here."

"Oh, no doubt, Princess," he agreed amicably. "But the rooming situation stays. Worry not, you can comfort yourself with the knowledge that this is also *different*, because you're my pet and I'm your owner."

Gritting my teeth to keep from responding, I climbed into the bed closest to the fire without another word.

Evander was almost eerily quiet on his side of the room. He didn't slurp his soup, didn't fidget, didn't even breathe loudly. Even in the silence, though, it was impossible to forget he was there. Tension thrummed in the air whenever he was around.

I didn't think he was lying about his intentions or his reasons for sharing a room, but I would have been an idiot to let my guard down entirely. So I forced myself to stay awake, my mind drifting to everything that was just said.

I would have been married right now if Evander hadn't stepped in. I thought back to all the nights Theo and I had shared a room on the way here, how we had forced ourselves to stop at just kissing. How we had drawn the line at sharing a bed.

How we wouldn't have had to do those things anymore.

Suddenly, I missed him so much it physically hurt. All I wanted was to lay my head on his chest, to feel his heart beating under the palm of my hand and let the rest of the world fade into the background.

To be anywhere in the world but here with a man who had taken me for reasons I still didn't understand.

CHAPTER 10

We had already stopped for our second break the next day when it dawned on me.

This would have been the eighth and final day of the Summit, the day my fate would have been decided, had things gone differently.

The day I turned eighteen.

If I were home now, my mother would have awoken me with the same long story about my birth that she repeated every year. My father would have told me all the things I had done that made him proud, though that list was likely to be short these days.

It was a momentous day in my family, the day we officially became responsible for our people, our holdings, our succession, everything.

But now, did they think I was dead? Missing? Was my family holding a vigil at an empty grave instead? Was my older sister drowning in even more grief? Were the twins still playing pranks and filling the house with much needed laughter, or had the weight of one tragedy after another stolen that from them?

Longing for my family washed over me in a palpable wave, settling onto my skin like a thousand needles prickling at the back of my...

Stars.

That wasn't longing. It was a warning.

Another storm was coming, this one significantly bigger than the little snowstorm that had made us so miserable the day before. We would need shelter well before we stopped for the night.

When I glanced up at the clear blue sky, a curse escaped my lips, and a sickening feeling of déjà vu overtook me.

Damn Socair and its stars-blasted ridiculous weather.

Was it worth the risk of revealing I knew the storm was coming? Was it worth the risk if I didn't? Kirill offered me his canteen, as he always did at breaks, and it steeled my resolve.

Even if I was willing to risk my own life, which I had done more than enough of lately, there were three dozen men here and only one I would have no real qualms about leaving to face the elements.

In Lochlann, the weather moved in more predictable patterns, storm clouds visible miles away. On the rare occasion I had sensed something the average soldier couldn't, a member of my family was around to make an excuse to stop.

Only Socair had put me in the position of claiming to have a stars-damned weather toe.

Where is Davin when I need him to pretend we're stopping early because his favorite brothel is nearby?

I took a deep, fortifying breath, bracing myself to be ridiculed.

"What time are we stopping for the day?" For a rare change, I addressed the question to Evander instead of Kirill.

He raised his eyebrows. "Overexerted yourself already, Lemmikki?"

I shook my head irritably, turning to Kirill to ask instead when Evander's voice sounded again. "We ride to Ryaya today, so not long after sundown if we make good time."

"We need to stop sooner than that," I blurted out.

Nicely done, Rowan. That was both convincing and very un-suspicious.

An uneasy silence fell among the men as they looked to Evander to see how he would take that assertion.

His gray eyes narrowed in suspicion. "Do we?"

I sighed, looking out at the sky and then back at him with resignation. "A storm is coming soon. A dangerous one."

"And you know this because..." He gestured for me to expound.

"Because I have a—" *Do not say weather toe. Do not say weather toe.* "An interest in weather. I've studied it extensively."

"I see. And how soon is soon?" It was impossible to tell if he was mocking me, but I answered anyway.

I studied the horizon ostensibly. "Two hours, at the most."

Evander's expression didn't flicker, and I knew I was going to have to do better than that. When he opened his mouth to speak, I prepared myself for his inevitable condescension.

But he didn't address me at all.

Instead, he spoke in a voice loud enough to carry, his amused gaze never leaving mine. "Kirill, where is the nearest inn?"

"Korov, my lord."

"Excellent. We'll stop there for the night."

Sounds of protest came from a larger portion of the men than I would have preferred. *If he changes his mind...*

"My lord," one of them complained. "Are you truly going to take the word of a woman—"

"Come now, men," Evander said. There was the condescension I had been waiting for. "The princess clearly has...feminine needs to attend to that she's too shy to say aloud."

A few uncomfortable laughs sprang up in place of the protests. Heat flooded from my neck to my cheeks, but I didn't argue. I couldn't, when it was getting us where we needed to be.

Evander eyed my pink skin with some curiosity before he finally looked away, spurring his horse forward and encouraging mine to follow.

Had he said that to humiliate me? Had it been to save face?

It hardly mattered if we were off the roads when we needed to be. At least, that's what I told myself to avoid giving into that temptation to punch him in his face, after all.

CHAPTER 11

Even with my warning, we didn't reach the inn before we were accosted by freezing rain and ground-quaking thunder. The small droplets pouring down from the sky grew bigger and bigger until the icy rain turned into small hailstones, battering down on the horses and us.

I pulled my hood lower over my head, bracing myself for the tiny stinging bastards. The poor horses whinnied, but they didn't slow down until we reached shelter at the stables.

A man ushered us into the barn, cursing under his breath as pieces of hail struck him. Taras took charge of his guards, helping the man sort out the animals into stalls, while the rest of us rushed back outside and headed to the inn next door.

We were drenched by the time we walked through the main doors.

Taras and the other men followed minutes later. They had barely closed the door behind them when a deafening roar reached our ears, like horses were galloping across the roof.

Glass shattered, and I skittered back as an icy sphere the size of my fist sailed in from the broken window, followed by another and another. Evander darted a glance at the hailstones before looking back at me. He cocked his head to the side, not unlike a bird of prey might search for its next meal.

"Oh look," I said flatly, raising my eyebrows. "The weight of my feminine needs has broken the window."

In spite of my mocking, I couldn't suppress a sigh of relief that we were sheltered from the worst of this storm. Especially when a couple of villagers stumbled in, one right after the other, sporting wounds from the tremendous hailstones.

The storm thundered down on the buildings and road until everything outside the broken window was covered in a blanket of white stones. Several more broken windows and injured villagers later, and there was finally a small break. Though the pressure in my spine told me we were in for at least one more surge like this before the night was over.

Awareness settled over me, and I spun to find Evander peering at me with suspicion.

"An interest in the weather?" he deadpanned.

"Yes," I said, before clarifying. "I mean, in addition to my urgent feminine needs, of course."

"Of course." His brow was furrowed. "Perhaps you'll make a useful pet after all."

"One can dream," I bit back sarcastically.

He chuckled under his breath before walking away to speak with the innkeeper, leaving me with Kirill. When he returned after only a moment, he handed a key to the guard and instructed him to take me to room twelve.

This time, there was only one bed, rickety and taking up most of the cramped space. Was I getting a room to myself tonight?

That made me almost as nervous as sharing a room with Evander, probably because this inn was far less reputable than the last one we had stayed at. I wasn't even certain the door had latched all the way shut.

I didn't have much time to dwell on that before a servant came to help me undress, this one tackling my hair with less fear than a dogged determination I had to admire. She left as quickly as she had come, and I didn't get a chance to ask her about dinner.

My stomach growled, and I was about to head out to ask whatever guard they had posted outside about food when the door swung open. I turned, expecting the maid again, but of course, it was Evander who walked in.

CHAPTER 12

Evander was carrying two bowls this time, and handed one nonchalantly out to me. He had changed into dry clothes, but his hair still hung in damp, tousled locks on his forehead.

My confusion must have shown on my face because he sighed.

"Once again, we are short on rooms, and even if we weren't, surely you didn't think I trusted you, or the rest of the tavern, enough to let you have a room to yourself?" He glanced significantly at the window.

"Where would I even go?" I sighed, more tired than upset at this point.

"With the common sense you've displayed thus far, the possibilities are limitless. Would you walk directly into a bear cub den, or simply hand yourself over to the nearest Unclanned?"

I barely suppressed an eye roll, taking the proffered bowl. "I suppose I won't bother to argue if you're that committed to sleeping on this floor."

There were more than a few spindly shapes crawling in between the uneven, dirt-covered planks.

Evander followed my gaze with distaste. "*You* are more than welcome to the floor, if you so desire it. Perhaps I could even get you a little cushion to curl up on like the estate cat has. Never let it be said that I am unkind to my pets."

I opened my mouth to argue, but he cut me off. "Need I

remind you that it was you who insisted on stopping early for the night? The inn we planned on stopping at was another soldier's inn, plenty of rooms with two beds. But *you* wanted to stop here."

"Need I remind *you* that we would likely be dead or...at least, seriously injured by now if I hadn't?" I lifted my chin.

He shrugged. "I'm surprised that bothers you, what with your lack of self-preservation skills."

"Well, as fun as it would have been to watch you get caught in that storm, I wasn't about to risk Kirill." I smiled savagely, and something flashed in his eyes too quickly for me to read. "Speaking of whom, if you'll point me in the direction of his room, I'm happy to stay there. Or in the stables, for that matter."

"How quickly you go from concerns about your propriety to wanting to jump into bed with one of my soldiers," he muttered darkly. "In any case, I doubt Kirill's wife would appreciate that."

My cheeks colored. I hadn't meant it that way, only that I didn't want to be in Evander's room. "I—"

"Unfortunately for you," he broke in. "I won't force my men to suffer through your company, and the stables are off limits for obvious reasons. So again, your options." He gestured gallantly from the bed to the floor.

At that exact moment, a small, fat rat emerged from a gnawed hole in the paneling of the wall. I suppressed a shudder. My older sister might have been a friend to all creatures, but I never could quite reconcile myself to rodents.

My gaze slid to the bed, which was looking more spacious by the minute.

As nervous as I had been to share his room before, he was one of the few men who had not been lecherous during the dances at the Summit, and even when he went to put me on the saddle had kept his hands firmly where they belonged.

"Fine," I snapped. "Just...keep your hands to yourself."

Evander arched a single sardonic eyebrow.

"Well, it would help if you had worn something less provocative." He looked pointedly at the misshapen outline of my ruffled nightgown. "But somehow, I'll manage."

I made a noise in the back of my throat that was definitely

not a stifled laugh because I would rather have died than laugh with Lord *Aalio*.

With an irritable sigh, I went to eat what appeared to be very watery stew with a fully intact slimy fish floating on top, one watery eyeball looking straight into my soul. I swallowed back a wave of nausea, reminding myself that there were food shortages here and people in this village who would be happy to have this meal.

Tipping the bowl up, I took a tiny sip. It was lukewarm and even worse than borscht. Immediately, a gag assaulted me. I clamped my hand over my mouth to keep the stew from coming back up, meeting Evander's eyes inadvertently.

He tilted his own bowl back in an obvious way, taking a huge sip. He didn't gag, and his features were so carefully controlled that I might have even thought he was enjoying it...except for the telltale watering of his eyes.

Still, I took the look for what it was. A challenge.

Not dropping his gaze, I held my breath and gulped the rest of my bowl down as quickly as I could. It was at least a nice distraction from how awkward it was eating alone with Evander in the tiny room with the bed we were both going to sleep in.

For as casual as he acted, his uncharacteristic silence made me wonder if he was feeling the weight of it as well. Or maybe it was just the impending knowledge of whatever awaited us at Bear getting to both of us.

My enslavement and whoever Evander's *she* was.

More than that, though, I couldn't help but wonder why Evander had actually stopped based on nothing more than the word of a girl he disdained. He glanced up from his soup to find me scrutinizing him, and raised his eyebrows.

Before I could help myself, the question tumbled from my lips. "Why did you believe me about the storm?"

"What makes you think I did?" he countered. "Perhaps I was only reading between the lines of your apparent shyness."

"Ah, yes." I nodded sarcastically. "That damnably reticent nature of mine. Then why weren't you surprised when the storm hit?"

"Maybe I was, and just not everyone wears every feeling they have for the entire world to see." His features were closed off enough that I might have believed him. Except...

"Maybe you're avoiding the question," I prodded.

He met my gaze for a solid minute before answering. "I don't pretend to have a superior understanding of the weather, Princess, and really, I had little to lose. If you were wrong, we lost half a day on the road. If you were right, we avoided both the inconvenience and the potential hazard of traveling in a storm."

I studied his features, but they were as aloof as ever. Why had he bothered answering, and why did I feel like it wasn't the whole truth?

The reason made sense, and I couldn't help but compare it to the way Iiro had risked his men in the same circumstances. Would Theo have done the same thing, if it had been his choice, or would he have reasoned the way Evander did?

I traced the outline of the lotus charm on my bracelet, wondering if I would ever have the chance to find out.

On that cheerful note, I climbed into the bed, keeping my back to Evander while I pulled the single, small blanket up around my shoulders.

I tried not to react as the straw mattress sank down next to me. There should have been at least a foot of space between Evander and me, but somehow it felt like much less.

He dragged the blanket over him, pulling it away from where I had it tucked under my side and allowing a draft to come through. I yanked it back, eliciting an irritable grunt from him.

After a few more rounds of that, Evander muttered what I was fairly certain was a curse in Socairan.

"Spending all day needling at me may not be taxing for you, Princess, but I would like to get some sleep."

"As would I," I gritted out. "So give me the blanket."

"There would be plenty of blanket for both of us if you would quit taking all of it. Have you always been this selfish?"

"If by that you mean, have I always put my own comfort above that of my self-proclaimed owner, then let's go with yes," I growled.

Another irritable huff, followed by a beat of silence before he tugged the blanket back once more. I debated whether my pride was more important than my sleep, and landed on a solid, resounding *no* before I shuffled the extra few inches that would allow us to share the blanket comfortably.

Though he had more or less gotten his way, Evander stiffened at my proximity, which was enough to make me feel victorious in this exchange. Even if I did have a long, uncomfortable night ahead of me.

Even if I did miss Theo and his warm, solid arms more than ever.

I fell asleep to thoughts of Theo, and I dreamed of him, too.

It was peaceful, imagining him next to me, how warm I would be in his arms. I leaned into the dream version of him, soaking up the comfort of his presence and the way he smelled like the air just before a thunderstorm.

I nuzzled my face into his chest, and his arms tightened around me.

"Theo," I murmured his name, and he froze.

I opened my eyes and looked up just in time to see Evander opening his. He clamped his hands on either side of me and practically threw me away from him, setting me on the far side of the bed that suddenly felt much, much too small.

"Do you mind, Lemmikki?" He brought his hands back to his sides before thrusting the blanket toward me. "You can have this. It's plenty warm in here now."

Humiliation spread through me. I was certain if the fire had been burning any brighter, it would have been plain to see the bright red hue of my entire body. Taking the blanket, I rolled over so I wouldn't have to face him anymore.

Der'mo, again.

CHAPTER 13

I spent the rest of the night so concerned about accidentally rolling into him that at least by the time morning came, I was too tired to feel awkward.

It helped that Evander had already left the bed and the room when the maid woke me up to leave.

The discomfort we had been spared was more than made up for on the road, though. An ominous feeling permeated the air, and it wasn't only the uncomfortable night that hung between us.

It only got worse when we finally reached the estate.

Nestled in the imposing mountain range was an expansive castle with the same domed towers I had seen throughout Socair, only instead of being garishly colored, these were patterned black and white.

My heartbeat thundered in my ears, my breaths came in short, white puffs of air. The Duke was somewhere in that castle, the man who had wantonly murdered his own people and mine.

What will he do now that I'm here?

It was a surreal feeling, realizing that in another life, my Aunt Isla would have been his wife, the Clan Wife of this estate. She wouldn't even have been my aunt, technically, if she hadn't married Uncle Finn, just my father's cousin.

Stranger still, she would have been Evander's stepmother. Maybe he would have been nicer then, some of her innate goodness seeping into him.

Though she had a solid temper to rival my father's, so maybe he would be the same arseling he was today.

It wasn't long before my apprehension about what awaited me edged out my slew of what-ifs. When we made it to the stables, Evander leapt down from his saddle and muttered something to one of the stableboys, who went running toward the castle.

"Now, it's my turn to tell you to keep your hands to yourself," he said, firmly grasping my waist and lowering me to the ground.

I shot him a confused look and the edge of his mouth pulled up.

"I just know how you feel about stableboys," he explained. "And Pavel here is much too young for you."

I glanced at the gangly boy at least five years my junior.

"I'll try to restrain myself," I said drily.

A younger man in the same black livery as the rest of the soldiers approached us. He clasped hands with Evander, Kirill, and Taras before his wide, gray eyes landed on me.

He was a cross of Evander and Taras, though he looked even younger than I was.

"Lady Mairi...eagerly anticipates your arrival," he said gravely.

"Thank you, Yuriy." All traces of humor vanished from Evander's features, replaced by wary resignation. "Come, Lemmikki."

I followed his stoic steps into the castle, reminding myself that no matter how ominous this felt, it wasn't permanent.

Whether it was Da' or Theo, someone was going to come for me.

Our footsteps echoed on the marbled floors up to the high, domed ceilings. Servants scurried past us in the halls, looking at me with expressions of confusion or horror. *Ah, something familiar, at least.*

We finally came into a room that was tucked away down the grand hall. A large window took up most of the far wall, while the others were covered in bookcases and a crackling fire lit the hearth.

"Stepmother." Evander greeted the small figure standing by the window.

Her narrow shoulders stiffened at the sound of his voice before she slowly turned around.

"What happened with the Summit? Your father has been concerned."

I wasn't sure what I had been expecting, but it certainly wasn't this. She spoke the Common Tongue as well as the nobles back home. Even her voice sent a pang of familiarity through my chest, making me realize how homesick I truly was.

When her gaze finally drifted from Evander to me, I was startled by the intense green of her eyes.

For a moment, I saw my sister staring back at me.

The woman reminded me so much of my home and my family and my people that it hit me with an unexpected ache.

"I had planned to have my pet brought upstairs and then was going to report to Father," Evander said smoothly. "I am certain he will fill you in."

The woman's gaze narrowed, and she ran her hand over a few loose strands of white hair on her head, as if she needed to smooth out some imagined imperfection.

It struck me that there was a slightly pink hue there too, almost as if her hair had once been red like mine. Had she endured all of the same prejudices that I had since arriving in Socair?

"And how did you manage to acquire a Lochlannian pet?" Disapproval emanated from her tone. Of me, or of the fact that I had been taken prisoner?

Evander hesitated only a second. "I collected on a blood debt against the Lochlann ruling family."

Lady Mairi's hawklike gaze sharpened as she honed in on me before turning back to Evander. "Your father's blood debt, you mean?" There was a warning in her tone, barely evident.

If her features hadn't given her away as one of my people, her failure to adhere to Socairan standards of female demurity would have. But to what end?

Was Mairi warning her stepson of his father's wrath?

If I hadn't been observing him for the past three days, would I have noticed the subtle paling of Evander's skin?

"Of course," he finally responded.

Icy tendrils raked down my spine, true fear settling in for the first time since I climbed into Evander's carriage.

As much as Evander had claimed I belonged to him, he was going to turn me over to his father? The man who killed my grandparents? Who did unspeakable things in a war that he started? A man who despised my people and who was, by every definition of the word, a monster?

Lady Mairi nodded like she was satisfied with that response, or relieved, even. "I'll let him know you're coming."

Evander nodded curtly, wrapping a hand around my arm and tugging me toward a different hallway.

I glanced back over my shoulder to try and catch one last look at the woman, but she was already gone. She had been impossible to read, but I hadn't sensed any outright hostility. At least, not toward me.

If I could find an ally in the Clan Wife, I might be safe.

There might just be hope yet.

CHAPTER 14

We made our way back to the main entry room, where Taras and Yuriy were waiting.

"Taras, please escort the princess upstairs." Evander's words dripped with something dark. "Put her in the room next to mine."

"In mother's old rooms?" Yuriy asked, casting me a suspicious look from the corner of his eyes.

Taras placed a hand on the man's shoulder and shook his head in one barely discernible movement.

"Come, Princess." Taras appeared to be nearly as thrilled about the idea as I was, but he dutifully tilted his head for me to follow. *Well, then.*

I shot one last glance at Evander, who was already heading in a different direction, his shoulders tense with the weight of whatever our encounter with Lady Mairi had stirred up in him.

Taras cleared his throat pointedly, pulling my attention away from the Bear Lord. He led me up a massive staircase and through a wide, arched hall with pristine gray stone. Black banners cascaded to the floor, each with the white bear symbol stitched into the center.

The dark colors lent the imposing hall an even eerier feel, matching just about everything else in this castle thus far.

It wasn't until we climbed yet another set of stairs that the decor went from being militant to something resembling a home. Portraits lined the walls, along with paintings of land-scapes or flowers, interspersed with artful sconces.

I tried to focus on those little details instead of the anxiety building inside me, the questions I wasn't sure I wanted the answers to. There was one thing I did want to know, though.

"Is Lady Mairi the *she* you were referring to when you spoke to Evander in the stables?"

He shot me a cool glare from the corner of his eye. "Surely even Lochlann teaches that eavesdropping is rude."

"Is that a yes?"

He ignored me, but his features gave him away. After another few minutes of terse silence, I blurted out the first thing that came to mind.

"You aren't terribly fond of me, are you?"

His eyebrow lifted, barely, the only flicker in his expression, but he didn't bother to deny it.

"Is it the hair? The lineage?" I needed the man to speak, to distract me from my spiraling thoughts.

Taras let out a sigh, his measured footsteps the only other sound in the spacious, winding hallway. He didn't respond until we reached an intricately carved wooden door.

"It is the chaos you bring," he said simply, opening the door to the rooms. "The maids will be up shortly."

He turned to leave without giving me a chance to respond, or even to ask what in the stars he had meant by that.

The room was, predictably, done entirely in black and white, though there was something decidedly feminine about this decor. It was in the damask pattern covering the walls, the black jeweled chandelier hanging overhead.

A white bear skin rug lay before an unlit hearth, and a massive four-poster bed took up half of the far wall, covered by a black crushed velvet canopy.

I shivered when a cold draft whistled in through the balcony doors, moving my hands up to rub my frozen arms.

I reached out to open the velvet canopy when a startled gasp sounded behind me, along with a thud and a splashing sound. I spun around to see a maid staring wide-eyed at my hair.

Of course.

Steaming water sloshed all over the floor from the bucket the woman had dropped, but she barely even noticed. Instead, she made a similar gesture to the one I had grown used to seeing Venla make back at Elk, the one I suspected was to ward off evil, before turning around to leave the room.

Several minutes later, another maid appeared. Rather than fear, she looked at me with something that bordered on fascination.

"My name is Taisiya. I'll help you bathe, Your Highness," she said, gesturing toward a small door in the corner of the room.

Her voice was lightly accented, closer to Evander's than Kirill's.

"Thank you, Taisiya," I told her, making my way toward what I assumed was the bathing chamber. "What happened to...the other one?"

Taisiya shook her head with a trace of exasperation. "She is...indisposed."

I couldn't help a small answering chuckle. At least someone in this castle didn't hate me on principle.

Maybe the Clan Wife would make two.

CHAPTER 15

When I was dried and in one of the soft, comfortable nightgowns that Mila had left me, I walked back into the bedroom to a roaring fire and a turned down bed.

The chandelier was lit, casting a glimmering light on the floor and walls that, combined with the flickering fire, gave the room almost a cozy feel.

For a prison, anyway.

Taisiya left, promising to return with dinner. All I could do was hope fervently it wasn't fish stew. Or borscht, for that matter.

The Socairans really knew how to ruin soup.

While I waited, I sank down onto the rug near the fire. The fabric was warm from the flames and I eagerly melted into the plushy carpet.

Leaning back toward the hearth, I utilized the heat of the fire to help dry my hair. If there was anything less fun than being stuck here to begin with, it would be waking up in a freezing pool created by my several pounds of hair.

When Taisiya knocked a solid rap on the door, I called for her to enter, my stomach growling in spite of myself.

But it wasn't dinner.

Instead, Evander stormed in, still dressed in his traveling clothes. He stopped in his tracks when he caught sight of me, lounging back to stretch my head closer to the fire in a lacy nightgown that was, admittedly, a little too fitted in certain areas.

I lunged forward, crossing my arms over my chest with all the subtlety of a drunken moose. Something broke through his mask for the barest fraction of a moment before he reverted to the dangerously calm expression he had been wearing when he walked in.

Fury burned behind his eyes, and tension radiated off of him in waves. It was a sharp contrast to his usual brand of casual arrogance, and I couldn't help but wonder if it had something to do with the meeting he had with the duke.

If it had something to do with *me*.

He cleared his throat. "I came to tell you I'm leaving tomorrow."

A quiver of panic shot through me, his words confirming my fears.

"Am I to be your father's *pet* now?" My voice was breathier than I meant for it to be.

"No." The word was a low growl.

I couldn't deny a small, unwelcome bit of relief. *Better the devil you know, after all.*

"Well, I'll try not to be too desolate in your absence," I said, trying for lightness.

In fact, I could use the time to try to get to know Lady Mairi, but I wasn't about to mention that to him. It was one of my rare good decisions, since his next words were on that very subject.

But he was in no mood for banter.

"I expect you to stay in your rooms."

I raised my eyebrows at the uncharacteristic order, and his face lost what little humanity it had left.

"Trust me, Lemmikki." His voice was like a sharply honed blade, pure, deadly, steel. "You will not enjoy the consequences if you disobey."

I studied him, from the taut set of his shoulders to the subtle savagery that lurked behind his casual façade, belatedly realizing I had been too quick to forget who he was and why I was here.

I nodded slowly, and he narrowed his eyes.

"My men will be watching."

I wanted to tell him that after sneaking out of the castle of the King of Lochlann, his guards didn't concern me, but that would only make him assign more to me.

Besides, perhaps I wasn't afraid of his guards, but I'd be lying if I said I wasn't just the smallest bit afraid of Evander right now. But I would die before letting him see that, so I forced a nonchalant expression.

"Inside these rooms you insist I stay in? That hardly seems appropriate," I chided.

A muscle ticked in his jaw, and he shook his head back and forth in a barely perceptible movement. "I told you at the Summit, you didn't have the sense to be afraid. Now would be a good time to remedy that."

He turned to go as quickly as he had come, leaving me alone with the ominous threat that almost felt more like a warning.

CHAPTER 16

True to Evander's word, one of his men was watching my door at all times.

But not my balcony.

Setting aside my misgivings, I surveyed my options for escape.

Evander's warning echoed in my head, but I wasn't about to waste my time playing the good captive in my rooms while he played puppeteer with my fate. Especially if there was a chance that Lady Mairi might be an ally of sorts.

So I found myself navigating a route from my stone balcony onto the roof of the castle, one of the perks of being on the highest floor.

A pang of longing went through me for my older sister. Avani and I used to do this same thing, usually to sneak out to the village taverns with Mac.

This time, though, I had a more serious goal in mind.

Since the highest levels were generally thought to be the safest, it was likely that Lady Mairi's rooms were here, too. If I could get to the other side of the castle, I might be able to find her, to talk to her and do...something.

Of course, there was always the risk of her reporting me to Evander — or worse, the Duke, but I couldn't just stay in my room and do nothing. In six months, Theo and Davin would alert Lochlann and my father would come here. And when he found out Evander had taken me, there would be war.

War meant casualties and poverty for Lochlann, even if I hadn't been concerned about my own family leading it.

Besides, I could always observe her for a while first to gauge her reaction.

I dug through my trunk until I found one of the older, stuffier dresses that had been altered to fit me at the Summit. The stitching at the seam was still loose enough that with a few good tugs, I was able to pry the two pieces of the skirt apart. Once I was certain that the skirts were wide enough for the climb, I headed out to the balcony before I could talk myself out of it.

A guard was making a round down in the courtyard below, so I leaned against the low stone wall and pretended to be looking wistfully out until he passed.

Amateur. The guards in Lochlann never would have fallen for that. At least, not after the first few times my sister and I had snuck out this way.

As soon as his back was turned, I heaved myself onto the wall, then stretched up to leverage the ledge of the rooftop. Angling toward the inside of the balcony, lest I fall several stories down, I swung a leg up over the ledge. The rest of me soon followed.

When I got to my feet on the roof, I half expected my father to be standing there waiting with his arms crossed over his chest, shaking his head and muttering "Damn it, Rowan," under his breath.

It was strange to think there was a time that would have felt like the worst possible outcome of an escapade onto the roof, when I would give anything for it to happen now.

Pushing those thoughts away and the sharp stabbing feeling that accompanied them, I ducked behind a battlement.

A frosty breeze whistled past, and I shivered. We were going to have snow again soon, but that was the least of my problems now. The wind would pick up throughout the day, and if I wasn't careful, I could easily be swept off the roof.

To be on the safe side, I waited a solid few minutes before scuttling across the roof, then assessed the balconies on the other side.

One of them was distinctly fancier than the others, far more spacious and decorated with rows of potted evergreen shrubs.

Even if it was the wrong balcony, it would be the easiest one to hide on until I could make my way into the hallway.

Decision made, I slipped from the roof down onto the balcony as quietly as possible, using one of the many plants for cover. I waited for several moments to be sure no one had seen me before finally peering through the glass door that led into the room.

The reflection of the snow-capped mountains behind me made it difficult to look through the glass, but everything appeared to be quiet and still. After a few more stilted heartbeats, I cracked open the door and quietly eased myself into the room, closing it behind me.

I had less than a second to feel relief at my successful break-in before a voice broke through the quiet, freezing me in my tracks.

And unless she spoke in a rumbling baritone, it was definitely not Lady Mairi.

CHAPTER 17

"Good morning, my dear." A deep, accented voice greeted me. "Why don't you join me for breakfast?"

Alarm bells sounded in my head, fashionably late as usual. I wanted to run as fast as I could and lock myself in my room like Evander had told me to do.

But it was too late for all of that.

Slowly, I looked over at a small table in the corner to find an older man sitting there, watching me with a wicked gleam in his eye and a smug grin on his mouth. The expression was so familiar, even on the aged face, that I knew who he was immediately.

It shouldn't have surprised me, knowing that the duke was likely to reside in this part of the castle as well, but I hadn't expected him to be in his rooms in the middle of the day.

One of many things I had been wrong about, as it turned out. I wondered if this would turn out to be the one that killed me, considering who this man was and everything he had done. I swallowed back a wave of bile.

There was less than a second for a battle of wills where I once more debated running back out the balcony, but none of that would matter now that the duke himself had seen me. Besides, where else would I even go?

"Good morning," he greeted casually, as if I hadn't just broken into his private chambers from the castle roof. "Won't you join me for breakfast?"

My heartbeat picked up its pace, and my mind reeled. *What*

kind of game is he playing?

He gestured toward the chair seated across from him and began scooping some of the food from the bowls onto the plate there.

"Please," he said, pointing at plates of poached eggs, bacon, and even biscuits. "I hate eating alone."

My traitorous stomach growled, eager for something other than the porridge I had eaten every day since arriving in Bear.

But the small, principled part of me had no desire to take a meal with the man who had ordered my grandparents' bodies strewn up the wall of their own castle. The man who had colluded with my other grandfather's own brother and sister to depose him and start a war.

Where is my family's blood debt in all of this? Aunt Isla's mother and despicable uncle had disappeared before they could pay for their crimes, but this man was here, alive and physically well.

Would it be worth it if sitting here helped me find a way out of this?

Easing myself into the chair, I waited for the questions to begin, for the accusations or the list of ways I would pay for this, but they never came. The duke only picked at his eggs, thoroughly enjoying every bite, smiling up at me now and then, as if it were the most normal thing in the world to have me in his room.

"Do eat, my dear," he said, gesturing toward my plate. "You won't want it to go cold."

Something was very wrong here, but I forced a neutral expression and picked up the biscuit, slathering some butter and honey on top. It was an effort to force myself to take a bite. The food should have been delicious, but doing something so casual as eating in the man's presence had my stomach churning.

The duke watched me carefully, without saying a word, which only made the tension in the room grow. *Is he waiting for something?*

"Thank you, Sir," I choked out, motioning toward my breakfast.

"Sir? What happened to Aleksander?"

Having never met the man before, I wasn't aware we were on such informal terms...but, whatever game he was playing, I decided to play along.

"Of course, Aleksander. My apologies--"

I stopped short when his features pinched together, and he darted glances around the room. When his eyes landed on me once again, the paranoid expression that had been there only seconds ago had already disappeared.

"Ah, good morning, my dear. I'm pleased you could join me. I do hate eating alone." A smile stretched across his face, as if he were seeing me for the first time again, and my chest tightened.

I forced a grin in return, though my mind was traveling to a dark place it hadn't visited in years.

For a moment, it wasn't Duke Aleksander sitting across the table from me, but Grandmother Bridget instead. She had forgotten the last time I had come to see her, though it had only been earlier that morning.

Her memory had been failing her for some time, but eventually she forgot my name, and then Avani's. Eventually, she even forgot who my parents were.

My eyes stung, and my stomach knotted.

The difference here, of course, was that Grandmother Bridget hadn't been a murdering sociopath before her mind failed her. When she forgot when or where she was, it was usually a peaceful place she returned to. One where her son was still alive or when she lived in the cottage by the forest.

Aleksander, on the other hand, had been ruthless and cruel. There was no telling who he thought I was or what he might decide to do about it.

"Do be sure to eat, my dear." He motioned toward my plate as he continued taking bites from his own.

I forced myself to pick up a slice of the bacon, conscious of the way he waited for me to take a bite. Once again, something that should have been delicious turned to ash on my tongue.

Was I really eating breakfast with the man responsible for the slaughter of so many of my people? Of my grandparents?

Did it matter if he didn't even remember the heinous things he was responsible for?

The question plagued me as I forced down the rest of my food, making small talk with a man who had no idea who I was, and would likely kill me if he found out.

I just hoped I wouldn't hate myself as much as I hated him by the time I left.

CHAPTER 18

In spite of my better sense and the way it made my skin crawl, I spent the next two mornings meeting the duke for breakfast. Both times were similar to the first; a haze of confusion and small bits of information that I hoped would lead to something useful.

On the second morning, I learned that Evander's mother's name was Yrsa and that she had died from an illness only a year after he was born.

When Aleksander spoke of her, it was impossible not to see his grief. Whatever sort of cruelty he showed in other areas of his life, he at least had loved his first wife. I cut our visit short that day when he went into a rage and grieved her death all over again, worried the noise would bring someone into the room.

It was equal parts terrifying and painful to behold. As I climbed out onto the roof, it struck me all over again how I had never wanted that sort of love.

The kind that would break you...

The kind that must have broken him. Was that what had made him so awful in the war?

I peeked out from behind the battlement to survey the courtyard below for anyone who might be watching. A gust of icy wind whistled past, carrying a few dead leaves and the last remnants of autumn along with it. The air smelled like snow, and the small tingling along my spine promised we would see that very soon.

My eyes caught on one of the figures, and I let out a low curse, straining harder to get a better look at him.

Sure enough, it was Evander.

He was speaking with one of his men, gesturing toward different sections of the estate before turning to head inside.

My knuckles went white around the stone ledge.

When *had* he returned?

Was he avoiding me? And if so, why did he bring me here to begin with?

Then my mind raced to the room I had left. The one where his mad father sat locked away, reliving his past, and I wondered what was truly going on. I thought about the way Evander filled in for his father at the Summit, how he spoke of him and never once mentioned that he wasn't well. I thought about the reputation that the clan had, their cruelty and violence.

Had Evander merely carried out the orders of his father? Or was he the one pulling the strings, hiding behind his father's name and reputation to do whatever he wanted?

My head spun with a thousand more questions that I wasn't sure I would ever get the answers to. Finally, I waltzed back into my room, shutting the door to the balcony and all the bitter thoughts from the morning out with it.

I wasn't sure why I decided to go back the next day. Was it morbid curiosity? Boredom? Belief that he would eventually tell me something useful?

I supposed the answer didn't really matter when the questions only came as I was climbing onto his balcony. I wished they had come sooner.

As soon as the duke saw me, he ushered me over to the small table where his breakfast was waiting. He, however, refused to sit down. Anger radiated off of him in waves as he stormed around the room.

"I've convinced the king to let us march tomorrow," he seethed.

I had become accustomed to going down different roads of his past with him, but this wasn't one I was familiar with. It also wasn't one that I wanted to travel down. Especially not when the king he was referring to had been dead for nearly two decades...killed not long after the war with Lochlann.

"Why so soon?" I finally asked, though I was terrified of the answer. There couldn't have been many marching orders after they came back from that.

Aleksander glared at me as if I should have known the answer, before ticking off the reasons on his fingers one by one. He slipped in and out of Socairan as he spoke, but I understood plenty. The things he said about my Aunt Isla, about my grandparents, my mother...

My stomach twisted, and I wanted to be sick.

I did my best to keep my features neutral as he made all manner of threats against my people, knowing that some of them he had actually carried out.

The longer he spoke, however, the more suspicious he became. Tendrils of fear rose up inside of me, and not for the first time, I wondered why the hell I hadn't just stayed in my rooms.

As soon as the opportunity arose, I ran to the balcony and practically leapt onto the roof in an effort to get away from him. Only seconds after I got my bearings, the sound of a door opening had me pausing.

A few voices muttered low, placating words until the duke was finally calmer, then the door was opening and closing once again.

"Good morning, my dear." He greeted someone with a kindly tone, as if he hadn't said any of the vile things from a few moments ago.

I wondered if this was how it always was at Bear. I hadn't heard a single whisper of the mad duke, only ones of his cruelty and strength. Did he still control the territory? Did the soldiers march on his whims?

Or was it his son keeping the cruel reputation of Bear alive?

CHAPTER 19

I hadn't been able to make myself go back to Aleksander's rooms the next morning. Or the one after that.

Our last encounter had been enough to make me want to bolt the door to the balcony all together. But staying in my rooms left me entirely too much time to be alone with my thoughts, something I worked hard to avoid most of the time.

Especially since Mac died. My mind had a tendency to travel in a loop back to the day we got the news, like if I thought about it hard enough, I could change what happened.

I'm going to check on the village this morning. He had announced it as he was leaving breakfast, pausing only long enough to plant a kiss on my sister's lips that made my father clear his throat and one of the twins pretend to gag.

Then he had never come home.

What if we had found a reason for him to stay? That was probably selfish, though, knowing that he had saved several lives in the house fire that took his.

This line of thought inevitably led me to my sister. Would Avani hate me when she found out I was still alive? Hate me for making her grieve twice for such a stupid, inconsequential reason?

Hate me for leaving her to deal with that grief on her own while I traipsed around the kingdom with Davin, even before we wound up here?

I blew out a sigh. I couldn't stay in this room alone any

longer, and I wouldn't go back to Aleksander. Instead, I went to open my door, finding Yuriy on the other side.

"Did you need something, Highness?" His lightly accented voice was polite, but distant.

I pondered his question, not actually having thought that far ahead.

"Yes," I said with more confidence than I felt. "Do you have a deck of cards?"

"I could send for one," he said uncertainly.

"Perfect. I need...someone to play a game of *war* with me."

His eyes widened. "I'm supposed to be standing guard..."

"And what better way to keep an eye on me than if I'm in the same hallway?" When he looked close to caving, I pressed. "Who knows what kind of trouble I might get into if I'm left to my own devices in that room for too long."

He sighed. "I suppose one game wouldn't hurt."

I beamed at him. He sent for cards and, as I had hoped, was loosening up by the end of the first game. We played a few more, and he was actually chuckling by the time an irritable throat-clearing interrupted us.

I froze, telling myself my heart couldn't be hammering in my chest, because I was definitely not afraid of Evander. Even if he had just caught me breaking his rather forceful edict to stay in my rooms. An edict that I had disobeyed in more ways than this one...

"Van." Yuriy hurriedly got to his feet. "Erm. Lord Evander, I mean. We were just--"

"Playing a game instead of guarding the princess?" he supplied in a deceptively calm tone.

"I'm hardly going to abscond in the middle of a game of *war*." I infused my voice with nonchalance.

"I wouldn't put it past you," he challenged.

"Please," I scoffed. "I play to win."

"Is she winning?" Evander raised his eyebrows at Yuriy, who nodded sheepishly.

"But I think she's cheating," he added.

Only a little. I made a face of mock offense, and Evander shook his head.

"Well, I wouldn't put that past her, either." He looked from me to Yuriy, then down the stairs and back again. "You may as well keep playing, then, if only to salvage your pride."

Yuriy looked hesitant, but eventually settled back on the ground while Evander disappeared into his room.

It felt like a win, all things considered.

CHAPTER 20

The weeks continued to tick by in a slow, tedious routine of waking and eating and counting the damask designs on the wall. Of which, there were one thousand, seven hundred and ninety-two.

I mostly obeyed Evander's orders and kept myself in my rooms, or just outside them in the hall. For someone who insisted they wanted me around for entertainment, Evander continued to make himself scarce.

Not that I was complaining.

I had convinced most of his guards to play games with me, and gradually, several of them seemed to relax. Dmitriy even taught me a couple of new games. Of course, on the rare occasion that Taras was assigned to me, he refused to budge.

"Highness, please return to your rooms." His ramrod-straight posture didn't falter, his gaze barely wavering from my doorway.

Returning to my rooms was the absolute last thing I wanted to do right now. There was far too little distraction to be had there.

"Or, you could please remove the stick from your--"

"Lemmikki," a voice chided from around the corner just before Evander emerged on silent footfalls. "Do try to refrain from harassing my men."

"But he makes it so easy," I protested.

A muscle in Taras' jaw ticked, and I couldn't help but smirk.

Evander heaved an exasperated sigh, reaching into the pocket of his cloak. "So, I suppose you aren't interested in these letters, then?"

I crossed the distance in three short strides, holding out my hand impatiently. "From who?"

"One from Lord Theodore and one from...your eunuch guard."

It took everything I had not to laugh out loud. Biting the inside of my cheek forcibly, I responded in a mild tone. "It was thoughtful of him to check on me."

"Indeed." He handed over two envelopes...two open envelopes.

"Did you read my letters?"

"That depends." He put a finger to his lips. "Are you a prisoner receiving letters from an enemy clan?"

I glared at him.

"You can pass any return letters along to Taras. I'm sure he would be thrilled to read through them before sending them along."

"Delighted," Taras intoned.

Casting each of them a look in turn, I spun around to go back to my rooms. Flouncing onto the bed in the spot with the most sunlight streaming in, I opened Davin's letter first.

To Her Royal Highness Princess Rowan Blair Juliette Pendragon of Lochlann,

Remember that time we woke up on the floor of a Socairan dungeon? I never actually thought we would top that, but you appear to have more of Gwyn's competitive streak than I ever gave you credit for.

I chuckled wryly.

His letter went on to detail a few amusing stories about misunderstandings with the customs and requested that I fill him in on the events of the Summit at my convenience so that he might have a better picture than the vague one Theo and Iiro had painted.

. . .

I hope you're happy because 'Lord' Theodore--who, by the way, alleges you were betrothed by the time you were taken--is even less amusing when you aren't around. Honestly, I'm not certain there is any fun to be had in the whole of Socair, though I suspect that's even more lacking where you are.

Only five months until the pass opens. Tellus Amat Fortis.

After ending it on the serious note with our family's motto, the world loves the strong, he had signed it, *Your most humbly loyal and obedient servant guard.*

I couldn't help but laugh, though my expression sobered quickly when I opened Theo's letter.

Rowan,

How is it possible to miss someone so much when you were only around them for two weeks? Already, I look around, expecting you to be there with your mischievous grin and an inappropriate joke waiting on your lips, and then I remember what's happened.

Iiro and I are doing everything we can to get you out of this situation, but if all else fails, I promise, I will get word to your father. One way or another, I will not stop fighting until I have you back in my arms.

All my love,

Theo

I had tried so hard not to think about everything I had walked away from at the Summit, but it came flooding in now. Memories of Theo and I tucked away in the tent during the rainstorm, the way he would reluctantly smile when he was exasperated.

The way he held me like he could keep me safe through sheer force of his will.

I read the letter a few more times before pulling out a quill and parchment from the desk to craft my own. I gave Davin a more detailed accounting of what had happened at the Summit, and assured him that I was all right.

Then I wrote back to Theo, and I was sure to include a couple small passages that would make whoever was stuck with the job of reading these letters wildly uncomfortable.

I hoped it was Taras.

CHAPTER 21

Another week went by, this one bringing a letter from Mila, but no news on when or whether I might actually be getting out of Bear. I hadn't seen Evander at all except for the two times in the hallway, and the men never had any information for me.

So, I finally decided to go to the arseling lord himself.

The house was quiet, almost eerily still with the wan shafts of moonlight dancing on the hallway walls. Yuriy was guarding my rooms tonight and appeared rather dubious about my plan.

"I just want to ask him something," I said.

The young guard hesitated, looking me over as if to assess whether I was a threat. I made myself look as harmless as possible, which wasn't difficult when I was only five feet tall.

Apparently, it worked, because he reluctantly nodded.

I hurried over to Evander's door, rapping lightly on the solid wood.

He opened it abruptly, and I found myself face-to-face—well, face-to-chest—with his bare skin. He was wearing nothing but a pair of soft-looking black and white tartan trousers and a matching long-sleeved shirt he hadn't bothered to button.

An unwanted memory assaulted me of when I had awoken pressed against said chest. My cheeks reddened, and I wrenched my gaze from the defined muscles peeking out of his shirt.

Not that his face was better, when his lips were tilted up in pure arrogance.

"Did you need something, Lemmikki?" Even when he should have been innocuous standing before me in his nightclothes, he still managed to thrum with tension, reminding me that danger always lurked just below the surface.

"Yes." The word came out a rasp, so I cleared my throat again. "Yes, I need to know what exactly your plans are, aside from keeping me locked up in that room."

Rather than step back, Evander moved forward, crowding me into the hallway, and shut the door behind him.

"As it happens, I was going to come to you in the morning, but I may as well tell you now." He dismissed Yuriy with a gesture before speaking again. "Clan Elk desires to meet to discuss potentially purchasing your debt."

Emotions flooded through my veins, almost too quickly for me to identify. Excitement. Relief. *Hope.*

"Is that possible?" I breathed.

"It isn't generally done, but it is not against clan law," he said neutrally.

"So..." I narrowed my eyes, not wanting to look a gift horse in the mouth but unable to shake the feeling I was missing something. All this time, I had assumed his end game was to take me, to punish me, maybe, or leverage me, but... "You went to all the dramatics of calling in this blood debt and now you'll just...give me back?"

"You sound disappointed." He leaned back against the wall, crossing his arms over his chest.

"More like disbelieving."

Evander heaved a sigh. "I told you once that Socairans live and die on propriety. Declining this meeting would reflect badly on Bear."

"So you have no intention of taking their deal?" I prodded.

"I didn't say that either." He shrugged. "We're still discussing terms of the meeting at this point."

"Such as?"

"Where we will meet, and with how many people. If--"

An idea came to me, a small thrill running through me.

"Am I going to this meeting?" I blurted out.

He eyed me with suspicion. "I would assume so, since you are the subject matter in question."

"Then I have a condition." If they were still deciding on

how many people could come, then I could see Davin. It was almost too much to hope for, when I was already getting to see Theo, but I hadn't seen my cousin in over a month, not since the day I left for the Summit, unsure of whether I would return.

Which had been a legitimate concern, as it turned out.

Evander arched an imperious eyebrow. "You're hardly in a position to negotiate."

I glared at him. "Then do it because you owe me for wrecking my life for what was apparently no more than your own amusement."

His lips parted in surprise...or maybe offense, and he blinked several times before responding in a voice that was colder than before. "What is it that you want?"

"I want to see my guard. To make sure he's all right."

He studied me for a moment. "I suppose there's no harm in making Elk's life more difficult by adding to our list of terms."

"All right." I turned to head back to my room before spinning back around. "There is one more thing."

"Yes?" The short word was clipped.

"I want a weapon when we travel." I wanted my dagger back, actually, but I knew a sword would be more useful and there was no way he would give me both.

He tipped his head back and laughed. "Of course you do. Anything else, Princess?"

I pretended to consider it. "No. Just those two things."

He gave me a considering look. "I'll give you a weapon when I'm sure you won't stab yourself with it."

Now it was my turn to narrow my eyes. *Condescending. Arseling.*

"I think I've proven that amply by now."

"Do you?" He let out a patronizing chuckle, making me wish I had a weapon right about now. "Tomorrow morning, we'll spar. If you beat me, I'll give you a weapon. But if I beat you, you have to answer any question I ask. Truthfully," he tacked on.

I deliberated. I had seen him in action twice now. Once in the sparring ring, and again with the Unclanned, and both times he had been a force to be reckoned with.

All ye need is one good opening to win. My father's words came back to me, making me weigh the situation a little more.

It was worth a shot, though I wasn't sure why Evander would bother.

I studied his inscrutable features. "Why not just ask me what you want to know?"

"Because though you're terrible at it, you seem inclined to lie."

Well, then.

"I won't give you any information on Lochlann. Or Elk," I clarified.

He rolled his eyes. "That would be boring, Lemmikki. I promise not to ask you for anyone's secrets besides your own."

That should have been comforting, but instead, it gave me pause. What could he possibly want to know enough to barter for it, if not to give him an edge on Lochlann or Elk?

This time, my hesitation was longer, but finally, I nodded. "Then I accept."

CHAPTER 22

The next morning, Evander and I stood in an indoor training ring in a building off the main estate.

I wore one of Mila's lighter dancing dresses, the sapphire one, so at least I had room to move, even if I had gone numb with cold on the walk over.

It was the most normal thing in the world to train with the men back home. I missed the energy of the sparring rooms; the loud clanging of training weapons, the grunts and laughs of the men fighting, the constant bickering between my cousins and me.

The spirit of competition and...fun.

One of those things was ostensibly lacking from this morning's activities, though I certainly felt competitive enough. Especially since this would make the difference in whether I was, once again, stuck on the road defenseless.

Evander had dismissed the few guards who were sparring when we arrived, leaving us completely alone in the large, open room. I couldn't decide which was worse: fighting under the weight of their scandalized stares, or being in here alone with Evander.

He unbuttoned his black military overcoat, revealing a thin cream colored tunic with black leather laces over fitted black trousers. Once he neatly folded the coat and set it to the side, he grabbed two wooden sparring swords...like the kind children learned with.

I leveled a look at him, and he leveled one right back.

Reluctantly yanking one of the swords from him, I moved to the center of the ring to begin warming up.

But Evander had other plans.

He attacked without warning.

Glaring at him, I sprang up from where I had been stretching out my frozen legs to deflect his blade. He nodded like he was reluctantly impressed, and a little triumphant thrill went through me.

Inwardly, I thanked Fia for starting out so many of our lessons the same way.

I braced myself for the same lightning fast attack he had used on Theo, but he kept a moderate pace as he swung his blade toward my torso, my neck, my legs, waiting to see how I would counter his movements.

The bastard was toying with me.

I parried his next hit, then went on the offensive. Keeping my features entirely neutral, I feinted toward his smug face before swinging my blade low, knocking it against his solid thigh with a thud.

Instead of looking irritated, a satisfied smirk played at the corner of his lips. He circled me before attacking again, this time with incrementally more speed than before.

"Playing games now?" I huffed.

His eyes sparkled with amusement. "What kind of master would I be if I didn't play with my favorite pet?"

I lunged at him, but he sidestepped, so I tracked his movement and tried again. And suddenly, we were dancing, our blades crashing into one another and echoing through the large space while we arched and ducked from each other's blows.

Well, mostly I arched and ducked. He didn't seem to need to employ any real acrobatics to evade me, nor was he too out of breath to critique me.

"You're dropping your elbow."

I picked it up, scowling as I went in for another hit.

"Watch your footwork," he barked, just as I overstepped and faltered.

The worst part was that I had heard all of these things before, from Fia or my father or even Gwyn, so I knew they were true.

All you need is one good opening. My father's advice had been sound, but Evander wasn't inclined to give me any openings, let alone a good one.

I picked up my speed, ready to attack him full on.

"Careful, Lemmikki. Your expressions give you away." Evander's pompous voice broke through my thoughts and I rolled my eyes.

"And what exactly are they telling you, right now, Lord *Aalio*?" I panted.

Evander chuckled and spun around, switching sword hands before knocking me in the back of the knees with his wooden blade. "That you're flagging already."

I growled as my legs buckled ever so slightly. Recovering myself, I spun farther from his reach, using the large room to put a little more space between us.

Our cat and mouse game continued for several more minutes, but he never bothered to reach the speed I knew he was capable of. And still, I was nowhere close to winning.

"Why are you dragging this out?" I accused.

"We need to test your stamina." He shrugged.

I stumbled, earning me a solid thwack in the side. Still, I got several good hits in, landing one on his shoulder, another on his lower back and finally on his shin. All of this was worth the hits he gave in return, of course.

I couldn't deny that it felt good to spar, even when my opponent was Evander. I had been idle for too long, and the adrenaline of exertion was settling over me like a glass of well-aged whiskey.

Which was the only excuse I had for what I said next.

"Maybe you should worry about your own stamina." I grinned at him wickedly.

Much to my delight, his eyes widened and he momentarily faltered, giving me an even better opening than before. I didn't waste any time before taking advantage of that and landing three solid blows.

He recovered quickly, though, and in the end, he was infuriatingly right.

My stamina was waning, my movements slowing, while he wasn't so much as breathing hard. A fact which he didn't hesitate to rub in my face.

"Well, Lemmikki, it would appear that my stamina is perfectly intact." His features didn't so much as twitch to betray his emotion.

I opened my mouth to respond, but he surprised me by picking up his speed just enough to knock my sword out of my hand with embarrassingly little effort.

"Stars-damned son of a mother-loving whore!" I spat out, my chest still heaving from exertion.

Evander raised both of his eyebrows for a change, choking on something that sounded suspiciously like a laugh. "Indeed. Let me know once you've recovered yourself and I'll ask that question."

I glared at him, shaking my head bitterly. It wasn't that I had genuinely expected to win, but he didn't have to be such a smug arseling about me losing my only chance to feel protected when the Unclanned were roaming the countryside.

"By all means," I gritted out, gesturing for him to go on.

"What were you really doing in the tunnels that day?"

Now it was my turn to raise my eyebrows. "That's hardly a secret. Why would you waste your one question on something Iiro already told you?"

He scrutinized me before responding with another infuriating shrug. "Humor me."

"Apparently everything I do is already for little more than your humor," I muttered.

He cleared his throat pointedly, and I sighed. Leaning against the railing of the ring, I gave him the truth, the blandest possible version of it. I even threw in one of the casual, arrogant shrugs he was so fond of giving me.

"My sister was grieving." Which was a mild way to say *hadn't left her room in months*. "I thought a good bottle of vodka might lift her spirits."

It was an awkward subject to broach, but Evander didn't say any of the unhelpful sympathetic things people usually offered up.

In fact, he scoffed. Outright. "You agreed to answer honestly."

"I...did answer honestly," I hedged.

"Really?" His tone dripped with condescension. "So you couldn't have, I don't know, gotten her a different gift?"

"Vodka is her favorite drink," I countered.

"What about sending someone?" he pushed. "Did you really need to accompany your guard?"

I narrowed my eyes. "And ask someone else to take that risk on my behalf?"

"And all of the other times you were in the tunnel? Were those for your sister, too?" He arched a disbelieving eyebrow.

Iiro must have mentioned that when he was recounting my story.

"Not all of them." None of them, to be exact. We had gone twice to get a fancy jeweled egg for Davin's lady friends, and several more times for vodka.

Evander nodded like he heard the part I hadn't said aloud.

He stood up straighter. "So you were happy at the castle, before you left? Getting along with everyone?"

Memories of my last conversations with my family crept into my mind. *Damn it, Rowan. Can ye not go five minutes without doing somethin' stupid?*

My mother, chastising me for not caring who I married.

Avani, refusing to leave the bed she had shared with Mac.

"My family is very close." The words came out more quietly than I intended.

"That's not what I asked," he argued.

"Well." I glanced away. "I already answered your one question."

Evander made a humming sound in the back of his throat. "But not truthfully, so it doesn't count."

What are we, children?

"I think I would know that better than you do," I snapped.

"Would you?" He let out a low, disbelieving laugh. "Because I'm not sure you and the truth are always on the best of terms. *I* think the truth lies somewhere in why a Lochlannian princess who grew up with everything at her fingertips decided to risk her life, on multiple occasions, for little more than a whim."

He took a step toward me, and I took a step back in spite of myself, as much to escape him as the honesty he was hurling in my direction.

But he wasn't finished.

"So tell me, Lemmikki, were you running away from something, or were you just that *bored?*"

At the words *running away*, my lips parted. All this time, I had been worried that my family thought Davin and I were missing or dead. But what if they thought, as Evander did, that we had left on purpose?

That would break them. It would break Avani.

"I don't know, Lord *Aalio*," I said quietly. "Is there a reason you turned out as empty as you did or are you just that bored now?"

His expression shuttered. "The latter, I suppose. In any event, you can have your weapon on the road."

I blinked, nonplussed. "Even though I didn't win?"

"I never thought you were going to win, Princess. I would have been an idiot for arming you if you did." He turned to lead us out of the building, calling over his shoulder. "I just needed to know what you were capable of."

Why did I get the feeling he was talking about more than my sparring skills?

CHAPTER 23

T he next few days passed sluggishly while I waited for news from Evander, who always seemed to be out when I tried to sneak over to his room, making an excuse to my guards.

He kept his door locked, not that I checked or wondered vaguely if he had another captive he was squirreling away in there.

It would certainly go in line with his winning personality.

In the meantime, Taisiya delivered several bundles of fabric, thick wools and velvets in shades of navy, emerald, scarlet, and gold, most with fur lining. Dresses.

I had been expecting one since she measured me, but there were several here. She had me try them on, one by one, to make minor adjustments. I never imagined I would be excited about Socairan clothing, but here I was.

Though, these didn't look like any Socairan dresses I had seen.

There was a thick inner layer that served as the base. One was cream, one black, and the third the shade of tree bark. All three had full sleeves that buttoned at the wrist and two buttons at the back of the neck, easy to reach, that pulled the fabric together.

Then there were interchangeable outer pieces, some that were corseted in the front and others that tied just under my bust, but every one of them was wide, layered, and divided for riding. There were nightclothes as well, and two practical, warm pairs of boots.

I was no stranger to pretty things, and these weren't spectacular in and of themselves, but what they represented had my lips tilted up with excitement. The need for warmer dresses meant I was going outside, and the divided skirts meant I was riding somewhere.

Taisiya quietly shook her head at the clothes, enough to solidify my suspicions that they weren't conventional for Socair and that she hadn't been the one to pick them out.

Interesting.

When she took the clothes back to alter them, I grabbed a heavy fur blanket and retreated to my balcony to watch the snow fall.

The grounds were strangely beautiful blanketed in white, considering they were the source of my captivity. But it was too still. Too undisturbed. No one here threw snowballs or built forts or snowmen or made snow angels.

Not like in Lochlann, where even the guards had been known to join in our epic snow battles. Of course, Gwyn was always a hair too competitive, generally singling out Gallagher as her primary victim. And as the years went by, Avani and Mac usually wound up tackling one another in the snow and getting...distracted. Davin and I lived for those showdowns, though.

Melancholy settled over me like a dense cloud, remembering those times when we were all happy and the entire world felt like it was in front of us. Before death and imprisonment and grief crept into our lives and refused to leave.

Something I had contributed to.

At least if Evander was true to his word, I might be seeing Davin soon. *And Theo.*

I couldn't stay away from the balcony, even with the bittersweet memories it brought. The crisp, cold air was as close to freedom as I came these days.

So that was where Evander found me two days later. His arrival wasn't unexpected, since Taisiya had dressed me in one of the new outfits, lingering in the room longer than normal until Evander came to fetch me.

"Put these on," he ordered without preamble. "It's time to go." His voice was strangely devoid of inflection.

"To meet with Elk?" With *Theo*. "Is my guard coming?"

He narrowed his eyes but nodded, and I took the proffered bundle, which turned out to be a pair of supple leather gloves and a black velvet cloak with shining white fur lining...and wrapped in the middle, a delicate rapier.

I gasped, and he raised an eyebrow.

"I told you I would give you a weapon."

"You did," I allowed. "But I didn't actually believe you."

He sighed. "Of course you didn't."

A slow smile spread across my face. I threw on the cloak and gloves, and Taisiya surprised me by helping strap the sword belt around my waist. She was strangely contemplative as she did so, her brows furrowed in deep thought until she finally spoke up.

"My Lord, might I be of assistance on the road?"

I darted a glance from her to Evander. His eyes were narrowed as he studied her for all of a handful of seconds before he answered with a curt, "No."

Taisiya looked as if she wanted to argue, but nodded instead. Was she being protective of me, or merely preserving her idea of propriety?

"Of course, My Lord. I only wanted to assist the princess to make your journey easier."

"There is no need," he assured her. "She has promised to be a good little pet, haven't you, Lemmikki?"

I rolled my eyes at him and thanked Taisiya.

She left, and Evander turned to me. "So, in your...extensive studying of the weather, have you gathered anything about today's?"

My heart skipped a beat at his placating tone. If he didn't believe me about my reasoning, would he question me on the truth? Just because I had never come across a fae hunter didn't mean they didn't exist, and Fia was not one for exaggerations.

He didn't seem inclined to push, though, so I opened myself up to that awareness of the weather, pretending to study the clouds outside the window.

"It looks like we're in for more snow, but there are no...erm...signs of a storm."

He examined my features with some suspicion before nodding, leading us out to the hallway. It was hard to stay anxious about what he may or may not suspect in the excitement of leaving.

I bounded out the door and down the hall, in part because I couldn't wait to see Theo, but if I was being honest, I was also just desperate to leave the castle. The black walls of my room and the cold stone of the balcony had been slowly driving me mad.

Evander led the way downstairs, and we were nearly to the front door when a figure intercepted us. Lady Mairi.

"Where are you taking her?" Again, there was a quality to her voice I couldn't quite identify, something that felt more sinister this time than it had before. Directed at Evander? Or me?

"Father has given me the freedom to take my pet wherever I like," Evander answered.

A thinly veiled way of telling her it was none of her business.

After the time I had spent with Aleksander, I had my doubts as to whether or not that was true, but right now, I was firmly in the corner of whoever was taking me away from these four walls.

So, I averted my gaze when he breezed past her, shuffling to keep up with his quicker pace. Taras, Kirill, and a few others were already waiting on their mounts, with two more saddled and ready to go.

Logically, I knew that I was still a prisoner.

But for a moment, I could almost pretend that I wasn't a captive princess at the mercy of Socairan men in a ridiculous power struggle that I didn't begin to understand.

CHAPTER 24

The horses here were fascinating to watch in the snow.

They didn't seem to care if the roads were icy or dry, if the snow was high or melted all together. They flew through the frozen terrain with a speed that I could never have expected from our horses in Lochlann.

Though, in addition to their natural abilities, they were wearing chained shoes that helped give them traction.

They also took little heed from us and seemed to set their own pace, excited about the roads we were taking. Or maybe they were just as happy as I was to leave the estate and its quietly suffocating walls behind.

Icy winds rushed past us, and it didn't even bother me that my cheeks and nose were red with the cold, or that I would likely have to share a room with Evander on the road.

But as excited as I was, Evander was more closed off than ever. Each mile further from the estate we rode, he became more and more sullen. Did it have something to do with the encounter with Lady Mairi?

Before I could help myself, I asked a question that had been niggling at the back of my mind for some time.

"How long have Lady Mairi and your father been married?"

I could swear his shoulders tensed, but he stayed silent, not even looking in my direction. For a moment, I wondered if he had even heard me.

"Twenty years," he finally said.

Twenty years? The answer caught me by surprise.

"So, right after the war, then?"

"Yes," he answered flatly.

My mind reeled. After everything...after a war that the duke started because my Aunt Isla wouldn't marry him, he had turned around and just married someone else from Lochlann instead?

Was it always his back-up plan? Did he meet her because of the war? Take her captive? If he was satisfied with any marriage from Lochlann, then why did he wage a war?

Thousands of innocent people had died in that war. My grandparents had died in that war. Lochlann was ripped apart because of it, and I could still see the scars it left in my parents all these years later.

I opened my mouth to ask another question when Evander went even more rigid in his saddle.

"Be sure your hair is tucked inside your hood, Lemmikki. And stay quiet."

My heartbeat thundered in my ears, but I didn't question him. The usually unflappable man seemed very...flapped.

I pulled my hood lower and did my best to ensure there were no stray strands of red curls peeking out. Our horses slowed their pace as we crept two by two through a narrow ravine.

The thing that had spooked Evander finally came into view, and I held my breath. Just off the narrow road was a campsite hosting close to twenty people, including three small children.

I sank down like I could disappear into my cloak. The last thing we needed was to anger them further by allowing them to see how much of an enemy I truly was.

That or, perhaps, they would all be just as terrified of my hair and urge us to leave more quickly. Without knowing, it wasn't a risk I was willing to take. So, for once, I listened to Evander and did my best to be as invisible as possible.

Six large men moved slowly to stand in front of the others in an attempt to shield them from view. All but the children had the telltale *B* carved into their foreheads.

Besklanovvy.

Evander's men didn't draw their swords, they didn't spur their horses into a run, they simply stood still and waited to see what he would order.

A small head peeked out around one man's leg, and blue eyes

stared up at us with a mix of curiosity and fear. A woman at the campfire spoke to him in rushed, whispered tones in one of the Socairan dialects, and he ran over to her.

Still, no one else moved.

Fear coursed through my veins. Fear for what Evander and his men would do to these people, who didn't appear to be a danger to us.

Fear for myself if I was wrong about that.

My hand went to my sword, both for my own protection and because I knew beyond a shadow of a doubt that I could not sit here while Evander or the other Bear Clan soldiers cut down innocent children.

Even if I didn't have a real chance of stopping them.

After a tense silence, Evander raised one of his hands.

"We wish to pass peacefully." The deep timbre of his voice echoed through the ravine, and the Unclanned tensed at the broken silence.

The six men looked at each other, muttering something amongst themselves before looking back at Evander again.

"Go in peace," one of the men responded through a thick accent.

Evander nodded, grabbing the reins once more, his grip on the tether binding our horses even tighter than before. He gently nudged his horse, leading mine to move cautiously forward, and the other soldiers followed.

I held my breath until we were back on the main road, worried Evander might change his mind.

Even then, I was haunted by the sunken cheekbones and jutting collarbones of the children who had done nothing to deserve that life.

CHAPTER 25

Everyone stayed quiet after the encounter with the Unclanned, making our journey through the Socairan countryside far more ominous than it had felt before. By the time night fell, there hadn't been a village for hours, and there didn't appear to be one on the horizon.

I was both surprised and relieved when we finally got off the road, stopping at a farmhouse for the night.

"The *Dedushka* here lets us stay in the barn in exchange for a few chores around the house," Kirill explained.

"*Dedushka*?" I asked.

"Grandfather," he supplied.

"Taras and I will chop wood tonight," Evander cut in, earning a pointed glare from the slighter man.

"We'll get set up in the barn, then," Kirill responded.

We stabled the horses, two of the men I didn't recognize offering to take care of them. The other six men and I headed to the barn.

Which smelled...like a barn.

A few cows mooed from their stalls, but Kirill led us past them to a spacious loft with plenty of clean hay. The mood was still somber from our encounter with the Unclanned. That, combined with the uncertainty and anxiety of the upcoming meeting, lent an oppressive weight to the atmosphere.

I tried to shake the feeling away, but watching the men

quietly unpacking their bedrolls or rigidly sorting out meal rations for everyone didn't help.

"Does anyone have a deck of cards?" I asked the room.

Good ol' Kirill came through, handing one out.

"Not another game of war, Princess," Dmitriy said, earning a laugh from the others.

"No," I said, grinning at the small shift the mood had already taken. "I feel like it's safe to assume you all have flasks?"

"We are Socairan, aren't we?" Kirill asked, pulling his flask from his pack.

Others followed suit, looking more and more interested in what we were going to do.

"Perfect." I flounced cross-legged on the hay, settling my skirts around me, and gestured for them to sit as well. A couple of them did, while two held back, watching me shuffle warily.

I arranged the cards face down in a series of circles, each one larger than the last.

"What's the game then, Highness?" This quiet question from Igor, the one I had mocked for touching my underthings.

"It's called Kings and Arselings." Saying the words out loud nearly stole my breath.

I hadn't played this game since Mac died.

It was one of his favorites, one he had taught us all. His adopted father had been the leader of the rebellion before the war, and had always insisted on staying close to the people, so Mac tended to be a little more in touch with the villagers than we were.

Including their tavern games, and the bawdy songs that Davin was so fond of.

Blinking back the unexpected wave of emotion, I focused on the men around me, who were a fair bit taken aback by the name of the game.

Someone choked on a laugh, and another man snorted.

I explained the rules, which were fairly complex for a drinking game, but no less ridiculous.

Drinking games, I learned, were extremely common in Socair, though this one was new to them. However, they got the hang of the game quickly. So quickly, in fact, that it was me feeling a bit tipsy by the time someone pulled an ace--or an arseling, for the purposes of this game.

Then again, I was a great deal smaller than they were and we had eaten pretty sparse rations on the road. Regardless, I knew I wasn't the only one who felt relieved that the oppressive weight from earlier had lifted just a little.

I examined the ace, pretending to muse aloud. "Has anyone ever noticed how the Arseling card looks an awful lot like Lord Evander?"

The words slipped out before I could stop them, and I cringed, bracing myself to be chided by the men. It was one thing when I was going back and forth with the Bear lord, but it was another to speak about him so openly and disparagingly to his men when he wasn't around.

The answering loud guffaws of laughter told me I needn't have worried.

On my next turn, I pulled a king. "That means I get to make a rule." I announced. "And I declare that Dmitriy here can't stroke his mustache until he draws a six."

The man in question was stroking his burly mustache as I spoke, but he hastily put his hand back in his lap. Play continued to my left, with Kirill drawing a four just as Dmitriy reached up to stroke his mustache.

"Drink!" I ordered, pointing a finger at him.

He happily obliged, and the next man, Reino, picked a card that allowed him to create an edict.

"I say that Henrik has to touch the princess' hair."

Silence fell as they looked to see how I would take that. All but Henrik, who had gone white with horror. He made the Socairan sign for warding off evil, and I laughed out loud.

"Touch it or I'll rub it on your face," I threatened, waving my loose curls in his direction.

A throat cleared behind me, a sardonic voice ringing out, "Quite the interesting time you're having, Lemmikki."

I turned to face him, the room spinning just a bit in my periphery. "Oh, look, Lord Arseling himself has come to join us. All hail Lord Arseling," I announced in a louder voice, dramatically bowing from where I sat.

Another round of laughter broke out, a couple of the men echoing "Lord Arseling" and bowing as well, while Evander shook his head in exasperation.

Behind him, Taras gave a long-suffering sigh, mouthing what

I was certain was the word "chaos." He ordered us to pack up the game, much to our equal dismay, saying something about not being too hungover on the road tomorrow.

Well, I supposed that was valid, anyway.

We all climbed into our bedrolls. Evander, of course, settled himself only a few feet away from me, and I didn't miss that he had positioned himself between me and the exit.

He radiated...something. Anger? Displeasure? Hunger? I was so tired it was hard to tell, but for once, I actually didn't care. I was going to see Theo soon, and Davin.

And even surly Evander couldn't rob me of that feeling.

CHAPTER 26

True to Taras' prediction, some of the men were a bit worse for wear the next morning.

And by some of the men, I meant me.

Fortunately, it wasn't nearly as bad as I had experienced in the past, just a delicate stomach and slightly more sensitive ears. It was worth it, though, for the way the soldiers were visibly more comfortable around me.

Even Henrik no longer shot my crimson locks shifty sideways glances.

It was bittersweet, the realization that life in Elk wouldn't have been as bad as I had worried about it being. All at once, the reasons I had for refusing to marry Theo felt childish and insignificant. Surely, those men would have come around, too.

Would I still have the chance to find out?

Fortunately, the ride passed relatively quickly, with the men joking on breaks between hard stints of riding. Dmitriy even gave me a few herbs he carried with him to help with the nausea. Even better, there were no more incidents with the Unclanned.

There were also no more drinking games when we stopped at another barn for the night, mostly because we had to spend the evening under the watchful glare of Sir stick-in-the-mud and Lord *Aalio*.

The moon was high in the sky the next evening when we arrived at the cabin where we would spend the night before heading to the border.

Though, what Evander had called a cabin was nearly half the size of the castle at the estate. Only where that was gray stone and spires, this was all sweeping windows and dark wooden logs.

"The cabin is prepared, so everyone can care for their own mounts tonight," Taras announced.

Kirill offered to care for mine, but I shook my head.

"I can do it," I told him. "Unless, of course, Lord *Aalio* is worried I'll abscond into the frigid night."

Evander raised his eyebrows. "If you want to be eaten by wolves or a rabid bear, by all means."

"The only rabid bear I see here is you." I smiled sweetly.

He ignored me, dismounting and leading his horse into the stables. I followed, putting my horse in the stall next to his. Kirill led his to the stall on my other side.

My massive mount towered over me by more than a foot, but I was determined not to let that dissuade me.

We both stood, staring at one another with our heads cocked to the side. Even though I wasn't the sibling that could communicate with animals, I already knew he was judging me.

Maybe it was the slight gleam in his eye, or the fact that he huffed in disbelief as soon as he saw me, but either way, I took it as a challenge instead of accepting defeat this soon.

Grabbing the stool in the corner, I climbed on top of it and flipped the reins over his head to begin the work to remove his bridle. His ear twitched, and he huffed an approving breath when I slipped the bridle off.

I whispered to the gelding while I was working.

"You know, Mother makes us take care of our horses back home. Granted, Avani is a little better at it than the rest of us, but that's understandable."

The horse pawed at the ground, and I took it as a sign to stop talking. *Rude.* Once I slipped off his bridle, I replaced it with a halter and secured him to the stall.

A nicker sounded behind me, and I grinned.

"Told you I've done this before," I said, moving on to the saddle next.

When I was finished unstrapping the saddle, I barely caught the thing as it slid off, knocking me from the stool. The saddle easily weighed forty pounds and was far heavier than the ones we used back home.

Stumbling over to the side of the stall, I heaved it onto the divider. At least only Kirill was here to witness my struggle. Evander had apparently left, so I would be spared his mockery for a change.

I was especially grateful for that fact when I used a little too much momentum and it went sailing over the other side.

A grunt sounded in time with the thud, and I froze.

"Lemmikki," Evander's deep voice was strained. "There are more creative ways to kill a man. I'd prefer my legacy not end because you can't hold on to a saddle."

He got to his feet, holding onto said murderous saddle with annoyance plain in his features. He placed it back on the divider, this time a little more securely.

My hand flew to my mouth, and I leaned back into the horse, trying to stifle a laugh. *Apparently, Evander had not left.*

Clearing my throat, I attempted a serious tone.

"I don't know. Having contemplated your demise thoroughly, I'm convinced that you absolutely deserve a mediocre death."

Evander didn't deign to respond to that, only walked out muttering something that sounded suspiciously like, *Where are the rabid bears when you need one?*

CHAPTER 27

The cabin was warm, with a fire crackling in the hearth and the savory scent of stew wafting in from the kitchen, surprisingly inviting and comfortable for its size.

A couple emerged from around the corner, smiles on their faces until they saw me. They both shot my hair surprised glances, clearly wary of my presence.

"Princess Rowan, meet Nico and Riina." Evander introduced us.

He must have been forgoing calling me his pet for their sake, since it sure as stars wasn't for mine.

"It's lovely to meet you," I added.

Their postures relaxed, though their smiles didn't return. We made small talk, and they filled Evander in on how they and the cabin were doing and the things that needed repairing.

Apparently, they lived at the cabin year-round, tending to it when Evander was away and taking care of him and his men whenever they visited.

Riina showed me to the room that Evander had declared was mine for the duration. It wasn't nearly as grand as the set of rooms back at Bear Estate, but it was infinitely cozier. A fire lit up the hearth, lending its warmth to the entire space.

A double bed made of dark wood and covered in several thick blankets and fluffy pillows rested against the far wall, with two small nightstands on either side. On the floor in front of it was a massive wool rug that stretched nearly to the two armchairs resting in front of the fire.

An enormous mirror stretched across the wall, giving me an unwanted glimpse at myself. Days of riding hard and sleeping in a barn were visible from the bags under my eyes and the even wilder, more volatile turn my hair had taken.

No wonder Riina and Nico had looked at me that way. Even if they weren't superstitious, my hair was terrifying, and this small basin of water was doing nothing to alleviate that.

If I showed up to negotiations looking this way, Theo probably wouldn't even want to bargain for our betrothal. And I wouldn't blame him.

I needed a bath, but there didn't appear to be a tub in this room or the adjoining privy.

My gaze snagged on the view outside the floor to ceiling window, and I gasped.

Even in the moonlight, pale, snow-capped trees and mountains stretched out as far as the eye could see. A small hut with smoke billowing from a chimney sat on the edge of a vast frozen lake that sparkled like crystals.

Footprints led from the door over to a large, black hole carved into the ice...I froze.

Der'mo.

Of stars-damned course there was a sauna, and a freezing body of water to go along with it.

Though I suspected I knew the answer by now, I poked my head out of my room to call down to Riina.

"Is there a bathtub somewhere nearby?"

"No, milady," she responded, confirming what I had already begun to suspect. "Only a sauna outside. We are about to go, if you would like to join."

We, meaning Riina and her husband? All of the men?

Did it matter, when that was my only option to be clean?

I stood immobile, debating that for all of about thirty seconds. As nervous as I was to see Theo tomorrow, I didn't want to compound it by smelling like a barn and looking like a lunatic.

So, sauna, it was.

Mila had told me about men and women sauna-ing together, but I still couldn't wrap my head around that concept, especially without her here to make it feel more normal. Or at least to laugh at me for being nervous about walking into a room full of naked men.

Because anyone would be comfortable in that situation...

"Come," Riina called back over her shoulder, gesturing toward the entrance to the sauna.

Removing her towel, she hung it up on one of the posts just outside the door, standing naked as the full moon above us and waiting for me to do the same.

Taking a deep breath, I squared my shoulders and ripped my towel off, placing it next to hers. I felt even more naked than the lack of clothing accounted for, since I had removed my bracelet and the chain with my ring also.

When in Socair...

The cold air bit at my skin and I shivered until Riina opened the door to the sauna, allowing the steam and warm air to wash over us. I yanked the door shut behind me, cognizant of Mila's warnings about the steam escaping.

Fortunately, I was fast enough that the thick billowing cloud hadn't dissipated around the men sitting further in on the benches.

Just around those of us standing close to the door.

Between the steam and the wan shafts of moonlight leaking in through the single miniscule window, it was too dark for me to really see much of anything. Hopefully, that was true for everyone.

I forced myself to believe that so I didn't cringe and run to the nearest empty seat. Instead, I walked with false confidence, keeping a stately pace behind Riina as she led us to a space on one of the benches. Waves of intense heat threatened to bowl me over as we went.

A sharp intake of breath sounded over the low hum of conversation, and I froze. Of course, I realized the men were in here, in theory, but somehow, I hadn't quite put together that Evander would be with them. He seemed to keep himself separate so often.

"Welcome, Princess." The jovial voice sounded like Kirill. "Have an ale!" A shadowy outline thrust a wooden tankard a respectful distance away from me, and I greedily reached for the liquid courage.

"Thank you, Kirill," I said, before chugging a rather long swig.

I reminded myself that it wasn't strange that a naked man just handed me an ale in a room full of other naked people, myself included.

Mila said it was practical. We were all here to get clean. That was it. Even Riina, who I could already tell was far more reserved than Mila, seemed entirely unfazed by the situation. She happily drank her ale and conversed with the men around her, and Nico certainly didn't appear to be bothered by her nudity around the soldiers.

I wondered how Theo would react to this situation. Of course, if he were here, I would actually die before getting in this sauna. Maybe the Socairans saw nudity as platonic, but I had a hard time applying that to the two of us.

"Doesn't being in a sauna offend your Lochlannian scruples, Lemmikki?"

I flinched at the sound of Evander's voice, closer than I was comfortable with him being to my naked self.

"Not as much as being kidnapped does," I muttered.

A few smothered chuckles sounded around us, and I grinned victoriously into my ale, taking another drink as a reprieve from the oppressive heat. Beads of sweat poured down my skin in warm rivulets.

Evander sighed. "Indeed. I just know how delicate your sensibilities are."

That got much louder snickers, probably because of the blatant lie. I got the sense he didn't want me in the sauna, which, naturally, only made me determined to stay in longer.

Even if I did feel like I might pass out and die at any moment.

"I find your smug face far more offensive than a few pasty man-butts," I said with false cheer. "But thank you for being so considerate of my needs."

Even in the dark, I could practically make out the semi-amused expression he always got when he couldn't ruffle me.

"If there's a pasty butt in here, it doesn't belong to a Socairan," someone said after a moment--Dmitriy, possibly--and everyone, even Riina, howled with laughter. Even Evander's dark, surprised chuckle joined in, and I couldn't help but laugh along.

Even if it was an unwelcome confirmation that the men could see me and my translucent arse just fine in here.

CHAPTER 28

We had either been in the sauna for minutes or several days. I couldn't tell.

Sweat streamed down my neck and back, and I could feel my hair inflating by the second. If this was going to become a regular thing, I would need to start braiding the whole unruly mass back.

One of the many masochists in here threw another ladle-full of water onto the hot stones, and the new wave of heat hit my face, sending another bucketful of sweat dripping down my brow.

Only my pride kept me firmly planted in my seat.

This is it. This is how I go.

For all my taunting about Evander deserving a mediocre death, it will be me, prisoner and second-in-line to the throne of Lochlann who keels over from a building full of hot rocks.

"Come on, Princess. Let's get you to the ice." Kirill's voice floated over from the direction of where Evander's had been.

I wondered again about how much they could see in the dark room but decided it didn't matter when I desperately needed a break. I gratefully followed him out of the sauna and into the snowy world outside, taking a deep breath of the crisp air.

The others emerged behind us, everyone besides Evander and the caretakers. I lunged for my towel to cover myself.

"Everyone, line up!" Igor shouted, and the men lined up on either side of me and Kirill.

"You'll want to keep your towel dry, your Highness." Kirill said, pointing toward a large rock by the lake. "You can leave it there if you like, when you jump in the water."

Igor yelled for us to go, and soon there was a line of naked-man-butts running away from me. One by one, they leaped over a snowy mound before jumping straight into the icy water, emerging as quickly as they went in.

I squeezed my eyes shut, my legs refusing to move. I had done this before, in the river with Mila.

It would be the same, right?

"I thought you were tough, Princess!" Dmitriy cackled. "Prove it!"

When in Socair...

I repeated the line over and over again, as I took off running wildly through the snow. Even when the gaping maw in the ice made me want to run in the opposite direction, I didn't falter.

But I did scream the entire way down.

As soon as I went crashing under the icy water, my lungs seized, and my limbs locked up.

For a split second, I panicked, just before breaking the surface and taking a gasping breath of air once again. Despite the shock to my system, I felt more invigorated than I had in ages.

The men all cheered and laughed from the shore as they wrapped themselves in robes. Someone had even thoughtfully left one on the rock for me near my towel. I threw the robe around myself, grateful for the coverage while I twisted the towel around my hair.

Part of me debated going back into the sauna to warm up again, but my attention was yanked in another direction.

"Hey, Princess! Come judge our butts!"

A cacophony of laughter erupted from the men at the guard named Paavo's request.

Surely, they don't mean their actual arses.

A sigh of relief escaped me when I saw they were all still fully robed.

The nine men stood in a line in front of strange indents in the snow. Even grumpy ol' Taras was there, looking extremely uncertain about having been caught doing something even remotely fun.

When I neared the indents and registered what I was looking at, I howled with laughter.

There, in the snow, instead of the angels my sisters and I would make, were nine perfectly shaped indents of buttocks.

"You have to judge. Which is the superior arse?" Dmitriy asked, and I laughed again.

It felt almost wrong to be laughing so much when everything was a mess, and I missed Davin more than I could put into words. I could perfectly picture him fitting in here, merrily sinking his butt into the snow and teasing me for being the reluctant judge of this unusual contest.

Was he having fun in Elk, or just homesick and miserable? At least I would get to ask him tomorrow, and hopefully go with him after that.

If Evander actually let me go free...

I shook the feeling off. There was nothing I could do about it now.

Instead, I made a show of thoroughly studying each individual indent, finally determining that the second from the left would be the winner.

The men shoved Taras forward, hollering and laughing. I was surprised to see a smile crack his usually hardened features. Picking a small branch from a nearby pine tree, I handed it to him with a dip of my head.

"All hail the victor!"

Taras' mouth pinched shut, but amusement danced in his eyes.

Kirill let out a bark of laughter and clapped his friend on the back while I took my opportunity to head inside. My toes were sufficiently numb, and the rest of me was quickly getting there.

I spun around to head back to the cabin, but instead collided with a steaming, naked chest.

"Lemmikki," Evander grunted as he took a step back, adjusting the towel around his waist that I had apparently knocked loose.

"Lord *Aalio*," I greeted in return, averting my gaze.

"You know, I wasn't afraid of your hair before, but I'd be lying if I said I wasn't now, after seeing it in the sauna..." he commented.

147

I narrowed my eyes, looking up at him to see his attention was fixated on a frozen curl that had escaped my towel.

While his own towel was now securely wrapped around his waist, another was draped across his shoulders, hanging down his back. It was unexpectedly modest, unless he was merely cold, but that didn't seem likely.

His hair was slicked back, all but one small wavy strand that insisted on hanging over his brow. I twisted my wayward curl around my finger.

"Well, you should...see your hair. It's disgusting." Even I knew how ridiculous I sounded.

He didn't call me on it, though. At least, not verbally. He only arched a single, skeptical eyebrow.

Instead of waiting around for any more delightfully uncomfortable interactions, I practically sprinted around him.

Now I just had to get to my room without running into any more naked men. *Easier said than done at this cabin.*

CHAPTER 29

Once I was in my room, I changed into the nightclothes Taisiya had packed. It was one of the new sets, leggings and a long, loose shirt in the same soft, patterned fabric Evander's had been in.

I was curled up in the chair in front of the hearth, using the heat from the flames and a fresh towel to dry my hair, when a familiar indolent knock sounded at my door.

Knowing full well who it was, I was tempted to ignore it, but curiosity had me padding over to the door and wrenching it open.

Evander stood there, in his nightclothes also, which struck me as oddly amusing. Had he decided to come here at the last minute?

"We should talk about tomorrow," he said without preamble.

He moved past me into the room, and I didn't have it in me to argue propriety when that ship had sailed.

"By all means," I muttered, gesturing to the small chairs near the fire before sinking into the one I had been using before.

He sank into the chair but didn't speak right away, instead taking a long sip of the drink he had brought with him while he stared into the flames.

Something in his expression was less guarded than usual, making me wonder how many imbibements he had consumed before this one.

The thought made me long for a stiff drink as well.

"If you're going to bring a drink for yourself, the least you can do is share." I held my hand out expectantly.

He raised his eyebrows but surprisingly didn't argue, passing the glass my way.

My fingers bumped against his as I took it from him, sending an uncomfortable zap straight through to my spine. I pulled the glass away a little too quickly, only barely managing to avoid spilling it.

I took a healthy swig, noting that the vodka was even better on ice. Or perhaps this was just better vodka, period. The smuggler had clearly been holding out on us.

When I was finished, I set the glass on the small table between us, not wanting to risk contact with him again.

Evander's gaze followed the motion, his lips twisting wryly.

"Tomorrow?" I prodded him.

"Yes. Tomorrow. While you've been busy playing drinking games and judging arse contests, I've been trying to plan logistics--"

My jaw clenched, and I cut him off. "While I've been making the best of being your prisoner, you've been racking your brain to ensure there was no way for me to go free, you mean."

He pursed his lips. "Try to remember that you have the capacity to start a war tomorrow. It might sound appealing to have Korhonan fighting to take you back, but I assure you, that will not end well for any of us."

It was almost impressive how quickly fury overtook my curiosity about why he was here. War was the last thing I wanted, and it was insulting that he thought otherwise.

"I'm sorry, are you actually telling *me* not to start a war right now? Maybe you should have thought of that before you *claimed* me, Evander."

Heat flashed through his eyes. Anger. Probably. *Surely.*

"I did think about it, Princess," he snapped, his frustrated tone a far cry from its usual calm. "In fact, it's all I have the luxury of thinking about most days."

"And yet--"

"And yet," he interrupted me. "I saw one of my enemies about to ally with another of my much more powerful enemies, conveniently located on either side of my clan's territory, and I did what I had to do to stop that from happening."

My jaw dropped, my rage mingling with a degree of shock. "So all of this was to stop me from marrying Theo?"

His expression hardened, and he nodded.

I saw red. Everything he had put me through, all for something that might not have even happened?

"You manipulative bastard!" I bit out each word. "I knew you didn't give a single stars-damned hell about that blood debt." I was all but shouting now, something I almost never did.

Evander sat forward in his chair, his features tight with an ire he had no right to. "I'm the manipulative one? You're so busy concerning yourself with what I had to lose from that alliance, have you stopped to think about who stood to gain from it? And how very conveniently that worked out for them?

"Here's a tip, Princess. When you want to figure out who's manipulating a situation, take a step back and figure out who benefits from it most." He put a mocking finger to his lips. "I wonder who stands to benefit if Lochlann allies with Clan Elk just as they're preparing to make a bid for the throne."

I thought about what Iiro had said, how some thought the monarchy should come back together. He had implied that Elk had the best claim, with their mother being the cousin of the late queen. But he hadn't said anything about pursuing it...

"That doesn't even make sense," I fired back, without revealing that bit of information. "If that's what they wanted, Iiro could have broached that subject before dragging me to the Summit. Stars, he could have just reached out to my father and asked. Theo didn't even mention marriage until the last possible opportunity."

He shook his head as if to argue, but I cut him off.

"Has it occurred to you that you're just seeing what you want to see because you hate Theo and you hate Clan Elk and you hate Lochlann, and honestly, is there anything you don't hate or anyone you don't instantly disdain, or is that illustrious honor reserved solely for me and the people I love?"

He scoffed at that. "Yes, I'm sure the time you spent with Theodore gave you ample opportunity to explore his character."

This again. "Is everything you've done about getting back at him for whatever the hell is between you two? Or is this because you want the throne instead?"

I hadn't forgotten the rest of that conversation with Iiro,

what he said about Bear wanting a claim as well, based solely on the size of their territory and their brute strength.

He laughed, but there was no humor to it. "No one with any sense wants the storms-blasted Obsidian Throne."

I narrowed my eyes again, scrutinizing him under the lens of everything I knew. Did he really not want the throne? Was this just another manipulation?

Or was it more personal than that?

"So, everything you've done is just about keeping Elk from getting something you don't even want?"

He didn't deny it, and for some reason, that did me in. I rose from my chair, fuming all the way to the door.

"I should have known." I shook my head. "This is just like the day you used me against him in the sparring ring. You treat people like toys, like pawns...like *pets*." That last word was soaked with bitterness. "I guess you were up front about that, at least."

I opened the door, ushering him out. "You can go now. Rest assured *I* won't be starting any wars tomorrow. You've done that enough for the both of us."

To my surprise, he actually left without another word. Instead of feeling victorious for finally being the one to leave him speechless, though, I just felt drained.

And more than ever, I longed for the peace of Theo's arms.

CHAPTER 30

S leep was impossible.

I spent hours wondering if this would be my last night as Evander's prisoner, how Theo would react to seeing me tomorrow, and if I might be back to getting married again.

When I finally dragged myself out of bed, I was somewhere between still angry about the fight from the night before and strangely chagrined. I knew Evander didn't really hate everything, had seen it in the way he was with his men. I also knew that as far as captors went, he could have been far worse.

Of course, he could have just *not* been my captor at all.

Still, he had agreed to this meeting. Maybe that meant he felt guilty about taking me and, in spite of how he acted, that he was going to let me go. *And maybe my weather toe will sprout wings...*

Regardless, I couldn't shake the butterflies beating their enormous wings in my stomach at the thought of seeing Theo in a few short hours. I took extra care with my hair, braiding the top section back from my face and deliberately not thinking about all the times Avani and I had done that for one another, though her curls were looser and easier to work with than mine.

I paired the cream-colored underpiece with the emerald corseted skirts to bring out the green in my eyes. It still felt odd not to don a matching tiara on days like this, but at least I had Theo's bracelet to complete my outfit.

Finally, I headed downstairs to have breakfast with the others.

Much to my delight, it wasn't porridge that awaited me in the kitchen, but instead, I was lured in by the buttery smell of biscuits. My mood immediately lifted when Riina pulled a tray of them out of the oven, plopping them onto a serving plate next to some butter and honeycomb.

I hadn't seen biscuits since my breakfast with the duke, and that had hardly been an experience worth remembering. At least I could enjoy them this time.

My mouth watered, the anxiety of the day somehow diminishing in the light of this unexpected surprise.

Dmitriy and Henrick groaned over the dish of butter, both of them looking as if they had found their one true love.

"Should we give you three a moment?" I teased, eliciting a laugh from the room.

"If you don't mind," Dmitriy said, not even bothering to look up from the butter dish.

Henrick blushed, and the reddening of his cheeks reminded me so much of Theo it hurt.

"It's been a long time since we've had butter," he explained, and whatever he saw in my expression had him expounding. "Milk can be put to better use if it's made into cheese. It lasts longer that way, and can be eaten on its own."

Understanding dawned on me.

I hadn't thought about that before. How much of a luxury butter could be. All at once, I felt extremely fortunate for the life I lived in Lochlann, though it was tinged with the bitter edge of guilt.

"Forgive my asking, but then why make vodka? Wouldn't the potatoes go further in a meal?"

A few chuckles sounded around the room, but it was Nico who answered me.

"Before trade ended, it was our biggest export. No one needs to make it anymore. It's a staple in nearly every cellar you come across."

That made me feel better about the vodka I had purchased, but only barely. It was my parents' refusal to trade that had led to the food shortages here. Even if it had been justified after the war, it was no easier to see the results of that decision.

Riina interrupted my thoughts by handing me a plate with

eggs, some sort of fried, gamey meat and one of the freshly baked bundles of perfection.

With my newfound knowledge about the sanctity of butter, I was careful not to use too much, saving the rest for the men. Instead of moving to the table with the others, I ate my meal at the counter.

It was partly because I was too anxious to sit, but mostly because the only open seat at the table was next to Evander.

While things were more relaxed here than they were at the estate, there still seemed to be an order to it all, a subdued nature surrounding meals that was probably something my mother only dreamed about for her uncivilized children.

I expected Evander to meet my eyes with his usual casual, unaffected air, but he avoided my gaze altogether. Maybe he was still upset?

Or could he possibly feel a hint of remorse?

When I finished my biscuit, I looked around hopefully for another one, but they had all been taken. It wasn't surprising, since there was a horde of hungry soldiers, and food was hard to come by.

I barely had a moment to be disappointed at the end of the biscuits when a plate slid into my field of vision. Evander's plate, with one warm, buttery biscuit sitting perfectly intact on it.

He didn't meet my eyes, didn't even turn his head as he walked by, but I took the biscuit for what it was.

A truce. For now.

CHAPTER 31

For the first time since he had taken me, Evander insisted we share a horse on the way to the negotiations. Then subsequently spent the next few hours complaining about it.

"Your cursed hair is in my face again."

"That means it's marking you as a victim. Beware."

With an irritable huff, he tucked the wayward strands back under my hood.

"You wouldn't have to worry about this if you hadn't insisted we share a horse." I was uncomfortably aware of every point of contact between us.

Though it was warmer this way, I would have preferred the distance. Still, at least we were back to some version of our usual level of animosity rather than the outright hostility from last night.

"No," he muttered. "I just would have had to worry about Elk taking you the second we got there."

"And the reason you took my sword after promising to arm me on this trip?" I asked, still bitter that he made me leave it behind.

"I can't very well have my prisoner showing up to negotiations armed." Evander tsked.

There was no more talking as we drew closer. But I didn't care, I could barely keep my seat on the horse as we approached, straining up in the saddle to try to see further. Evander groaned and tensed behind me, but I ignored him.

It was difficult to see the camp through the trees, but tendrils of smoke wafting through the air told me we were close.

A thrill ran through me when I made out the first tent, a large swath of fabric suspended between the trees.

A little further and I could make out several smaller tents, hung in a similar fashion. Then the sound of voices reached us, and I already recognized at least one of them.

As we neared, achingly familiar figures emerged from the larger tent, and my heart leapt to my throat. The horse hadn't even pulled to a stop when I went to catapult off of it, but Evander stopped me with a solid arm.

"Wait," he growled in my ear, keeping his arm firmly clamped around me while nodding toward Dmitriy and Taras.

They dismounted, going to exchange words I couldn't hear with the other guards before disappearing into the main tent. My gaze flitted from Davin, whose face was carefully blank, though his fists were clenched, and Theo, who stared with open hostility at Evander's arm.

After an eternity, the guards emerged once more, giving Evander a nod.

When he finally gave me the go ahead, I jumped off the horse, taking off at a sprint. Davin surged forward to meet me halfway, pulling me into an enormous hug and spinning me around. I threw my arms around him, barely cognizant of the people around us.

My cousin. My best friend. The closest thing I had to home on this side of the world. His black hair was longer than usual, and he had several days' worth of beard, but he was still unmistakably one of my favorite people in the entire world.

I hadn't even let myself dwell on the possibility that something had happened to him, but seeing him here, alive and well, made me realize that somewhere in the back of my mind I had doubted I ever would again.

Just when I wondered if I would lose my composure in front of a few dozen guards and Lord Arseling, Davin set me back on my feet.

"Well. It seems you've gotten yourself in quite the pickle this time, Row," he joked.

I chuckled, but before I could respond, my gaze landed on Theo. He was standing only a few feet away, looking at me with an inscrutable expression in his hazel eyes.

He was even more perfect than I remembered, with his square jaw and broad shoulders and soft, kissable lips. I made a hesitant move toward him, and he closed the distance between us, wrapping his arms solidly around me.

Somehow, I had forgotten how warm and comforting Theo's arms were. He enveloped me inside them like he could shield me from Evander, from this situation, from the entire world, and I greedily soaked it up.

His heartbeat was steady against my ear, and I buried my face in his chest, happy to hide from reality until the sardonic clearing of a throat interrupted us.

"You're awfully cozy with my pet, Korhonan, and you know I don't like to share."

Theo stiffened, but it was Davin who spoke.

"And you're awfully cocky for someone who stole the Lochlannian King's favorite daughter." His tone almost sounded joking, as it had with me, but there was the barest edge of steel underneath that reminded me Davin was heir to the most powerful holdings in all of Lochlann, even if he generally let people forget it.

Still, I had to bite back a laugh. *My father's favorite?* More like his problem child, but I wasn't going to undermine my cousin's threat by arguing.

Davin went on. "Either you're arrogant enough to believe you can withstand a war against our people even when the first one failed, or you're too stupid to realize it will come to that. So, which is it? Arrogant, or stupid?"

"Davin," I chided, easing out of Theo's arms.

Usually, my cousin was the one who kept his head, but I got the feeling he was intentionally needling at Evander to gauge his reaction...which was substantially less murderous than I expected it to be.

If anything, suspicion coated the lines of his face. "This must be the eunuch guard you've told me so much about."

Davin blinked, but he didn't skip a beat or even look to me for an explanation.

"Mhmm," he agreed, nodding slowly. "That is me. A...big ol' eunuch."

I pinched my mouth shut and turned my head subtly away to keep from laughing. Theo did a valiant job of keeping a straight face, though his eyes widened briefly. Fortunately, another familiar voice broke in before we lost it all together.

"Welcome Princess Rowan." Sir Arès, Mila's father and Duke of Lynx, had agreed to mediate, something I was sure she had a hand in. "Lord Stenvall. We should be on with negotiations sooner than later. Daylight is escaping us."

We headed to the tent, but not before I heard Evander's growl sound behind me.

"My, my, Lemmikki. It would seem you've been keeping secrets of your own."

There were furs spread out on the ground of the tent around a small fire. Everyone took their seat, and it finally hit me that someone crucial was missing.

"Did Iiro not come?" I asked no one in particular.

There was an uncomfortable silence until Evander spoke up. "You had your terms, and I had mine."

I made a sound in the back of my throat. "I just hadn't realized your terms were quite so petty."

Davin choked on a laugh, and Arès shot me a paternal look to be quiet. I obliged him, settling on the ground between Theo and Davin. Arès gave a brief opening spiel about how there would be no weapons or threats tolerated. This would be a peaceful negotiation, which he would arbitrate.

"Clan Elk, please state your desired terms."

"Clan Elk desires to purchase the blood debt of Princess Rowan." Theo went on to give a fairly exorbitant sum, along with a list of goods and even services Elk was willing to provide.

While he was speaking, he fiddled with the charm on my bracelet, his fingers grazing the inside of my wrist, as if to remind us both that there was still hope for us. Warmth spread from my wrist to encompass my entire body, chasing away the cold of the day.

It baffled me that Iiro would go to those lengths for me, but

Davin's face made me wonder if he hadn't maneuvered that, negotiating recompense from Lochlann on his parents' behalf.

It would certainly be cheaper than war, I supposed.

Evander looked at me, then Theo before answering. "A generous offer. Or, it would be, if you weren't planning to ally with the princess and vie for the throne."

Arés' eyes widened slightly.

Evander put a mocking finger to his lips like he was contemplating. "So I think I'll keep her, Korhonan."

Theo's face was like a thundercloud, but he kept his composure. "At the Summit, you said you didn't want a war. What exactly do you think is going to happen when Lochlann finds out you have her?"

Evander laughed darkly. "I don't want a war, but I'd sooner fight one on my own behalf than yours, which, by the way, were my only two options when you and brother dearest decided to cart the storms-blasted princess off to a Summit. Tell me, what did you think was going to happen when you locked her in a dungeon and then coerced her into marriage?" His tone was deceptively calm, but a tempest brewed in his eyes.

"It wasn't like that," Theo growled.

"It doesn't matter," Evander snapped back, losing a bit of that calm. "How do you think they would have seen it when they found out? I might have taken her as my prisoner, but at least I had the decency to keep my hands off her."

"That's not what it looked like to me," Theo spat, his body tensing as he stared at Evander.

I stiffened. "He hasn't *touched* me."

Theo looked at me apologetically, taking a deep breath before continuing. "Regardless, it's not like we had a choice when she came stumbling into our territory."

Evander and Davin both scoffed in disbelief, and I shot my cousin a warning glance.

"No choice?" Evander asked, shaking his head. "You couldn't have hidden her? Storms, you couldn't have pretended she came intentionally for a potential alliance and then sent her home when the 'negotiations failed'? You couldn't have done *literally anything* but put her life in the hands of a Summit and create a political nightmare for us all?"

Theo hesitated for a fraction of a moment, long enough for me to consider Evander's words as well.

"Word would have gotten out," Theo finally said.

That was valid. I knew enough about court life to know they would never have been able to keep it a secret. That was why I hadn't fought harder to begin with, and the way the gossip had spread through the guards at the Summit only drove that point home.

"And when it did," Theo went on. "What would Clan Bear have done?"

Evander's closed off expression was evidence enough. He knew Theo had a point, even if he was unwilling to outwardly acknowledge it.

"Exactly," Theo responded. "You would have used it as an opportunity to undermine and attack us. It's always the same with you, Evander. You put people in impossible situations, then judge them for making the only choice they can."

Evander's face paled, his features going tight with fury and maybe even shock.

"So that's how you've justified it to yourself all these years? Whatever helps you sleep at night, old friend." Bitterness coated his words. "The fact remains that even if part of what you say is true, every asinine decision you and your brother made would have led us directly to war with Lochlann, a war that Clan Bear would be situated directly in the middle of. And just like back then, you're lying to yourself now if you think Iiro didn't plot any of this."

His words hung in the air for a moment before Theo let out a long breath.

"Not everyone is as underhanded as you are, Evander."

"Is that so?" In spite of his outburst a moment ago, Evander's tone was casual now, his face a mask of deadly calm. His churning gray eyes were the only sign that the rest was a ruse.

"I might even believe you, except..." Evander looked pointedly at Davin. "Except that Clan Elk has a history of lying for their own gain."

My heartbeat thundered in my ears, and I tried to quell my panic. That's what his *secret* comment was referring to. I would have guessed that we hadn't sold the eunuch thing well enough, but he seemed to know more than that.

It wasn't that I was scared of Evander, exactly, but he had already proven that he had a ruthless nature and wasn't above using someone for his ends. I didn't want Davin to become the next pawn in his games, not when my cousin was safe where he was, and Theo had promised me he would stay that way.

I risked a glance at Arès, who was glancing between the two men with skepticism. Instead of commenting, though, he merely held out a hand.

"Enough. We are not here to hash out every past wrong, only to focus on a solution for this single situation. Clan Bear, do you have a counterproposal?"

Evander's gaze went to where Theo's fingers were still brushing against my wrist. "The only way Princess Rowan is going back to Clan Elk is if she agrees never to marry into it."

Theo opened his mouth to respond, but Arés held up a hand.

"Lord Stenvall has stated his terms. It is my advice that you take them under consideration before making a reply. You are the heir and last in your family line. I am certain your brother would not want this decision to be taken lightly."

Theo nodded, his knuckles white, his muscles straining under the weight of his anger.

"Tensions are obviously high," Arès added. "I think it's time we take a break. It's safe to say each clan knows what the other wants. We will reconvene in the morning to see if we might reach a compromise." He said the last part as if he were dubious about it.

Me, too, Arès. Me, too.

CHAPTER 32

As much as I hated to give up what little time I had with Theo and Davin, it was more important to figure out a way out of this mess. With a rushed explanation, I followed Evander as he stalked away from the main tent to where a few of his guards were setting up a smaller one.

"You have got to be kidding me," I hissed. "I told you last night, you do not get to treat me like your puppet and you sure as stars don't get to tell me who I can marry."

"Actually, Lemmikki, I do," Evander stopped, but didn't turn around. "And rest assured that when my clan's safety hangs in the balance, I will."

"You know that my family will come for me," I said, my tone bordering on pleading. "Why trade the threat of war for the guarantee of one? We could have worked out a treaty."

"There was no time, and once again, you fail to see the bigger picture." He shook his head. "There would have been war either way. Just the idea that Lochlann is allied with Elk would have been enough for most of the other clans to cave, then the upstanding Iiro would be sitting on the Obsidian Throne. And my father would never let that stand."

"Your father or you?" It was hard to picture the man I ate breakfast with leading a war at this point. "Is this all about power?"

"Is that what you believe?" He finally turned to look at me, his gray eyes probing mine.

Even as I said it, the words rang false. Evander had made it clear that he was interested in protecting his clan, but the kind of power and responsibility that came with ruling an entire kingdom was a different sort of beast. In spite of Iiro's claim, it wasn't one that I could see Evander grasping for.

Aleksander, perhaps. Back when he had control over his mind...

When I didn't answer, he shook his head. "Think what you will, Lemmikki, but I don't trust Iiro further than *you* could throw him, and I won't risk my clan on his dubious word."

"What about my word?" The words were out of my mouth before I could stop them.

He raised his eyebrows, and I took it as encouragement to go on.

"What if I agreed to wait to marry Theo until we could speak to my father? No one wants another war, least of all, Lochlann." As I spoke the words, I wondered at how true they were.

Was Evander right? Hadn't Iiro said he believed in Elk's claim to the throne, but that Bear opposed it? He had seemed to want to solve things diplomatically, and Theo had said more than once that they wanted to avoid a war.

Evander looked contemplative, but then he fixed me with a calculating gaze.

"You talk about trust, Lemmikki, but I'm not the one who has been lying."

I chewed on the inside of my lip, knowing he was talking about Davin and not wanting to give away more than he had figured out.

"Davin is a eunuch guard, is he?" he prodded when I didn't respond.

"All right." I spread my hands out. "You got me. Davin is...intact, as far as I know."

"Lemmikki." He said the word like a warning, leveling a look at me.

I took a breath, bracing myself as I exhaled my next words. "He's my cousin."

"Hmm?" He pretended not to hear me, and I scowled.

"He's my cousin!"

"You don't say." He was using his condescending arse voice now.

I narrowed my eyes at him. "How did you know?"

"Other than the fact that he speaks like a noble and shares a name with your uncle's only son?"

"Davin is a very common name--"

"Indeed." He said the word too agreeably, and I knew a rebuttal was coming. "And are there many Davins who you travel alone with? Who you openly embrace in front of your betrothed?" Evander spoke slowly, ticking the points off on his fingers.

I was already opening my mouth to argue when he laid down his final reason.

"And who happen to have lips shaped exactly like yours?"

I clamped my mouth shut. *What a ridiculous, inconsequential thing to give us away.* No one but our parents had ever even noticed the subtle similarity, the unremarkable lips that were slightly bowed on top and fuller on the bottom, just like Da's and Uncle Oli's.

"You know," he continued when I didn't respond. "I'm less offended than I am impressed. I didn't know you had that kind of conniving in you, though I did wonder what compelled someone as contrary as you are to bother to stand in front of the Summit and even keep your mouth shut for as long as you did. If they were holding your cousin over your head, however..."

I didn't deny it, and he scoffed. "Iiro is even better than I gave him credit for. And these are the people you want to go back to? Are you certain? The same ones who wanted you to be, what was it Iiro said, *amicable and accommodating?*"

I had nearly forgotten that Iiro said that in front of Evander at one of the many horrid dances.

I tilted my head, peering at him with mock confusion. "As opposed to the one who took away my future, my only family here, my fiancé, and claimed me as his pet? Yes, I'm quite certain."

Evander only shrugged, though the motion was strained. "If you say so, Lemmikki."

Shaking my head, I stalked back into the negotiations tent and planted my forehead firmly against Theo's chest.

He wrapped his arms around me, leaning down to kiss the top of my head.

"Tell me now, Rowan." He took a deep breath through his nose, his entire body rigid with whatever was bothering him. "Are you being treated--?"

I pulled back abruptly.

"He isn't hurting me, Theo." I made sure to meet his gaze. "I promise. He wouldn't do that."

His eyes narrowed slightly in what I could only assume was suspicion.

"What is it between you two?" I asked quietly.

He looked between me and Davin with a sigh. "It's...complicated. He wanted me to keep a secret from Iiro, and that wasn't something I could do."

Knowing Theo's loyalty to his brother, I wasn't surprised that he wouldn't keep a secret from him, but I was a bit taken aback that something like that had led to the level of animosity they had now.

Then again, he had said it was complicated, and now was clearly not the time or place for that story. A beat of silence went by before my cousin spoke up.

"Well, at least we can all agree that this is going splendidly." Davin's sarcastic tone made me smile, in spite of myself.

"Absolutely. I couldn't imagine a more agreeable negotiation," I said, turning to face him.

"I daresay this might even be the beginning of a true friendship betwixt the clans." He nodded enthusiastically. "They should honestly be thanking us."

"Indeed. Indeed." I laughed.

Theo smiled, and I gave his bicep a little squeeze.

"Well, I'll be damned." Davin raised his eyebrows. "I wasn't sure there was a personality underneath all that muscle, Theodore. It's nice to see that my cousin brings out something other than the brooding in you."

Theo let out a long sigh before turning to me. "I'll give you a moment with Davin while I take care of a few things."

"All right." I nodded, dropping my hand from his arm as he left the tent. "I'll come find you later."

Davin groaned as soon as he left. "Don't make me go back with him, Row. He's so...moral and *noble* all the time. It's boring."

"Sorry, Cousin, but you have to." I smiled wanly.

Davin's usually solidly carefree mask slipped to reveal concern, but I cut him off before he could argue with me.

"You are free while you are in Elk, Davin. And you're safe. I can't risk you coming with me, if Iiro would even agree to it."

"Before, when you said he wasn't hurting you..." He scrutinized my features. "You have heard the rumors, haven't you? The guards say he's slaughtered entire villages at his father's whims."

I swallowed, in spite of myself. Evander hadn't hurt me, and didn't seem inclined to, but I would be lying if I pretended not to notice the brutality behind his eyes, the way he could bring it out and put it away at will.

"All the more reason for you to stay where you are," I finally said. "At least, for now. We only have four more months, and that's if no one gets through the rubble first."

He shot me a doubtful look. "Even if they knew we were here, how long would it take to dig through that? That tunnel was demolished." He leaned in, pitching his voice lower. "Which is odd, don't you think? If it had been the storm, wouldn't just a few rocks have tumbled in?"

"Maybe..." I tried to follow his line of reasoning.

"How bad was the storm, even? Bad enough to shake a mountain?"

I thought back to that day, the pressure I had felt, the awareness of the raging winds outside. They had been tame compared to the one that hit us on the road to the Summit.

"No," I shook my head. "Not bad enough for that. So what? You think someone shut us in there on purpose?"

It was dangerously close to what Evander had implied.

"Not someone..." He glanced significantly outside the tent, and I bristled in spite of myself.

"You can't think Theo did this," I whispered.

"Of course not," he said dismissively. "The man is obnoxiously upstanding and, whatever his faults, genuinely seems to care for you. His brother, on the other hand..."

I shook my head in disbelief. "You honestly think he shut us in there and just, what, hoped we didn't die?"

"No," my cousin countered. "I think he shut us in there and carefully left the supplies we assumed were for the smugglers.

Did you know that up until three months ago, they weren't even patrolling that tunnel?"

A sick feeling churned in my stomach. "How do you know that?"

"Like I said, guards talk."

I opened my mouth to respond when an imperious voice cut through the tent cloth. "Lemmikki?"

I let out a long, frustrated sigh, but headed toward the outside of the tent.

"What does that even mean?" Davin muttered.

"It means...pet." I risked a glance at his face.

His features were drawn tightly, his cobalt eyes flat in a rare show of fury. "We're getting out of this stars-forsaken kingdom if it's the last thing I do."

CHAPTER 33

E vander insisted I stay near him for the duration of the evening. Now that we were at the negotiations, he reminded me more of the man I had met at the Summit. Calm and condescending as always, but also endlessly calculating.

It was clear that he wanted everyone here to remember that I was his property.

We eventually made our way to the campfire, lulled by the smell of roasting meats over the fire. A freshly slaughtered boar was lying nearby, as well as a bucket of fish, covered in snow and ice.

I took one of the skewers with the boar meat and was on my way to sit by Theo when Evander's commanding tone rang out once more.

"Lemmikki."

I gritted my teeth, spinning around to face him.

"What?" I asked sharply.

He raised his eyebrows, giving me a look to remind me he held the power to agree to these negotiations or abandon them.

"Yes, Lord Evander?" I amended, my tone dripping with honey. "Is there something I can do for you?"

"You can fetch me a skewer and take a seat." He gestured to the space on the log next to him, and a muscle ticked in my jaw.

Theo and Davin wore twin expressions of indignation, and

177

even a few of my friends among Evander's guard were struggling to conceal the disapproval in their eyes.

But I could play his games for now, if there was even a chance of him letting me go tomorrow.

Arès himself handed me a skewer, also shooting Evander an exasperated look. "Like a child with a toy, that one," he muttered under his breath.

I snorted, and he smiled openly.

"You know, I thought Mila had a knack for getting into trouble, but I do believe you rival her."

"One does what one can," I said wryly, making my way back to Evander.

I thrust his skewer at him and sank onto the log beside him. Davin wasted no time coming to sit next to me, practically scowling at Evander the entire time. Theo took a seat on the log to Davin's left, though he looked decidedly irritable about it.

I examined the meat on my skewer, then looked over at Theo. "So, is there a special fork for this? Or is it okay to just sort of...go for it?"

He flashed me a dazzlingly handsome smile. "No. No forks for these. But I'm sure you'll find your own way to do it, regardless."

I laughed then, and Evander stiffened beside me.

"I'm sure I will," I replied, ignoring the obnoxious man to my right.

Theo went back to his food, and I couldn't help but watch him. It was like finally exhaling after holding my breath for too long, like putting on a cloak when I hadn't even realized how cold it was outside. Unexpected warmth and comfort from the elements around us.

I had missed him, and it had been easier not to dwell on how much until he was here again. My smile faded when I realized that what I suspected about his brother would hurt him deeply.

Davin and I exchanged a look, but said nothing.

After a few minutes of mostly quiet eating, listening to the hum of conversation around us, Evander upended the wooden mug in his hand to show that he was out of medovukha. He opened his mouth, likely to tell me to refill it, and I twisted to glare at him.

I have played your games already today, I tried to convey in that single look.

He held my gaze in a silent contest of wills.

When I quirked an eyebrow, he closed his mouth and shrugged. The barest edge of his lips tugged up before he rose to refill the drink himself.

"I don't like the way he treats you." Theo leaned over and spoke in a low tone once Evander was out of earshot. "Like he owns you."

"Well, technically..." Davin chimed in. "Thanks to your little trip to the Summit, he sort of does." He gave him a derisive salute before getting up to get more food.

I bit back a laugh at Theo's long-suffering expression as he moved over to occupy Davin's vacant seat. He reached out to tuck a strand of hair behind my ear, and I melted into his touch, heat flooding through me at the contact.

His hand trailed down my shoulder, to my wrist and the bracelet resting there.

"Do you remember why I gave this to you?" he asked in a low voice.

"Hmm." I pretended to think. "Something about rare, complex, difficult to keep alive."

He shot me a crooked grin. "And all of those things are still true. But you forgot beautiful."

"You never said beautiful." I raised my eyebrows for emphasis.

"Well, I was definitely thinking it. I'm thinking it now, too." The firelight danced in Theo's eyes as he looked into mine.

For a moment, everyone else faded away and it was just the two of us. It took everything in me not to lean in and kiss him right then.

Then I felt the force of Evander's glare before I even saw it, his gray eyes alit with something like a warning. Gritting my teeth, I whispered to Theo.

"Go to bed early tonight. I'll come to your tent."

"Rowan, I want to see you, but I don't want you to put yourself in dan--"

"I won't. I'll be fine," I assured him.

He reluctantly nodded as Evander came back, effectively

throwing a bucket of cold water over whatever moment we had found ourselves in.

Aalio.

We all stayed by the fire after dinner, and tensions began to lessen between the clans. Though they still sat on opposite sides of the fire, several of the Elk and Bear guards were talking and laughing and telling stories.

Some of Evander's guards chimed in to ask questions, mostly Kirill, and a few of Theo's guards seemed to have gotten chummy with Davin. Even Arès joined in to say a few things about Mila, and for a minute, I could almost forget we were all here to decide whether or not I would still be a prisoner tomorrow.

Though he said little, Evander's presence next to me was almost as loud as the rest of the camp.

There was a deceptively casual expression in place of the one he had let slip earlier, but he was crackling with the force of his ire. I was in no mood for his raised tension, not with everything I had at stake here.

"Will you be stopping on your way back to the estate to attend to *your* feminine needs, or is this mood a coincidence?" I mumbled out of the side of my mouth.

Apparently, it was louder than I thought, because Kirill choked on a laugh, but Evander just shook his head mutely, an incredulous expression breaking through his aloof facade.

After that, I did my best to ignore him. One by one, the men trickled to bed, including Theo, who came over to press a kiss to my forehead, much to the delight of Evander.

Eventually, only four of us remained.

"Princess Rowan, where might you be staying tonight?" Davin asked like it had just occurred to him, but something in his expression made me think he had been waiting to address it.

I took a bolstering breath. "In the tent with Evander, if I had to surmise a guess."

I looked at the man in question for confirmation, and Evander gave a single curt nod.

"Hmm. Is that so?" Davin's false congenial expression met

Evander's ever composed one. "I believe I'll sleep there as well, then, as two guards are certainly better than one, when your safety is in peril. Wouldn't you agree, Lord Evander?"

Evander raised a sardonic eyebrow. "Indeed, Eunuch Guard Davin."

There was a stilted pause. I still hadn't explained the lie to Davin, or that Evander actually knew the truth about who he was. Though, judging by the look on my cousin's face, he had figured it out.

I took a sip of my medovukha to hide my smirk.

"We generally just go by guard, but never let it be said that I'm not adaptable," Davin spread his hands magnanimously. "If this is the custom in Bear, I suppose I should revise my address for you to Arseling Lord Evander."

It had been a mistake taking a sip of my drink. I barely leaned forward in time to spew the entire mouthful out on the ground instead of in my cousin's face, choking with the force of my laughter.

"Incidentally," I said between gasping for breath, "that *is* what he prefers to be called."

Kirill hid his laugh under the guise of a cough, and even Evander seemed to struggle to stay so serious.

"Well, if it hadn't been evident before..." he muttered, clearly referring to the fact that we were cousins. "Sleep where you will, *Guard* Davin."

Victory.

I grinned at Davin, relishing in this small moment where the weight of this situation didn't feel quite so heavy with my best friend by my side.

CHAPTER 34

Davin and I headed to the tent a short while later, and Evander actually seemed inclined to give us twelve whole minutes to ourselves before following.

"Dare I ask why you're telling people I'm a eunuch?" Davin looked more amused than anything.

"It was better than saying you were my cousin?" I shrugged.

"Was it, though?" He tilted his head thoughtfully.

"Well, it was pointless, anyway. Evander knows now."

Davin made a thoughtful sound in the back of his throat, laying out his bedroll in the middle of the tent.

"So...do you two share sleeping quarters often?" The complete lack of judgment in his tone was one of the many, many reasons I loved my cousin.

"No," I sighed. "Not often."

He pursed his lips, nodding. "Something you'd like to share, Row?"

"That would be another no."

"All right, then. Would shared sleeping quarters also have something to do with how you became engaged to *Theodope*? Because you know, that's really not a reason to get married."

I laughed out loud at the ridiculous name. "You *would* say that, but still no. I'll admit, it started as a necessity," I paused, realizing what that likely meant if Iiro had been plotting this entire thing.

Did it change anything? My feelings for Theo were the same,

but would I have considered marrying him if I hadn't been forced into it, staying here in Socair amongst people who hated me, cut off from my family for half the year?

"But then?" Davin prodded, laying back on his blankets.

"But then," I thought back, remembering the way he had begrudgingly softened over time. How he had held my hand every night until I fell asleep, fought for me at the Summit. "But then I realized I like him. A lot." I leveled a look at Davin. "The question is, why don't you?"

"I don't *dislike* him." He shrugged. "It's his brother I don't like."

A common sentiment, it seemed. Though Iiro hadn't been all bad in the end, I knew he loved his brother and his wife.

"Stars," Davin interrupted my line of thought, running a hand through his hair. "I just don't like anything about this place. The food or the weather or the strangely proper women."

I laughed again. "Oh, I see what this is about. Did your lady friend have enough of you?"

Davin put a hand on his heart in mock offense. "Take that back at once. You know that never has, nor ever shall happen to me."

I shook my head, sitting down on my bedroll next to him. "Indeed. What is it, then?"

His features morphed into something more serious. "Honestly, it isn't any one thing. I just...miss Lochlann. Don't you?"

"Yes." The word was barely a whisper. "I can't believe we're about to be gone for another festival." I had never missed one in my life before all of this, but now I will have missed both Autumn's and Winter's. Maybe Spring's as well.

"And the epic snowball fights." He chuckled. "Even if Gwyn does hit way too hard. I think I still have a welt she left from last year's battle."

"I miss..." I paused, about to say something funny when the truth came rushing out instead. "I miss our family."

Davin scooted closer to me, putting an arm around me. "So do I, Row. So do I. But--" He cut off abruptly, shaking his head.

"What is it?"

"Nothing."

"It's obviously something," I prodded.

"Just." He sighed. "What if you do marry Theodore? Will you even be going home then?"

"Of course. I..." I trailed off. I doubted, somehow, that Socairan ideals allowed for women travelling without their husbands, but surely that would be the exception. It would have to be. "Of course," I said again.

"Have you even considered what situation you might be marrying into? That you might be playing right into their hands?" Davin paused, meeting my eyes before continuing like he wanted to gauge my reaction. "That it would be better to be free, to get to go home, with a certainty, even if that meant...leaving Theodore here."

I sat up a little straighter. "You want me to let Lord Arseling tell me who I can and can't marry?"

"Stars, Row. Of course, I don't, but I want you to think seriously about our options here and what's most important to you."

I thought about the rolling hills of home, the family I missed every single day, and I couldn't entirely deny the truth in his words.

But, leave Theo? Never see him again? Just sit back while he married someone else? The thought made my food churn violently in my gut.

"I need to talk to Theo," I breathed.

Davin made a disbelieving face. "*Talk* to?"

I swatted at him. "Yes, talk to. And even if it weren't, remind me how many women I have helped you sneak out to see?"

"Well..." He trailed off, like he was about to try to explain how those two things were different and realized he had no actual reason for that. "Fine. Fair point."

I smirked. Now all we had to do was wait for Evander to fall asleep.

CHAPTER 35

It felt like an eternity before Evander finally fell asleep.

Davin, true to his word, took a trip to the latrines to distract the guards while I eased out of the back of the tent. With his bedroll being positioned between mine and Evander's, we hoped my absence wouldn't be noted.

I darted between the trees and behind a couple of tents until I finally found the one Theo had pointed out to me earlier.

Theo was relaxing back on his bedroll next to a low burning lamp when I slipped into the tent. A slow grin spread over his mouth, and I practically hurled myself into his waiting arms, burying my face in his chest once more.

"I missed you, Rowan," he whispered into my hair, squeezing me tighter and suffusing me with his warmth and goodness. "I was afraid something would happen to you before I could come. That I might never hear you say something inappropriate again."

A laugh escaped me in a huff of air.

"And I was beginning to think I would never again see your scandalized blush, but here we are." I smirked, looking up at him.

Then the smile died from my lips, remembering part of why I had come here.

"What is it?" he asked.

I took a deep breath, steeling myself. I couldn't ask him outright about Iiro, not when he had just told me that he couldn't keep anything from his brother and Davin was going right back to live under Iiro's thumb, but maybe I could get some answers.

"Why were you patrolling the tunnels that day?" I started with something relatively innocuous.

He furrowed his brow, but answered. "Because smuggling activity had increased lately. Why?"

"Why not wait outside the tunnel, where it was easier to waylay them?" My tone was conversational, but I wasn't sure it was fooling him.

He peered down at my features, as if trying to decipher where I was going with this. "Iiro thought it would be better if we made sure they weren't stashing the goods somewhere inside."

Once again, all roads lead back to Iiro.

"Did you know, when we left for the Summit, that marriage was an option to save me?"

"Where is this coming from?" he finally asked me outright.

"Just the things that Evander said--"

"Evander," Theo scoffed under his breath.

"I know you hate him, but was he wrong?" I asked quietly.

"I told you before, he just likes to needle at people, Rowan." There was a trace of exasperation in his tone. "He practically admitted that Bear would have attacked if we hadn't called the Summit."

I stared up into his golden-green eyes. "But did you know?"

He took a breath and ran a hand over the blond stubble growing on his chin.

"Yes. I knew. I just wasn't sure it was what either of us wanted at first, and then later, I didn't want you to feel forced into it." The sincerity in his tone was unmistakable.

Whatever Iiro had done, I was more sure than ever that Theo had been as much a victim of his brother's manipulations as I was.

"Which happened anyway," Theo tacked on. "Is that what this is about? Are you trying to tell me you no longer...desire to marry me?"

My conversation with Davin resounded in my head, but I wasn't ready to go there just yet.

"Have you thought about whether you still want to marry me?" I held my breath, half wishing I never had to hear his answer, but I needed to know.

We both did.

"I heard what Arès said about your obligations to your clan," I added. "At the very least, we would have to wait until the pass opened and got word to my father."

His expression softened, and he brought up a hand to cup my cheek. "Rowan, I told you once you were the girl I chose for me. Did you honestly think a few months would change that?"

"It might not just be a few months, though," I said quietly. "If we can't come to an agreement tomorrow, if Evander won't release me, it could mean years of negotiations or...war. Can you wait that long to marry someone? To...continue your line?"

Though I had teased him about blushing earlier, it was my cheeks that were flooded with heat at that last question.

Worse than the embarrassment was the uncertainty that crossed his features.

"I told you, I'm not going to stop fighting for you, Rowan," he said tenderly. "For *us*. I don't want anyone else, for marriage or...continuing my line."

There it was. The adorable, sexy reddening of his cheeks that made me want to drop this entire line of conversation and pretend I had never brought it up. But I owed it to both of us not to.

"And what about what Iiro wants?" I forced myself to ask.

"Iiro...wants me to be happy." He sounded less sure than I would have wanted, and my heart sank.

"Iiro wants you to be successful," I countered, my voice thick with emotion. "And somehow, I doubt that involves putting your entire life on hold for a captive princess you may never even get to marry."

"What are you saying, Rowan?" Theo's expression faltered.

"I'm saying that neither of our lives belongs to us, not really. That we may not be in a position to make or keep promises. I'm saying that if things don't go our way tomorrow..." I couldn't finish the sentence.

He leaned forward, putting a hand under my chin. "Then we'll just have to make sure that things *do* go our way tomorrow."

It was amazing how that single point of contact could fill me with so much relief. I hardly realized how much I had grown to rely on Theo's constant presence to chase away the chaos in the world around me until it wasn't there anymore, but I had missed it, craved it, even.

I stared into his hazel eyes, and saw my own longing reflected there. All at once, I was tired of talking. What more was there to say, anyway, that wouldn't sound like a preemptive goodbye?

Without another thought, I pressed my mouth into the hollow of his throat. His small noise of encouragement was all I needed to skate my lips around to the side of his muscular neck.

He whispered my name before flipping us in one fluid motion. A thrill ran through me, and my breaths quickened as he supported himself on one solid arm tucked under my head, staring down at me with an intensity that made my head spin.

Lowering himself, he pressed his lips to mine. Slowly at first, and then with a need that matched my own as his hand caressed my hip. A gradual heat spread over me with each singular point of contact.

Stars, I missed this.

Theo tasted like the first sip of warm tea after a day in the snow, like hope and warmth and a refuge from everything the last few months had wrought. I wrapped one arm around his back while running the other through his hair, pulling him closer to me.

His free hand roamed my body, sending awareness coursing through every one of my limbs. I returned his kiss with urgency, conscious of every single minute we didn't have together, that we may never have. His lips glided from mine to the sensitive spot below my ear.

"I love you, Rowan." The words came out in a single urgent breath.

I opened my mouth to respond, but it was a different, far colder voice that spoke instead.

"When you get to a natural stopping point, feel free to join me in our tent."

My eyes flew open while the rest of me froze. Theo's weight disappeared from my body in an instant, as he blocked me from Evander's view.

Several rapid breaths passed before I shuffled over for an

unobstructed view of Evander standing in the entryway to the tent. His entire being thrummed with barely pent-up rage.

But he wasn't the only one who was angry. My face warmed, and I sat up defiantly.

"Well, we're hours away from that, at least." As soon as the words left my lips, I heard the way they sounded, but I refused to take them back.

Even when Theo squeezed his eyes shut. "Storms, Rowan."

The lines of Evander's face tightened. "Do not test my patience further tonight, Princess." He bit out each word.

Theo got to his feet, placing himself firmly between Evander and me.

"Can you honestly blame her?" he demanded. "What exactly did you think was going to happen when you took my betrothed?"

"She's not your anything anymore." Evander's voice dripped with violence.

"She's not yours, either," Theo snapped, fury emanating from each and every taut rippling muscle in his body.

Evander raised a single eyebrow, but his usual sardonic humor was nowhere to be found. "According to the Summit, she is. Unless you'd like to disagree with our illustrious leaders?"

I moved between the two men, placing my hands on Theo's chest, gently moving him backwards. The last thing we needed was for one of them to let this go too far.

Tension pulsated through the tent, a decidedly less fun variety than that of a few moments ago. Finally, Theo bit out a curse.

"I'll escort her back to your tent." He placed a hand on my lower back.

"You will stay here unless you want to derail our currently peaceful negotiations," Evander contradicted him coolly.

Theo visibly warred with himself before I sighed.

"It's fine," I growled. "I'll go." It was strangely reminiscent of the day at the Summit, but instead of the fear I had felt that day, the only emotion coursing through my veins now was rage.

Theo's eyes searched mine. I gave him a small nod, moving one of my hands on his chest up to his cheek to offer whatever reassurance I could, given the circumstances.

His jaw twitched angrily beneath my touch, but he only hesitated briefly before closing the distance between us, kissing me on the forehead.

"I'll see you in the morning, Rowan."

I turned without another word, glaring at Evander the entire time. Once again, he was forcing me to walk away from Theo, and once again, I hated him for it.

CHAPTER 36

Evander took the long way back to our tent, leading me far enough away from the guards to be out of earshot.

He was breathing harder than the short walk accounted for, furious puffs of air that dissipated in the moonlight. "Is this what you meant when you asked me to trust your word? That you would sneak away like--"

"Like a woman who was ripped away from her betrothed and hadn't seen him in a month? What exactly did you think was going to happen when you put me in this situation?" I echoed Theo's question.

My own breathing wasn't nearly as steady as I would have preferred, but that was understandable, considering what he had interrupted.

He gave a disbelieving snort.

"The situation *I* put you in? Don't you mean the situation you put yourself in?" Evander shook his head, derision seeping from every inch of him. "Better yet, Princess, what about the situation you put me in? Don't you think all of our lives would have been a lot easier if you had just stayed your reckless arse in Lochlann? Or kept your storms-blasted mouth shut at the Summit?"

I saw red.

"The Summit where men were voting for me to die, you mean?" I hissed at him.

"Only two men there were stupid enough to vote against you

until you insisted on insulting them." Evander stepped closer, the weight of his fury nearly knocking me backwards.

"You were--" I began before he cut me off.

"*Never* going to vote against you." He enunciated each word. "Which you would have known if you had been paying even half the attention you needed to. Who do you think was reminding them all of the cost of war against us? If you had kept your mouth shut, this all--"

I crossed my arms and took a step closer to him.

"Would you honestly have sat there and listened to them insult your whole--"

"Yes!" he fired back. "If it meant keeping myself and the people I cared about safe, I absolutely would have sat there and listened to them insult myself and my family and my cat, for all I care. Even your precious Lord Theodore would have, and for once, it's not because he's a coward, but because we were raised to have a shred of self-discipline, something you could stand to learn."

My limbs were trembling now with the force of my frustration at having everything I had ever done wrong hurled in my face yet again. I couldn't bring myself to care about the biting air or that anyone in a five-mile radius could likely hear us at this point.

"Theo really was right," I yelled. "You can never let anyone forget about their mistakes. Perhaps one day, we might all aspire to be as perfect as you are, kidnapping women who have done nothing to you and terrifying your own clansmen. Murder any children lately?"

I wanted to take the words back as soon as they left my lips, even before Evander took a step backwards as if I had physically slapped him.

I opened my mouth to say something, anything, but Evander shook his head, his expression going even more frigid than it had been in the tent. When he finally did speak, his voice was laced with acrimony.

"The only *child* I have ever had any desire to murder is you." He disappeared on silent footfalls into the forest, and it was worse, somehow, than if he had stormed away.

CHAPTER 37

Davin was asleep by the time I returned to the tent, and I had no desire to wake him and recount my joyous evening.

Even still, as hard as I tried, sleep eluded me. And was made even more impossible when Evander pulled his bedroll on the other side of mine and lay there wide awake like a beacon of fury.

The next morning was no better than the night before. Once again, he insisted I bring his food and sit next to him, all with barely a word or glance in my direction. Theo glared at Evander as he walked over to press a warm mug of coffee into my hands.

"Mmm," I said, doing my best to ignore Evander's glowering presence. "Thank you."

Theo frowned. "You look unwell."

"You really should work on your compliments, especially given the short amount of time you have with which to woo me these days." I meant it as a joke, but if anything, his frown deepened.

With a wary glance at Evander, he sat next to me on the log, taking the seat Davin had occupied yesterday.

"Is that what's bothering you? We still have a whole day of negotiations." His hand went to my wrist, tracing the outline of my bracelet and sending warm shivers all the way to my spine.

I started to lean into him before Evander cleared his throat pointedly. It really was too bad I didn't still have that sword.

Arès opened up the negotiations once more.

"From yesterday, we can surmise that Elk is willing to purchase the blood debt, which Bear finds inadequate. Bear is willing to release Princess Rowan only if there is no chance at a marriage, which Elk has informed me they will not agree to. Do we have counter-terms today?"

Theo huffed out a breath. "I could propose a thousand counteroffers and Evander would still say no because he doesn't want to give her back as long as keeping her is punishing my clan."

Evander's eyes cut to me, then to Theo. "I can assure you, I'm quite keen to be rid of her. Keeping her is more of a punishment to *me* at this point than it is you. But I won't risk Bear."

There was a strained silence where they glared at each other.

I tried not to react to what he had said, and the way it cemented something inside of me that said I was constantly more trouble than I was worth, to my family, to everyone. It shouldn't matter that he felt that way, too. If anything, I should be grateful for it.

That thought gave me the push I needed to speak up. "I'd like to make a counteroffer."

Arès deliberated for a moment, likely because it was unheard of for women to speak during clan business. Also, I had no clan here, but I was the closest thing to a representative for Lochlann.

Besides, Mila was his daughter, and she was plenty outspoken, so I knew he wasn't quite as strict on that as some of the other dukes.

He nodded slowly.

I dipped my chin in thanks before speaking. "I have offered to Lord Evander that though I will not allow him to dictate whom I marry, I am willing to delay a marriage to Lord Theodore until such time as an arrangement can be made with Lochlann to agree to non-retaliation and to maintain their current armistice."

Theo looked over at me, a mixture of hope and concern warring in his eyes. I tried to convince myself that this would be the best solution. After all, a longer betrothal was not the same thing as being stuck in this perpetual limbo, so Iiro should be fine with it.

And if he was plotting something, this would effectively stand in his way.

"Four months isn't so long," I said softly to Theo and his expression softened. "Besides, this way, we can do things right and have my family there."

Turning to face Evander once again, I studied his features for any sign as to what he was thinking. He had almost appeared to be considering this last night before the topic of Davin came up. This morning, he was completely unreadable, though, as his gaze flitted between me and Theo and even Davin.

Finally, he looked at Arès. "I will agree as long as Bear has a guarantee that Elk will neither involve Lochlann in their bid for the throne, nor make any move against Bear in same said bids for the throne."

"You're being paranoid, Evander," Theo argued. "For the last time, Iiro is *not* making a serious bid for the throne. You act as though he's ready to rally the clans and storm your castle this very month."

"I would never put anything past your brother," Evander bit back.

Theo opened his mouth to argue again, but Arès stepped in. "If Iiro truly has no immediate designs on the throne, then where is the harm in promising?" His tone was so carefully neutral, I couldn't be sure if it was an accusation or if he was merely advising Theo not to act rashly.

Theo looked thoughtful for a moment, his gaze traveling from Arès' to mine.

"That seems reasonable," I offered.

I didn't doubt Theo's intentions, but with this arrangement, Iiro's motives would be made evident. He chewed the inside of his lip thoughtfully.

Before he could respond, there was a commotion outside the tent.

The sound of voices drifted toward us, and I spun around to see what was going on. Arés was the first to leave and investigate, returning only seconds later to grab Evander.

The Bear lord looked back at me, his eyes narrowing.

"Stay here," he demanded before leaving.

Theo rushed to the exit next and cursed under his breath at whatever he saw.

"Go," I told him. "We'll be fine."

He debated for a few seconds before nodding and disappearing out into the forest.

My heartbeat thundered in my ears, and a million questions ran through my mind. Davin and I shot one another a pointed look before we rushed to peek out of the tent.

Was it more of the Unclanned? There were plenty of Lynx soldiers to protect us, but would it be enough? Where were the rest of the men from Bear? Would they even get here in time for a fight?

As soon as I saw the familiar black-and-white uniforms, the tightness in my chest eased.

It was just Evander's men. Only a lot more of them than we had traveled with.

Evander's shoulders were tense, and his hand twitched toward the hilt of his sword as he faced the soldiers. Kirill and Taras moved to stand on either side of him, both of them wary as well.

What in the stars-forsaken hell is going on?

CHAPTER 38

The majority of the new soldiers stayed at the border of our camp. The men from Lynx had all lined up with their weapons drawn, effectively blocking them from coming any closer.

Only one of them was allowed through. He marched directly toward where Evander stood with his soldiers. Theo and Arés stood just behind him.

Davin and I emerged from the tent to meet them. I wasn't going to sit back and wait if my life was about to be flipped upside down yet again, and my cousin apparently felt the same.

We reached them at the same time as the Bear soldier. He handed a sealed envelope to Evander, who scanned the letter before crumpling it in his hand.

While his expression remained calm, I knew better. Agitation radiated off of him in waves.

"These negotiations are over." His voice was eerily neutral when he spoke. "We will return to Bear immediately."

My blood froze within my veins. I tried to meet Evander's eyes, but he refused to look in my direction.

"Is this some sort of game you're playing? Was this your plan all along, to taunt us?" Theo gritted the questions out through clenched teeth as he took several steps closer to Evander.

Pure, unadulterated anger rippled through the air as the two men stared one another down.

"Oh, Korhonan, I do wish I had planned to inconvenience

you. It would have made this unexpected bit of news far more pleasant." Evander gestured to Kirill and his other soldiers in the camp, who immediately began tearing down our tent and packing the few things we brought with us. "But, as you have always been so fond of reminding me, the Clan Duke's word is law, and my father has ordered us home."

Theo shook his head furiously. He muttered under his breath in Socairan, including a few potent curses. A bitter laugh escaped his full lips and he stared at the sky.

"I'm not sure how you did it, Evander, but—"

"Enough." Arés cut Theo off. "It doesn't matter who did this. The reality is that we were only here at Bear's discretion. If they have decided to sever the negotiations, that is in their purview."

Davin took a step closer to me, and I grabbed hold of his arm to keep myself steady. My mind was spinning. I had always known it was a possibility that I would have to go back, but I had made the mistake of hoping.

There was no way his father was alert enough to make this edict, right? Was it Lady Mairi, then? Why would she want to keep me at Bear?

Or was Theo right? Could it have been some ploy of Evander's? To give us false hope and then rip it away?

Looking at the man now, I knew that wasn't true. He had been just as surprised as the rest of us, and nearly as unhappy.

"Samu, please tell my father that we will ride home immediately." Evander's voice broke through my thoughts. "Once we collect our things and the rest of the Bear soldiers standing by, we'll be on our way."

The man cleared his throat uncomfortably and Evander's eyes narrowed.

"We were ordered to escort you back, My Lord."

The look that crossed Evander's features was murderous.

"Well then," he said flatly, turning his attention back to Arés and Theo. "I suppose that ends our time together. Do give my regards to Iiro."

Theo bristled, his fists clenching at his sides as he stood there shaking his head.

Davin pulled me into a hug. "Remember, Row, whenever Lord Arseling is ordering you around. You're a princess of Lochlann. Every one of them is a plebian compared to you."

I choked on a laugh that might have been closer to a sob, and he reluctantly backed away, making room for another goodbye I was nowhere near ready for.

Theo's expression was pained, and his breaths came in pants. I rushed into his arms, burying my face in his broad chest and feeling it rise and fall rapidly beneath my cheek.

"This isn't over yet, Rowan," he whispered into my hair, wrapping his arms around me so tightly I could hardly breathe. And I didn't care.

This was all happening too quickly. All I wanted was for time to stand still so I could disappear into him. Lose myself in his touch. Ignore the rest of the world and the trouble that had never seemed to stop chasing me since I set foot in this stars-forsaken kingdom.

A calloused finger lifted my chin, forcing me to look up into his hazel green eyes. There were no more words. Instead, he pressed his lips to mine, his warmth flooding through me and over me.

I deepened the kiss, not caring if anyone watched or was scandalized by something the Scarlet Princess was doing, once again.

I didn't care, because this kiss felt too much like a goodbye, and no matter what I told myself, no matter what I had told Theo the night before, I hadn't truly been prepared to walk away from him.

The sound of boots crunching through the snow pulled my attention away from him, and we both tensed as the new soldier Samu approached.

"If the prisoner is quite finished." He looked pointedly at Evander, stopping just shy of issuing an order.

Evander clenched his jaw, gesturing sharply toward the horse with his chin. I clung tighter to Theo's hand before forcing myself to step away, severing all contact. Suddenly, it felt far colder than the wintry day accounted for.

As I passed him, Arès placed a hand on my shoulder and gave it a gentle squeeze.

"Take care of yourself, Princess." I took the words for how they were meant: a warning. *But, from what, exactly?*

Each step was filled with lead as I made my way toward Evander. He took off without a word, just expecting me to follow him like the pet I was. And what choice did I have?

He stopped abruptly at his horse, lifting me on top of it and mounting behind me.

As soon as the other men were on their horses, we took off at a breakneck speed. I couldn't look back.

I couldn't watch Davin and Theo fade away.

Not when I didn't know if I would ever see either of them again.

CHAPTER 39

The ride to the cabin was nothing at all like the one here had been. There was no conversation, no joking between the men. Silence fell over us like a thick, oppressive blanket.

Evander sat at my back emanating the most tension of all, at least some of which was clearly still directed at me. Which was fine, since I had plenty of anger to spare for him as well.

I couldn't quite make sense of what had happened, and I couldn't very well ask him about this in front of the men. But I damned well planned to get some answers when we stopped.

We finally arrived at the cabin, long enough to collect our things and retrieve the men who had stayed. Evander escorted me in stony silence to my rooms, declining to follow me inside.

So I followed him instead.

He turned irritably just in time for me to shut the door behind me, standing against it. Though he raised his eyebrows, there was nothing playful about the expression in his furious gray eyes.

Suddenly, I wasn't quite sure how to begin. I looked around his room to stall, long enough to register that it was surprisingly cozy, all warm fabrics and rich brown wood to complement the black-and-white tartan theme.

Then Evander solved the problem of how to begin for me.

"Bold move, shutting yourself in with a wanton murderer of innocent women and children." He didn't look at me while he spoke, busying himself with neatly folding his clothes for his pack.

I shook my head slightly, my voice quiet when I responded. "What did you expect me to think?"

There was a stilted pause while he placed the pile in his bag. "Honestly, Princess, there are few things in this world I care less about than what you think."

"And why would you, when I'm just your pet?" I said bitterly.

"Why, indeed," he muttered, finally turning to me. "What exactly did you need?"

"I want to know what the hell just happened back there," I gestured vaguely behind me. "Was that what you meant when you said you had to entertain their negotiations, that you would orchestrate this?"

His fingers went to massage the bridge of his nose. "I didn't orchestrate any of this. My father--"

I held out my hand to stop him. "For all that you talk about other people manipulating me, that lie rolls off your tongue pretty easily, doesn't it? We both know your father likely doesn't even remember I'm here."

Evander's eyes widened and his lips parted. I had thought it wasn't possible for him to look any angrier, but he was proving me very wrong.

"What do you know about my father?" His words dripped with scorn, giving me a moment's pause.

But not enough to still my tongue. "I know that he didn't send that letter."

"You don't know anything," he corrected. It was an order, a threat, every bit as much as it was an argument.

"I--"

"You. Don't. Know. Anything," he repeated, biting each word off more forcefully this time. "And if you could bring yourself to display even incrementally more sense than you have in the past, you will remember that."

A sharp rap on the door interrupted us, one of the soldiers saying we should go before we lost more daylight. Evander crossed the floor until he was directly in front of me, so close I could practically feel the fury radiating off of him.

I froze, refusing to give up my ground, even as he reached

toward me, even as his hand came perilously close to my waist, his fingers brushing against my side.

His breath was coming in angry huffs while mine didn't seem to be coming at all. Something that felt almost like fear, but just a shade more dangerous, danced down my spine.

Then Evander's hand closed around the door handle, and he twisted it.

I had no real choice but to move or be shoved out of the way as he pulled the door open, so I reluctantly stepped aside.

He stormed down the stairs, sending Kirill up to watch over me as I hurriedly packed my own things. When we finally made it to the stables, I headed directly toward the horse I had ridden before, but Samu stopped me.

His features were pinched in disgust, and he closed his hand around my wrist like he thought I was at risk of escaping.

"Why does the prisoner take such liberties?" he asked Evander. "Surely she is not given her own horse."

"Because she's a hindrance to the movement of any man whose saddle she rides on," Evander answered. "At a time when there is more Unclanned activity than usual."

"We have plenty of men now," the guard said. He kept his tone respectful, but was pointed, nonetheless.

Evander sighed. "I don't care where she rides, Samu."

"Artyom," Samu called. "Take the Princess."

A man nearly as big as Kirill nodded, leering openly at me. I forced myself to stand my ground, to not show any discomfort or fear, even though that man's lap was the last place I wanted to spend the next few days.

It wasn't as though I had a choice, and I got the feeling he would enjoy my unhappiness a little too much.

"No," Evander barked, unapologetically contradicting himself. "She can ride with Taras."

I tried to hide the relief coursing through me.

To think, I might have complained about being the uptight man's companion only a few hours ago. I thought he might protest, but Taras surprised me by stepping closer without hesitation. He helped me onto his saddle almost protectively, even ensuring he stood between the men and me to block off their view as I was mounting.

Perhaps that butt contest award had softened him.

Or perhaps, like me, he now realized that I was not a threat to Evander. To anyone.

I was just a prisoner with rapidly dwindling hope of ever being anything else.

The next few days passed with interminable slowness.

There was no conversation or drinking games with the men. Everyone kept their eyes forward and their backs straight. When it came to stopping for the night, only brief words were exchanged while rations were passed around from one person to the next.

Even Kirill said little, though he and Taras slept on either side of me each night.

Evander hadn't uttered a single word to me since we left the cabin. No barbed remarks. No thinly veiled condescension. Just icy silence.

Everything felt cold and dark and bleak, and it wasn't just the impending snowstorm headed our way. It was deeper than that. Something sank down into my bones that I couldn't shake, that I couldn't laugh my way through.

I missed Theo. I missed Davin. I missed home.

It occurred to me that I was more alone than I had ever been, more lost. I still had no answers about whether Evander or his father or someone else was pulling the strings.

And then there was Lady Mairi.

None of it made any sense, and solving that mystery was the only thing keeping me from spiraling completely into myself. For the first time, I understood why Avani hadn't left her bed in months.

CHAPTER 40

I was right about the bed.

For weeks after we returned, I buried myself deeply into the blankets, emerging only when it came time to eat or bathe. Taisiya was kind as she brought my meals, even if she was a little distant.

There were no letters. Theo and Davin were probably just now back at Elk, and Mila likely thought that I would be there, too. I supposed we had both been overly optimistic, but that didn't feel like a mistake I would make again any time soon.

A few times, the guards knocked on my door. Dmitriy even asked if I was interested in playing a game, but I could barely bring myself to respond. I probably should have been making more of an effort since this was likely to be my life for the foreseeable future, but I couldn't quite see the point.

Not when I was starting to doubt that I would ever see my family again. Clan Bear might kill me out of spite when my father came for me, and even if they didn't, how long would it take to negotiate my release?

Unless, of course, Theo married someone else.

The thought made me physically ill.

I had meant what I said to him. He couldn't put his life on hold for me, and we both knew Iiro wouldn't let him. That didn't change the sick feeling that accompanied that realization.

Now that I was stuck here, I had as good as lost him.

One day, when it was well past lunch but not nearly time for dinner yet, there was a solid knock on the door.

"It's Kirill, Your Highness."

I called for him to enter. His face was a little too neutral as he strode in, holding out an envelope in his hand.

"What does it say?" I asked suspiciously. There was no point in either of us pretending he hadn't seen.

"You'll just want to read it," he said quietly. On those ominous words, he turned to go.

The letter was addressed in handwriting that had already become achingly familiar, even before I saw the stamp of Clan Elk. Dread pooled in my stomach as I ripped it open.

With good reason, as it turned out.

Dear Rowan,

I hardly know how to write this letter. I know now what you were getting at in my tent. About all of it.

I couldn't, in good conscience, hold you to a betrothal made under those circumstances, even if it weren't for everything else standing in our way.

Pain lanced through me, both at what he was saying and as an answer to the sadness seeping through his words. He knew. He knew about Iiro, and he was as much as admitting it to me.

I wish that I could explain this in person, but it has not been possible to arrange another meeting. And honestly, Rowan, I'm not sure I would have the strength to leave you again. It nearly killed me watching you ride away, and now...now this.

I see now that you were right when you said that neither of us is in a position to make or keep promises to the other, but please allow me to make one more.

Davin will be safe, and I will see that he gets home to Lochlann, no matter what.

Love, always,
    Theo

I read the letter several more times, searching for anything I might have missed, but each time shattered me a little more than the last. He had said he wouldn't hold me to the betrothal.

Did I want to be held to it?

Could I marry into his family, knowing that I would be under the thumb of the same man who had maneuvered all of this?

I didn't know, but it hardly mattered now. As he had so aptly pointed out, everything else was standing in our way. Before I could lose my nerve, I sat down to pen him a letter in response.

I told him I understood, thanked him for taking care of Davin, added some platitudes that sounded nothing like me. Wrenching the door open, I shoved it in Kirill's hands before burying myself in the covers once more.

Tears stung at the back of my eyes, and all at once, I missed my mother so much it physically hurt, as if my chest were collapsing in on itself.

I rarely cried, but when I did, she was always there, bringing me a pastry and running her fingers through my curls while I devoured it.

There were no pastries here.

No mothers. No Theo. No comfort or hope.

Just me and these blankets and endless, yawning days with nothing but my own tumultuous thoughts for company.

CHAPTER 41

Days or weeks passed in this same manner before I awoke one evening to the door crashing in on its hinges.

I couldn't dredge up much of a reaction. What was one more brush with death after the past few months?

It wasn't death, though. It was worse.

Evander crossed the room to my bed in a few long strides, stopping when he was close enough that his knees nearly brushed the side of the mattress. His features were calm to the point of being cold, but frustration simmered behind his eyes.

"Are you ill?" he demanded.

I blinked once at him, refusing to move from where I was nestled in the pillows. "No."

"Are you plotting something?"

Other than his untimely demise? I didn't have the energy to spit that at him, though, so I responded with another curt, "No."

His eyes narrowed in suspicion. "Then why have you not left your rooms?"

"The rooms you ordered me to stay in?" Though the words were contrary, my tone was flat.

"An order you have never followed."

"Well, now I am. Congratulations. You finally have an obedient captive princess." I rolled away from him, facing the other wall. "If there's nothing else you require, feel free to see yourself out."

There was a long pause before he spoke again.

"Tell me this isn't you mourning your ill-fated relationship." Derision coated his tone.

I spun slowly back around to face him, going so far as to sit up.

"Are you actually mocking me right now for the grief that *you* caused?" I didn't wait for him to respond before I went on.

"How exactly did you expect me to feel, to deal with any of this? You took me from my only family here, from a man who loves me. You took the hope that I could see my family again when the pass opens, that I could hug my sister and tell her I'm all right.

"You have taken *everything* from me, and now you want to mock me?" I clamped my mouth shut, looking away. That was more honesty than I had planned on giving.

"Trust me, Lemmikki, I haven't come close to taking everything from you." Fury edged his tone, and I found an answering anger rising in myself.

"Am I supposed to thank you for taking me but not killing me?" I scoffed when he didn't respond. "I might be a cliché, Evander, but I am not the only one here. Another brutal Socairan Lord. What the hell do you even have to be so angry about, anyway? Shouldn't you be happy? You got what you wanted, and all it took was destroying a person's life."

"And I would have done—have done—far worse to keep my clan safe," he snapped. "Keeping a single person somewhere she's been unharmed for a handful of months really hardly rates at all."

"Sure, I'll just be unharmed here for a few months, and *losing my fiancé*!" I shouted.

A humorless laugh escaped his lips, and he looked at the ceiling as if it held some answer he was searching for.

"Oh, so this *is* about that," he said, looking back at me. "The severing of the very deep connection you managed to make in...Was it even a full two weeks?"

"Just because you're a shriveled-up broken shell of a person who is incapable of loving anyone or anything outside of himself doesn't mean you get to apply that to me," I said, narrowing my eyes.

"And just because you're a naive, spoiled brat who has never had to make a single storms-forsaken difficult decision in her life does not mean you get to apply your narrow outlook of morality to me." He spat the words, and it was my turn to laugh.

I shook my head, making a sound of disbelief in the back of my throat. "You talk about difficult decisions like you did this for some greater good. Tell me, Evander, if this was about something other than spiting Theo or Iiro or Clan Elk or Lochlann or *me*, why lead your people straight to a war?"

He looked at me then as if I were nothing more than a foolish child.

"You keep saying that, but have you considered how unlikely it is that your father will attack the very place where he believes his daughter is being held?"

I had, actually, considered that. "When you have no proof that I'm alive and no way to get him any? I know my father, and he will tear this kingdom apart brick by brick until he finds me." And if he didn't, my mother would.

"Even on the threat of *his favorite daughter* being killed?" The corners of his eyes pinched, and I couldn't tell if he was patronizing me or if some part of him rebelled against what he had said.

"I'm hardly his favorite," I muttered bitterly. Probably quite the opposite at this point. "But when he finds out I'm being held captive? He still won't hesitate. My father was Captain of the Guard before he was King. It's no secret to him that there are things worse than death."

The words hung between us, coating the air with a hostility so thick I felt physically suffocated by it. Evander's tempestuous eyes met mine, his mouth quirking into an expression I couldn't quite read.

"And is this?" His tone was quiet, dangerous, like the whisper of a sword sliding from its sheath. "Worse than death?"

Tension stretched between us, a precarious cord poised to snap, and I swallowed.

"It doesn't matter," I finally said quietly. "It only matters what he will think. And what he will do because of it."

"I see." Evander stepped back, turning to go. "Well, Lemmikki, wars take time, even for the indomitable King of Lochlann. So settle in, because we have months yet to think about that."

The door slammed shut before I could think of a response,

and I cursed. At least his visit had accomplished one thing. Instead of being depressed, I was furious now and determined to find a way out of this and away from him.

Volatile or not, I would have to return to see the duke. I felt guilty for taking advantage of his situation, even if he was a terrible person, but I was desperate enough to try to persuade him to let me go.

As usual, his son had left me no choice.

CHAPTER 42

I t was a few more days before I worked up the nerve to visit Aleksander again.

Steeling myself, I entered his room through the glass doors on the balcony. The duke was already sitting at the breakfast table. He rubbed his hands over his face and through his hair, the movements jerky and agitated.

I had evidently not chosen the right day to return.

A voice in my head told me to leave, to be smart for once and try again another day, but the more prominent voice reminded me that my options were limited.

So I warily perched onto my usual chair across from him. Aleksander's attention snapped to me, and he sat back, crossing his arms.

"You think you can just come here after what your daughter did?" He scoffed. "That I will protect you?"

I furrowed my brow. *Who does he think I am?*

"I don't have time for this today. I need to clean up the mess that family of yours made. I will give you my decision in the morning." With a gesture, he dismissed me and went back to his cup of coffee.

My mind reeled. I debated leaving quietly but couldn't make my feet move.

Before I could talk myself out of it, I found myself asking a question. "Who is my family?"

Aleksander set his mug down. He looked up at me with a

condescending expression that reminded me so much of Evander that for a moment I nearly forgot that I should be afraid.

"Who are you?" the duke asked in the same calm, lethal tone that his son sometimes used.

He had never asked for my name before, always calling me 'my dear' instead. So, I took a moment, trying to decide on how best to spin this before eventually settling on the truth.

"Rowan, Sir." I tacked on the honorific in an attempt to stay in his good graces while I got to the bottom of this. "We have been having breakfast together every--"

"Rowan!" He roared and flew to his feet in one swift motion, knocking the table over in the process.

Belatedly, I realized how thoughtless it had been to say that name to him. He was currently existing in a moment when my grandfather still lived. And I just told him I shared the enemy's name.

Der'mo.

I scrambled backward, trying to inch my way closer to the balcony, but he moved to block the way, turning to examine my footprints in the snow.

The look on his face was murderous, and I internally berated myself for never making better decisions.

"Spy," he said, barely above a whisper. "Lochlann spy!"

"No! No, Sir. I am not a spy, I'm--"

"Do not lie to me!" He was shouting now, his olive-colored skin flushing with red. "Why are you here?"

The duke stomped closer, and I barely stumbled out of the way as the main door came swinging open. Lady Mairi strode in on quick, purposeful footsteps. She glared at me with suspicion before turning her attention on the duke.

"She is a Lochlann spy!" he yelled. "Send for my guard. She never would have gotten in if it weren't for that village of traitors!"

"My darling, there are no more traitors--" Lady Mairi started, and Aleksander cut her off.

"Do not question me! Bring me my guard! Now! Everyone in Korov will burn for this!"

I looked from the duke to his wife, and a thousand tiny pieces came together all at once.

My gaze roved over her soft, nearly white waves, the bare

hint of pink that still tinged them, down to her strangely familiar green eyes, and then to her mouth.

My hand came up to rest on my lips and the small arch there, the one Evander had pointed out that Davin and I had in common.

Lady *Mairi* had the same one.

"You think you can just come here after what your daughter did? That I will protect you?"

Aleksander's words echoed in my mind and the room felt like it was spinning. Was the daughter he referred to the woman he was supposed to marry? Was this Aunt Isla's *mother?*

"Ava?" The name was a whisper, but I may as well have shouted it from the rooftops for all she was concerned.

Her face went from shock to fury within seconds. She fled to the hallway, practically screaming for the guards.

I stood frozen in place, looking desperately for a way out, but Aleksander blocked the balcony, and Ava blocked the door. And even if I could have gotten past them, they had both seen me in the duke's rooms.

It was too late.

There was nowhere to go.

CHAPTER 43

Aleksander began pacing back and forth across the room, spitting curses my way every few seconds. I barely noticed. My mind was still struggling to accept the information in front of me.

Ava...

Aunt Isla's mother had disappeared during the war, shortly after trying to kidnap Isla to come here. Everyone had assumed she died, an entire generation gone in one year; first, my grandfather, then his brother, and his sister...

Ava entered the room again, followed by Samu and another soldier, and I felt so impossibly stupid for not seeing it earlier.

When her plans to marry her daughter off had failed, Ava had stepped in to take her place.

Even in her cool, assessing gaze, I saw my cousin Gwyn sizing up an opponent for battle. I saw Gallagher studying different herbs, trying to understand their medicinal properties. I saw Aunt Isla when Uncle Finn was teasing her too much.

And the letter that never made sense, the one that pulled me away from Theo. Away from Davin. Evander had been ready to let me go, and Aleksander had no memory of my being here.

But Ava...

"You," I said softly, looking up at my great aunt.

Her features twisted in anger as she glanced between her husband and me before calling toward the door.

I had been so lost in my own thoughts that I hadn't noticed

Aleksander's abrupt silence. He was now sitting on an armchair, his brows furrowed in confusion.

"Sir, you called for us?" Samu asked, but Aleksander didn't respond.

Before I could think of a lie, anything to get me out of this, Ava spoke up.

"His Grace caught the princess attempting to escape. Take her to the courtyard to be punished."

"What?" I protested. "I wasn't trying to escape! I was," I scrambled for something that didn't sound as ridiculous as, *having a regular breakfast with the duke no one else knew about* or as incriminating as, *trying to take advantage of his mental state to orchestrate my release.*

Samu's mouth was set in a hard line. "How exactly did you wind up in this room, if not in an attempt to escape?"

I squeezed my eyes shut and clenched my fists at my sides. There was nothing I could say.

"Fetch the guard who was supposed to be watching her," Samu ordered his fellow guard.

The younger soldier left while I tried to piece my thoughts together.

Which guard was assigned to me today? I hadn't even peeked into the hallway before heading to my balcony, not wanting to seem suspicious.

It was less than a minute later when the soldier returned, Yuriy at his heels. Yuriy's eyes widened when he realized I wasn't where I was supposed to be, but he recovered with a neutral expression quickly.

"You were on guard outside the prisoner's rooms?" Samu asked.

"I guard the princess' rooms most days, yes, including today." Yuriy's tone was bland, like he was discussing the weather, but I hadn't missed the way he went out of his way to restore a small bit of dignity to me.

A muscle ticked in Samu's jaw. "And were you aware she was out of those rooms today?"

Yuriy looked from my face to *Ava*'s furious one, then the duke, who was trying to hide his confusion under a mask of affront, and finally back to Samu's cold, waiting expression.

The guard might have been adept at schooling his features,

but weeks with Lord Evander had taught me to search for the nuances I might have missed before. So I saw the exact moment he opened his mouth to lie, and realized in that same instant that I couldn't let him do it.

The duke was volatile at best, and Samu had not shown a shred of kindness or mercy since I met him. Ava would be furious at whoever thwarted her attempt to punish me, that much I already understood about her.

I would not let Yuriy pay for my choices or my mistakes. Weren't plenty of people doing that already?

"No, he didn't," I barreled over him. "I used the balcony. I was only trying to explore," I added in a quieter voice.

But the glint in Ava's eyes told me I had already dug my own grave. The entire room seemed to hold its breath while she looked at Samu.

"Remind me, what is the punishment for attempted escape of a prisoner?" she asked.

"Twenty lashes, My Lady." By the terse way he addressed her, I wasn't entirely sure he was more fond of her than he was the rest of us.

"Let's make it thirty, since the stakes are considerably higher."

"That could kill--" Yuriy broke in, but Samu silenced the younger man with a look.

"Is this your will, Your Grace?" Samu asked.

Ava went to kneel before the duke, placing her hands on his and speaking to him in Socairan.

The duke looked between his wife and me with some confusion before nodding, uttering a few harsh-sounding words. I didn't need a translation to know that he had just agreed.

The open horror on Yuriy's face said it all.

CHAPTER 44

P ublic floggings had been outlawed in Lochlann for some
time now.

Of course, they were common enough in Socair to
have a special designated post for them, right in the middle of
the estate grounds.

That's where Samu chained me.

My hands were stretched above my head, and I had just
enough room to touch my feet to the snowy ground. They hadn't
even bothered to remove my dress, which was unfortunate, since
the deep green was one of my favorites, reminding me of my
father's eyes and my mother's trees and everything that represented home.

Distantly, I knew that wasn't what I should be worried about.

Yuriy had said this might kill me.

Did people really die from whipping? I didn't know.

I knew that it hurt.

Badly.

Yuriy wasn't here now, though. Perhaps they had taken him
away for punishment, after all. I hoped not.

Still, I was not without an audience. A vast crowd of soldiers
looked on, some I recognized. Though their faces were largely
carved into neutrality, I saw defiance there, too, and even
concern.

Of course, others were openly mocking, leering, waiting to
relish this moment and watch as the embodiment of everything

they hated and blamed and disdained was punished for the perceived sins of my people.

Waiting to watch me break.

And then there was Ava.

Violent shivers took hold of my body, but I knew it had nothing to do with the icy wind. I took a few deep breaths through my nose and swallowed back a lump of fear, my hands shaking so badly that the chains rattled together. Fia's words returned to me. *To give them a reaction is to give them power.*

I would not scream.

I will not scream.

But even after the sharp crack of a whip rang out in warning, I was unprepared for the blinding pain that followed. The leather sliced through the back of my dress and into my flesh in a single vicious stroke.

A strangled gasp tore from my throat.

Ava came to stand in front of me, the indifference of her features somehow more terrifying than malice would have been. I searched her eyes--my sister's eyes--for any hint of humanity, but there was nothing.

Her voice was even emptier when she spoke in a tone too low for the surrounding crowd to hear. "In the unlikely event that you survive this, remember that there is nowhere in this kingdom I can't reach. Whenever you consider breathing a word about anything you think you know, I want you to think about your precious cousin in Elk, and how much he might enjoy this same treatment."

A bitter cold seeped into my bones.

"Why do you hate me?" I gritted out.

"Your family took everything from me. I merely hope to return the favor one day." Her mouth tightened into a thin line, and she turned to walk away before I could respond.

This time when a crack rang out, I was prepared--or I should have been, but the second lash was so much worse than the first.

I still didn't scream. Not quite. But there was no part of me that believed I would hold out for twenty-eight more.

Crack.

My back arched in protest, and I squeezed my eyes shut against the sight of the blood-spattered snow around me.

At least Evander wasn't here. The last thing I needed was for him to gloat over one more thing I had done wrong. *Look at you, Lemmikki, the cliché spoiled princess already crumpling under a few lashes. How very expected.*

Imagining his taunting made me square my shoulders and lift my chin. I tried to glare at Ava, but I couldn't see her past the unwelcome tears blurring my vision. The next lash made me regret even that small rebellion.

By the sixth lash, I was screaming.

I stopped counting after that. Fury and agony crashed over me in wave after wave with each haunting crack of that stars-blasted whip. The chains were the only things holding me upright.

I lost all sense of time, of my surroundings, until a familiar, arrogant voice cut into it all.

"Playing with my pet, Stepmother?" Evander's voice was colder than the icy ground beneath my feet.

The whip stopped in its relentless pursuit, though the pain remained. Rivulets of blood seeped from the wounds on my back, soaking through the fabric of my dress.

I told myself that the break from the lashes was the only reason I felt the slightest bit of relief. Not from Evander's presence. Not when he was the entire reason I was here to begin with.

"I was merely seeing that your father's orders were carried out," Ava responded. "Your prisoner tried to escape."

"Did she, now?" Black boots stepped into my field of vision, and I forced my gaze to travel upward until I was glaring into his eyes.

I hoped he could feel half the accusation I was throwing his way, hoped that for once in his arrogant bastard life, he wasn't pretending there was nothing wrong with the way he had claimed my life with all the importance and forethought of claiming the last piece of bacon at breakfast.

"It seems I can't leave you alone for five seconds, Lemmikki." There was an undertone to his words, something my pain-addled brain couldn't quite make sense of.

I couldn't form a response. Only my ragged breaths sounded in the space between us.

He leaned down closer to me, speaking in a voice almost too

low for me to hear. "If you can't hide the defiance in your eyes, at least have the sense to close them."

The tone was mocking, but there was more to his words.

A threat? Or a warning? He cut his eyes over to Ava, and I surmised the latter. He wanted me to act cowed? In front of this woman who wanted nothing more than to see it?

Absolutely the stars-damned-hell not.

Evander grimaced like he could read my thoughts, straightening to his full height.

"What were my father's exact words?" he asked in a louder tone, directing the question at someone behind me.

Samu spoke up. "He said, give her the appropriate punishment."

"And how many lashes has she had?"

"Twelve, My Lord."

A muscle ticked in Evander's jaw. "Twelve lashes for a tiny slip of a princess when twenty is standard for a grown man, and a soldier, at that. I would say that's more than...appropriate."

He turned to address the onlookers. "Besides, we wouldn't want her to die before we have the chance to use her against our dear neighbors, would we?"

I caught Ava's assessing gaze, the way it moved between Evander, me, and the crowd who was murmuring in agreement. In spite of myself, in spite of every obstinate piece of me, I forced my eyelids to shut before she could see the hatred stirring in them.

When no one responded, Evander spoke again. "Of course, we could always fetch my father, but I would hate to trouble him with something so trivial. Wouldn't you, Stepmother?"

Another murmur went through the crowd. Could they hear the violence beneath his words as easily as I could?

"Of course," Ava responded at last, but something in her tone sounded too victorious for my liking. "One more, then, for her to remember this by."

For the first time, an expression broke through Evander's distant mask, pure murder overtaking his features.

"N—" he started to protest, but the crack of the whip drowned out his words as my back lit up with renewed agony.

Another scream ripped from my throat. Spots blackened my vision, but I fought to hold on to consciousness. The clinking of chains sounded, and I collapsed into a heap on the frozen ground.

Then Evander was there, one hand on each of my arms, trying to help me stand.

"No." It was one word. All I could manage.

No, you will not help me.

No, I will not look weak in front of that woman.

Just. No.

A slow breath escaped him. "For once in your storms-blasted life, Rowan, choose your battle wisely."

Rowan. Had he ever called me by my name before? My brain was fuzzy, my mind swimming, but I had no recollection of ever having heard the two clipped syllables said quite that way before.

There was an unexpected note of pleading baked into his usual condescension. That, coupled with the fact that I wasn't entirely sure I could move, is all that had me nodding my head.

The motion of him lifting me to my feet was too much, pulling at the excruciating wounds on my back and churning my insides.

His grip tightened as I tilted forward, and then my world went black.

CHAPTER 45

A strange, high-pitched sound woke me up. Meowing?

Had I fallen asleep in Avani's room? The palace cats were always seeking her out.

That thought felt wrong somehow, though. Wrong, and strangely painful.

Besides, the pillow didn't smell like hers. It was smoky and earthy and a little bit sweet, distinctly masculine. I shifted, and agony pulsated across my back.

That's when I remembered.

Socair.

The whipping.

Someone tipping a vial down my throat, bitter and full of herbs. Fading in and out of consciousness with each fresh wave of white-hot pain while my wounds were cleaned.

Then finally, nothing.

None of that answered the question of where I was, though. I forced my bleary eyes open to find silvery moonlight glinting off unfamiliar dark-paneled walls.

Meow. An orange, fluffy shape pranced across my field of vision.

"Hush, *Koshka.*" Evander's voice was wearier than I had ever heard it.

I tilted my head enough to find the man in question sitting at an expansive black desk with a low burning lamp, wiping a hand over his brow. I dug for some of the anger I kept simmering in the back of my mind for him, but it was like I had tapped that well completely dry after the flogging.

Or maybe it was just impossible to be furious with anyone who looked as drained as I felt.

I couldn't help but take this rare chance to observe him without his constant scrutiny, to take in the tired set of his shoulders and the way the arrogance seemed to bleed from him now that no one else was around. Even his black hair was rumpled, like he had run his hands through it one too many times.

He stilled, sitting up a bit straighter.

"It's not polite to stare, Lemmikki."

So much for the absence of his scrutiny. I had so many questions scattered in my foggy brain, but somehow, I found myself commenting on the least important one.

"You have a cat," I helpfully observed. My voice came out as a hoarse rasp, my throat still raw from screaming.

"The estate has a cat," he corrected.

I craned my neck as far as it would go from my position on my stomach, hissing out a breath when pain seized me once again. It was worth it when my gaze landed on a small pallet and an earthenware bowl on the floor.

"So that water bowl is for you, then."

"You really shouldn't waste your strength on talking," Evander said dryly.

I didn't want to think about my strength, or lack thereof, though. The cat in question hopped up into the bed like it owned the place, shooting me a suspicious glance.

"Oh, look. The *estate* cat seems to be quite at home in your bed." I tried for a casual tone, but the words came out gritted between my teeth as a spasm hit my lower back. "Speaking of which, why am *I* in your bed?"

At least, I assumed this was his room. It felt like his room.

My thoughts were confirmed when he didn't argue.

"I have to keep you close, seeing as you're an escape risk now." There was a false note to his words, like even he didn't believe what he was saying.

"Right. Lest I go running off at any moment." The sarcasm fell flat when my voice broke on the word *running,* because I wasn't sure if I could even turn over, let alone run.

I was in the land of my enemies, completely vulnerable. Even though Evander had already seen me at my absolute lowest, I still desperately hoped he chalked it up to my ravaged throat.

A beat of silence passed between us, long enough for me to wonder why I had argued at all. The truth was, I wasn't sure I could bear the thought of being alone in my room this way.

When a fresh wave of agony assaulted me, I sucked in a breath and buried my face in the pillows.

The sound of Evander's chair scraping across the floor rang out in the silence, followed by footsteps drawing closer.

"Injuries like this--lash wounds--are rarely as bad as they feel." How would he know? "I'm sure you'll be back to scaling balconies in no time."

I tilted my head in the other direction to face him.

He plucked a vial from the nightstand and uncorked it before pressing it into my hand. "For the pain."

"What about Yuriy?" I asked, lifting the vial awkwardly to the side of my lips and swallowing the contents with a grimace. It wasn't nearly as bad as Aunt Clara's tonics, but it was plenty disgusting. "Is he?"

"He's fine," Evander answered. "He's the one who came to get me."

And Evander had then come to get me. Why?

I didn't have the energy to ask him, to try to make sense of whatever half-truth he would give me.

He took the empty vial from my rapidly numbing fingers and set it on the table before heading back to his chair.

"Are you sleeping there?" I asked.

"I have work to do," he said quietly.

I sucked in another breath, and I told myself it was from the pain, not the blind panic that overtook me at the thought of being alone in this room. Evander assessed the expression I was too exhausted to hide, then gestured toward his desk.

"So I'll be *here* all night, working." He turned back to his papers.

"Oh." I tried to nod, but it pulled at my back in a single searing, unbearable motion.

Neither of us spoke after that. I just listened to the perpetual sound of his quill scratching and waited for the medicine to pull me under.

My dreams were of darkness and pain, of being stuck in a tunnel with no light and no end while Ava chased me with a whip. Of mine and Davin's family sobbing in the royal mausoleum.

Of black skies and storms that drowned out the sound of my sister's cries.

Of an emptiness so vast that it sucked in all light, leaving me alone in the cold.

The scenes repeated, an endless, interminable cycle until a low voice pulled me out of the abyss.

"Lemmikki, wake up. You're dreaming." A warm hand clasped on my wrist, and I jolted into consciousness.

My heart pounded in my ears, and I struggled to take in enough air.

"Breathe, Lemmikki."

I tried to obey the voice, but I was freezing, shivering so hard that my teeth rattled. The sound echoed strangely in my head.

The hand disappeared from my wrist and went to my forehead, then my neck. I leaned into the coolness just as it abruptly disappeared.

"*Der'mo*. Taras! Send for the healer!" The voice sounded panicked, but that couldn't be right. Evander was never anything but calm.

Another tremor racked my body, sending white-hot pain tearing through my back. I tried to cry out, but my throat was too raw, and it came out a whimper instead.

Darkness claimed me in fits and spurts, voices fading in and out of my consciousness, none of it quite seeming real.

I heard my mother, singing a soft song in the lyrical language she rarely spoke.

My father's deep brogue, *Rest, mo bhobain. Yer troubles won't run away in the night.*

Theo's determined tone, telling me he would fight for me.

Fight.

"Fight, Lemmikki. You're stronger than this." Somehow, that voice felt the furthest away of all.

But I wasn't sure that was true anymore.

Hadn't I been tired of fighting for a long time now?

"She's getting worse. She needs—"

The next thing I knew, there was warmth seeping into my bones, stilling my tremors. I gravitated toward it like a dying leaf toward the sun, greedily soaking it in. Finally, a deep breath, then another, deep enough to inhale that smoky, earthy scent again.

Then nothingness.

CHAPTER 46

I was sleeping on a rock.

A warm rock.

My fingers traced the ridged outlines, and I tried to force my eyes open, but they felt like they had been glued shut.

Until the rock moved, heaving up and down and bringing my entire body gently along.

Oh, no.

My hand froze, and I finally managed to pry my eyelids apart, confirming what I had already begun to suspect. It was well into the night, but the roaring fire in the hearth gave more than enough light to see by.

Enough to see that my face was crushed against a broad, tan chest, my fingers resting on the cords of a solidly muscled bicep.

Hazy memories came to me. My raging fever. Slipping in and out of consciousness. And Evander, one hand on my head and the other on my lower back, holding me firmly against him until my spasms and my shivers died down.

I lifted my gaze to see a strong jaw covered in a couple days' worth of stubble, but that didn't seem right. Evander was always clean-shaven.

There was no mistaking him, though. His dark lashes were spread against his cheek, his hand tucked beneath his head while his chest rose and fell in even motions.

I was fully on top of him, my stomach pressed against his, my feet tucked between his ankles.

It could be worse. He could be awake right now to witness my humiliation.

Although, that would hardly be new for either of us, if my foggy recollection of my fever was accurate.

I shifted, and my back groaned in protest. The motion tugged at my clothes, and I glanced down to see that I was wearing...very little. A thin cream-colored shirt that was several sizes too big, the black laces loose and untied. They were closer to framing what was there than they were covering it at this point.

Perfect. Heat flooded my cheeks.

Determined to move myself before he woke up, I braced my hand against the bed and wrestled my other one from where it was tucked behind Evander's back, gritting my teeth and ignoring the burning from my wounds.

I was so focused on accomplishing what should have been a pretty insignificant goal that I didn't notice the pattern of Evander's breathing change until two strong hands came on either side of my waist.

Carefully avoiding the lashes on my back, he eased out from under me, twisting me until I was propped up next to him.

There was a momentary flash of agony when my back came into contact with the pillow, soft as it was. I hissed a breath through my teeth, but the pain subsided once I adjusted. It was unexpectedly tiring, all of it, and my head fell back against the cushion while I surveyed Evander.

He put a hand on the back of his neck, looking as close to uncomfortable as I ever thought I would see him.

"The healer said you needed warmth, but with your back..." His voice was gravelly with sleep.

"Of course, I..." My voice came out a croak, and I trailed off, not really sure how to finish that sentence.

What did you really say in a moment like this?

His eyes were bloodshot, deep purple bags under them making me wonder if this was the only time he had slept in--

"How long was I out?"

"On and off for three days."

Three days? Had he stayed in the bed all that time while I slept wholly on top of him? I struggled to reconcile this man with the one who had expected praise for not having killed me yet.

"And you were here that entire time?" I verified.

He nodded, features carefully blank. "Your fever was spiking, and nothing could bring it back down. So it was me or an untimely death."

Did I imagine the defensive note to his tone?

I opened my mouth to tell him a fever probably wouldn't have done me in, but closed it when I remembered that was how his mother had died. It certainly wasn't impossible, even if my fae blood did make me a bit more resilient.

This was at least the third time he had stepped in to save my life when, by his own admission, he wasn't averse to killing when necessary.

Why, then?

I answered my own question aloud.

"Well, that would have been a waste of a perfectly good political prisoner, and a bit of a mess for Bea—" I cut off with a cough, my parched throat giving out on me.

"Here, you need water." Evander twisted around, presumably to get some from the side table, but I suspected it was also to hide the strange expression crossing his features.

The movement gave me an unobstructed view of his very unclothed back, and a gasp escaped my lips.

White lines crisscrossed his skin, contrasting deeply with the smooth tan around them. They varied in thickness, and some of them had healed cleanly while others were knotted...like perhaps they hadn't had time to stitch themselves back together before they were broken open again.

He froze, his shoulders going taut.

"Are you, too, an escape artist?" I kept my tone casual, not wanting to make it worse for him.

He turned back toward me slowly, though his posture remained rigid.

"Something like that," he muttered.

Curiosity crept in through my fatigue. If floggings were common here, did that just mean he was more rebellious than most? But how early did that start? Some of those scars had looked too old to be from his time as a soldier.

Before I could question him—if I even would have—he pressed the cup of water into my grasp. I brought it to my lips with trembling hands, cursing the residual weakness from the fever. For a moment, the only sound in the room was my overly loud gulps as I downed the entire glass.

My wrists burned where the cup brushed against them, and I realized they were raw, chafed from the cuffs. On my left wrist was a mostly healed puncture wound from where the lotus charm had pierced my skin.

Perfect. I should have taken it off when I read Theo's letter, but I hadn't been able to bring myself to rid myself of what little comfort I had here.

Just one in a long line of lapses in judgment.

I looked away from the damaged skin, and several beats of silence passed between Evander and me.

He didn't remind me that he had specifically warned me against leaving my rooms, and I didn't remind him that I wouldn't be here at all if it weren't for him.

What were you supposed to say when someone first put you in danger and then rescued you from it several times over?

My body solved that problem for me with an enormous yawn. I belatedly covered my face with my hand, wincing when the motion pulled at my back.

"I'll go so you can rest."

"No." The word escaped my lips before I could stop it, but I didn't try to contradict myself.

I didn't want to be in this room alone when Ava was somewhere in this house, probably hoping her punishment had killed me. Possibly planning to try again.

I didn't want to be alone. Period.

And stars knew it was far too late to argue propriety.

He let out a slow breath, searching my features before speaking in a carefully neutral tone. "You want me to stay?"

Holding his gaze, I nodded, slowly.

After only another moment's hesitation, he pulled a book from his nightstand and settled back against his pillow. He looked exhausted, and part of me wanted to tell him to get some rest, too.

But another, less reasonable part couldn't deny that I felt better knowing he was keeping watch.

After all, he appeared to have a vested interest in keeping me alive, even if his reasons for that felt a little murkier every day.

CHAPTER 47

E vander was gone when I woke up.

My heartbeat pounded in my chest, and I cursed myself for caring. For believing that he would stay. For feeling safer when he was around even though he was my *owner*. For--

My next thought cut off abruptly as one of the doors to an adjoining room opened, and the man himself emerged. He was clean-shaven and wearing fresh clothes, his hair still damp from the bath he had clearly just taken.

I tried to hide my shaking hands, but his gaze took in everything, as usual.

"Shall I have Taisiya draw you a bath as well?" His tone was carefully neutral. "You can't immerse yourself entirely, but I'm sure she could work something out."

A flush crept into my cheeks. I was sure I was disgusting, coated in three days of fever sweat.

"That would probably be for the best," I agreed.

He nodded, his features still grim, then went to murmur to someone in the hallway.

Soon, servants were marching in with steaming buckets of water. It was a wonder I slept through it the first time, but then, I had always been a hard sleeper.

Taisiya came in, sympathy peeking through her stoic exterior as she held an arm out to help me to my feet.

Evander was already seated at his desk, his quill scratching busily away, so at least he wasn't witnessing my many valiant attempts at standing. I finally managed to get out of the cushy bed with only twice the amount of agony I had been in before, so I counted it a win.

Once we were in the lavatory, my eyes darted toward the outer door. Taisiya followed my gaze, and she helped me out of my clothes--or what I assumed was Evander's shirt, rather--and into the copper tub, before going to lock the door.

I sat in only a few inches of water, but she gently helped to rinse me off with steaming water from the buckets she had nearby.

My fingers clawed at the edges of the tub when the first stream of hot water hit my wounds, and I sucked in a hiss of air through my teeth. Taisiya murmured something comforting, a phrase I had heard more in Lochlann than here. She must have spent time around Ava.

The thought made my breaths come more quickly.

"Nearly finished," she murmured, attributing my anxiety to an uptick in pain.

I tried to reason with myself. It wasn't like everyone who had been around Ava was a terrible person by association. Gradually, both my panic and the fresh wave of pain ebbed away until I found the water almost soothing.

After that, she helped me from the tub and positioned me in a low-backed chair near a wash basin before engaging in the exciting process of washing my several tons of hair, so I wouldn't get soap in my wounds.

No part of the experience was remotely soothing, but I couldn't deny how good it felt to have clean hair once again.

Of course, as soon as the thought crossed my mind, she rubbed a salve on my lacerations that made me wish I had learned more Socairan curse words. I was clutching the sides of the wooden chair in a death grip by the time she was finished securing a breathable linen cloth to my back.

Finally, she brought out one of my warm sets of nightclothes to wear. I eyed the fitted garments with apprehension before shaking my head.

"Another shirt, please."

She pursed her lips, then seemed to think better of it when she caught sight of my bandage. Nodding, she slipped through the door and returned a moment later with another of Evander's shirts, this one in black.

I breathed a sigh of relief when the loose fabric settled around me, rolling the sleeves up before we headed back to the main room.

Evander looked up when I entered, and his lips parted slightly before he closed them again. I didn't have the energy to be embarrassed when he had seen so much more by now.

Besides, the black shirt was markedly more modest than any of Mila's nightgowns. It hung past my knees and was opaque enough to hide what was underneath.

"I see you've helped yourself to my wardrobe," he finally said.

"It seemed like the least you could do, even if you were magnanimous enough not to *take everything from me*." I did my best impression of his serious voice, and a muscle ticked in his jaw, either because he was trying not to kill me or because he was trying not to laugh.

I decided to believe the latter.

"One of many things in my life I'll come to regret, I'm sure," he said sardonically, returning to his work.

Taisiya led me to a chair by the fire, then proceeded to alternate working a wide-tooth comb through my hair and using a towel to dry it. I wasn't sad to see this lengthy process interrupted by the arrival of food, though I was sad that I only had broth while Evander had actual food.

As Taisiya was clearing our bowls away, something occurred to me.

"Where's your manservant?" I asked Evander.

He was already crouched back over his paperwork at his desk, brow furrowed in concentration.

"I don't have one," he responded distractedly.

"Why not?"

"Because I can bathe and dress myself without assistance." Well, that sounded pointed. "And because I don't like people unnecessarily in my space. The maids come in for heavy cleaning once a week, and that's more than enough."

Considering the way he had gone to great lengths to keep me out of his room, his answer made sense. I surveyed the room, where everything was exactly in its place, with the newfound knowledge that he was the one who kept it this way.

I couldn't help but contrast it with my room back home, the way I had frequently bounded out the door with my cosmetics still strewn haphazardly across my vanity and a discarded pile of dresses on my bed.

Speaking of bed...I looked longingly at the fluffy black-and-white pillows, dismayed to realize how much the simple acts of bathing and eating had worn me out. With a grunt, I went to push myself out of the chair, wincing as pain tore through my back.

Evander looked over, but I waved him off, picking my way to the bed. It was another excruciating moment before I was propped up, by which time my lacerations were on fire.

"There's another vial in your drawer." Evander pointed toward the nightstand.

I made a face. Not only was the tonic disgusting, but it gave me strange, vivid dreams and the uncomfortable feeling of trudging through mud.

"Or," I countered, "you could share some of that vodka I'm sure you have stashed around here somewhere."

It was a reasonable assumption since he always seemed to have a glass of it nearby. He raised an eyebrow, but reached into his desk drawer to pull out a silver, engraved flask.

Wordlessly, he walked it over to me, releasing the stopper before handing it over.

I took a long sip of the cool liquid, relishing the burn as it glided down my throat. I was right.

This was better than tonic already.

CHAPTER 48

Evander and I reached an uneasy truce, wherein neither of us mentioned the fact that we were sharing a room, let alone a bed.

Although, given the lengthy awkward silences between us and the way he perched close enough to his side of the mattress to roll right off, I could surmise he wasn't thrilled about either of those things. Which made sense, given what he had said about his space.

Of course, that once again begged the question of, *Why?*

He couldn't have possibly believed I was an escape risk, in this shape or otherwise. I suspected he kept me here for the same reason I didn't argue about staying.

For my safety.

I had thought perhaps my fear of Ava striking again was unreasonable, but I wondered how likely Evander thought it was if he was willing to keep me in here.

Perhaps I was right to be afraid.

I wasn't sure what to think about any of that, which was an all too common feeling these days.

Neither of us spoke much during the day. For Evander, it was because he was usually working. The sound of his quill scraping against parchment was the constant backdrop to my life as he modified ledgers or wrote letters at his massive desk.

Of course, it was eerily neat, not a single paper or ink pot out of place.

In my case, I just found that I had less and less to say. Most days, I drifted in and out of sleep, frequently closing the curtains around Evander's bed and shutting the world out for hours at a time. Even then, my waking hours gave me entirely too much time to think.

About my family.

About Theo.

About this strange new normal and how long it could possibly hold.

And, my personal favorite, about the long line of exemplary decisions I had made to land myself here, in Ava's clutches.

The only distraction was when Kirill, Taras, or Yuriy came with daily reports or updates, or even sometimes to just have a drink with Evander at the end of the night.

They came to see me as well, and Taras even brought a deck of cards with him.

More shocking still, he settled onto the foot of the massive bed, crossing his legs. I would have thought he would die at that breach of all that is proper, but then, it wasn't like I was offering to get *out* of bed.

"Finally willing to sacrifice your pride?" I taunted.

He gave a rueful grin. "I'm just hoping it will be harder for you to cheat from bed."

I didn't bother denying it. "Well, the joke is on you, because the blankets make it easier to hide cards."

"I knew that's how she was doing it!" Yuriy called from across the room, much to Kirill's amusement. Evander just shook his head, not pausing from whatever he was doing.

Taras quirked an eyebrow, dealing out our cards. I sat up as gently as I could and crossed my legs, pulling the covers up high enough to cover the scandalous shirt. I could probably have reverted to my own nightgowns now, but there wasn't really much point when there was an endless supply of comfortable cream or black shirts at my disposal.

At least today's was black.

We played a few hands before he spoke again, his voice pitched low. "You could have let my brother lie for you."

Evander's quill stopped, then started again. I swallowed.

"She would have punished me anyway." I was pleased to hear that I sounded more casual than I felt.

That *punishment* was one of the many things I tried not to think about every day.

"Perhaps," Taras allowed. "But not as severely. Men take the brunt of the discipline here."

"I never could have done that," I said softly.

"I know that," he said. "I suppose what I'm trying to say, badly, is, thank you."

"Yes, well." I cleared my throat. "Watching you lose to me at cards is really all the thanks I need."

Fortunately, he took my cue to let it go, and we continued with our game. Where he did, in fact, lose to me at cards.

And I only cheated a little.

Though I was grateful for the occasional company, I still couldn't bring myself to leave this bed or the safety it had come to represent. When they convened in the sitting room, I stayed under the comfort of the black canopy.

Still, they always left the door cracked to the sitting room where they were, almost as if to let me know I was welcome to join them whenever I wanted.

Or maybe just so their voices would interrupt my new favorite pastime of sleeping.

Of course, sometimes it was useful.

This morning, the men were giving reports while Evander did his usual morning workout routine. Even if I hadn't been able to see him, the measured huffs of his breath sounding between each push-up would have given him away.

All that was visible through the crack in the door were the well-defined muscles of his arms and half of his torso as he lowered and then raised himself from the ground in endless repetition.

Kirill had just finished telling Evander about more Unclanned sightings from the other side of the room when Taras chimed in, his voice low. I strained my ears to listen, barely making out Lady Mairi's name.

My heartbeat thundered in my chest. Evander froze, then sat back on his knees. Someone threw him a towel, and he wiped the sweat from his face and hair before responding.

I studied every nuanced expression in his face, terrified of what mention of her could possibly mean.

"Not a word," he panted out, still out of breath from his workout. "The maids say she has been ill again."

A dark, bitter laugh came from Yuriy. "More likely, she's just waiting to strike."

"A snake, hiding in her den," Taras added.

Evander nodded gravely. "Just keep your ears to the ground. If she's planning something, we need to make sure we know about it."

He turned his head toward me, and we locked eyes for a moment, long enough for me to know that he had known I was listening and had let me hear anyway.

Because he wanted to make sure I had the sense to be afraid of her?

Or because he wanted me to know that I wasn't alone?

After over a week of being in Evander's room, the *estate* cat finally started venturing closer to me. He rotated between sleeping at the foot of the bed and lazily sunning himself in the window nearest me.

For supposedly not belonging to Evander, the cat certainly didn't seem to leave his room very often.

He was fairly adorable, as far as cats went, with a small, squashy face, wide eyes, and long orange hair that stood out starkly against the black backdrop of Evander's room.

"Here, kitty kitty."

"I wouldn't." Evander's voice floated over from his desk, but I ignored him and tried again.

The cat's ears perked up, and he leapt onto the bed, rubbing his body against the poster near my feet.

"Come here, kitty," I tried again, pleased when purrs rumbled from him as he inched closer.

But when I reached out to let him sniff my hand, something Avani insisted animals liked, he growled and bit me. I snatched my hand back from the little fiend, who looked entirely too pleased with himself.

"*Koshka*," Evander's tone was mock chiding as he spoke over his shoulder. "It isn't polite for one of my pets to bite another."

I narrowed my eyes, but let the comment slide. "*Koshka?*" I asked, trying out the word on my lips. "Is that a name?"

He sighed, angling to face me. "You really do need to learn at least some of the language, Lemmikki. It means *cat*."

"You named your cat, *Cat?*" I shot him an incredulous glare.

"I told you, he's not my cat."

I snorted a laugh. "Lie to me, but don't lie to yourself."

Evander raised his eyebrows in a challenge. "What an interesting sentiment, coming from you."

I ignored him, and he returned to the issue of the language.

"You should at least try to learn something."

I curled up a little further into one of the overly plush pillows, signaling just how eager I was to begin. "Aren't there like a hundred different dialects? That feels unnecessarily complicated."

He leveled a look at me. "There are five, but most people you'll meet have at least a working understanding of the Old Socairan."

"Then why don't you just all converse in that, if it's so easy?"

"Because when it comes to our armies, the words that tend to differ dialect-to-dialect are the important ones, and better yet, they mean the opposite of each other."

He sighed. "Can't very well have soldiers arguing about whether their commander meant left when he said *vaseo* or whether he intended to say right but slipped into his old dialect. So somewhere along the way the king decided the military would speak the common tongue."

"Then I see no need to learn a different language. It's not like I spend a lot of time out in the villages." I wasn't sure why I was so opposed when I had exactly nothing better to do, except that it felt too permanent. Too...something.

Evander made a sound of disapproval, but I cut him off when he opened his mouth to argue.

"I'm quite spent now," I announced. "Be a good little owner and close those curtains."

He glared at me for long enough that I began to think he wouldn't, long enough that I warred with myself on whether it was worth the pain just to do it myself. But, he crossed the distance to the bed and snatched the curtains closed, breathing out a series of increasingly irritable curse words.

"Well, I understood that just fine," I said loudly enough to carry. "See, I know all the Socairan that I need to know."

Evander's irritable sigh said more than words would have.

I didn't care, though. I was back in my dark, comforting cocoon, right where I wanted to be.

Where I planned to stay for the foreseeable future.

CHAPTER 49

An intense tingling along my spine wrenched me out of a deep sleep, and for once, it wasn't from the flogging.

A storm was coming.

I gently peeled the covers off myself and padded out to the balcony, looking out in the direction I felt it from. The Masach Mountains.

It was freezing out here, especially barefoot and wearing only Evander's shirt. My skin tightened, pulling at the scabbed over skin on my back.

At least, the cold had a numbing effect as well. I tried to let the icy temperature seep all the way through to my soul, soothing my frayed nerves while I watched the dense, dark clouds roll down the mountains.

Is it storming in Lochlann?

Avani hated storms because they scared half the animals in the palace. I wondered if she was cursing this one now, especially without me there to warn her.

I hated having no way of knowing what she was going through in my absence. *Because* of my absence, and Davin's.

Leaning forward, I placed my fingers on the snow-covered stone of the balcony's edge, imagining for a moment that I was home. That this was Lochlann snow. This was the balcony in my bedroom.

Today would be the Winter Festival. I had left the castle for Hagail nearly two weeks before we went in the tunnels, so I had been gone for...over four months. That was longer than I had ever been away from home.

Away from my family.

"Lemmikki?"

I jumped at the sound of Evander's voice, closer than I expected it to be.

When did he even open the door?

His tone was oddly hesitant, though whether that was because he rarely sought me out or because I was standing on the frozen balcony half-dressed, like a crazy person, I wasn't sure.

Nor could I bring myself to care.

"What is it?" he asked, coming to stand next to me.

I stared out at the tempest clouds churning like the waves on Loch Morainn. If I stared hard enough, I could almost imagine that I could make out the snow-covered hills of home on the other side.

All the somber, bitter thoughts I had tried to ignore the past weeks came crashing down on me, and I found myself answering his question with more honesty than I intended.

"You were right, you know." I shook my head, risking a sideways glance at him.

He raised his eyebrows for me to expound.

"You asked me why I went in the tunnel..." I looked back out at the mountains and the storm brewing over them, taking a deep breath. "At first, maybe I was just bored, but that last time...I *was* running away." I paused, swallowing.

"Before I left, Avani hadn't left her room for months. The weight of her grief...it settled over the castle until I felt like I couldn't breathe, let alone joke or laugh or even grieve myself."

Guilt gnawed at my insides for complaining about my sister and what she was going through, but I couldn't seem to stop the words from spewing forth.

"I lost my first brother when he was only a baby, before I even got to meet him. And it was sad, in a distant sort of a way. But Mac." I swallowed back the sudden lump in my throat. "He was everything a big brother should be. Protective and funny and kind. No one's pain could trump Avani's. I know that, but the rest of us were grieving, too."

Evander didn't interrupt me, didn't ask questions or make

placating comments. I could almost pretend he wasn't there at all, and it gave me the courage to keep going.

"And my mother wanted me to choose a husband, not just to marry, which I was willing to do, but someone I could be in love with." I scoffed. "But who in their right minds would want to go through what Avani did? Not to mention the entire stars-damned war my family managed to kick off *because* of love."

A memory came to me, of the day I told Theo this same thing. He had told me that love was a ridiculous reason not to want to be with someone, and I had almost believed him.

But here we were, and love certainly hadn't done either of us any favors.

I swallowed, continuing. "So, I told her to choose for me. It was one of the only things we've ever fought about, just days before I left."

I finally turned to meet his eyes, the exact same pale shade of gray as the storm clouds in the distance. They were pinched with an emotion I couldn't quite name.

"I *was* running away in that tunnel," I said. "When it caved in, I wasn't half as scared as I should have been, because in some ways, being forced to come to Socair felt easier than going home."

I realized how true the words were after I said them out loud, and warm shame flooded my cheeks. "And now my family probably thinks Davin and I are dead, and we may never see them again. And it's all my fault."

There was a beat of silence while we both looked out at the mountains again, toward Lochlann.

"You couldn't have known that the tunnel would close in," Evander finally responded, taking a step closer. "And whatever your feelings on it, you had no choice but to go to Socair when that happened."

"That's not what you said before," I reminded him.

"I say a lot of things," he muttered. Then, in a stronger tone, "You will see your family again, Lemmikki. You said yourself your father would come for you."

I huffed out a laugh, but there was no humor in it.

"I've seen your men fight, Evander. How many people will die before that happens?" Lochlann had a vast army, but it wouldn't matter if they were bottlenecked at the pass. "Who do you think will be leading that charge? My father. My uncles. My cousins."

I turned to face Evander again.

"And you?" Icy dread stole the breath from my lungs, my words emerging as barely a whisper. "Will you lead your men to the mountain pass?"

He searched my gaze before nodding slowly. "I would have no choice."

I squeezed my eyes shut.

"But I don't intend for that to happen," he added softly.

I forced my eyes open, looking at him once more.

"Then what do you intend?" There was less accusation in my voice than a quiet curiosity. "When you took me, did you honestly plan for me to stay here forever?"

"I didn't *plan* anything." He shook his head. "I just...panicked. Though, in fairness to me, I have tried to give you back twice now."

I sucked in a surprised breath. "Twice? What was the second time?"

"I sent a letter to Iiro after—while you were recovering. It had my father's seal and stated that we would agree to the terms decided on at the negotiations, if they were still inclined."

Nervous energy coursed through me, and for the first time, I truly felt the cold. "And what did he say?"

Evander blew out a breath. "He declined."

"Oh." Some part of me had already known that, but the words came to assault my already battered soul, nonetheless.

At least I knew where I stood, though. At least Evander had given me honesty, this time.

In a way, we were both victims of our own mistakes. The difference was that I had planned to meet that smuggler for weeks, whereas Evander had made a split-second judgment call that came back to bite us both.

It didn't excuse what he had done, not by half, but I couldn't entirely fault him anymore, either. Not after everything.

"Well then, I guess we're both stuck in this."

Weirdly, the thought made me feel a little less alone.

CHAPTER 50

Despite my protests, Evander did, in fact, begin teaching me Socairan, and he wasn't remotely subtle about it.

He took every chance he could to replace a word in the common tongue for a Socairan one.

"Lemmikki, could you perhaps have your *kilpi* drawn any other time than right when I'm going over estate taxes?" He huffed an irritable sigh, not bothering to look up from the stack of papers on his desk.

He had a point, as the several maids bringing buckets in tandem were certainly distracting, but I wasn't about to tell him that.

"Perhaps tomorrow, but I keep such a tight schedule these days. I'm afraid I have to get my bath in before my nap," I glanced at the clock. "Which is in a strict half hour."

Then, later that evening, "Lemmikki, *kertoa* Kirill to bring me the trade log from the South."

"Why don't you *kertoa* him yourself?" I called from the bed.

"Because I'm busy and you haven't left that bed all day."

I wanted to use my back as an excuse, but truthfully, it felt worse when I went too long without moving. So, with a sigh, I obliged him.

The worst offender, though, was the following morning.

Evander's breakfast plate sat on his desk, but mine was nowhere to be found. Though Evander still ate simply, there was usually a biscuit or two and a slice of meat along with our porridge.

"Where is my breakfast?" I asked suspiciously.

He gave me a bland smile. "I have instructed Taisiya not to give you anything that you didn't ask for by name."

I narrowed my eyes at him. "Now you're holding out biscuits on me? I think this is worse than you taking me prisoner to begin with."

He let out a dark chuckle as I marched to the door to find Taisiya, reluctantly deciding my stubbornness did not outweigh my desire for *pechen'ye*.

The worst part was that his unwanted teaching methods were obnoxiously effective. By the end of the week, I understood several Socairan words and phrases.

That evening, Kirill and Taras came, per usual. But instead of just reporting to Evander, they had something for me, too.

Kirill presented three letters, two for Evander and one for me. At first, I was excited, thinking it must be from Davin or Mila. Though Davin's letters carefully avoided mentioning Theo these days.

But Davin would have died before using the Elk seal, and the navy-blue antlers were unmistakable.

Theo.

A nervous flutter went through my gut. It had been easy to forget the rest of the world shut away in Evander's room, but seeing this letter filled me with remorse. How would Theo feel if he knew I was sharing another man's bed, however platonic it was?

Then again, what choice did I have?

Did it even matter, after the way we left things? What more was there really to say?

My mouth went dry, and suddenly I needed to know what was in this letter. Right now.

I shooed the men from the room to read in privacy. Evander shot me a sideways glance, but let up at Kirill's not-so-subtle headshake.

Dread pooled in my stomach, and I ripped the letter from the envelope before they had even shut the door.

My eyes flew across the words.

Rowan,

I am sure you have heard by now that my brother has declined the terms of your return. He is concerned that if we are not able to marry, your presence will only serve as a distraction.

A distraction from what? My heart beat a staccato in my eardrums, a warning that I wished I could heed. But I kept reading.

He has resumed talks with Ram.

There it was. Galina. The niece to the Duke of Clan Ram, the girl he had been all but engaged to before I came along.

My attempts to sway him have been unsuccessful.

All I can think about is you telling me you didn't want this feeling, the kind of love that motivated people to go to war. I thought it was silly, at the time, but I would be lying if I said I didn't think about those words every day when it takes everything I have to avoid doing just that.

For all your comments about Socairan society, I have never wished things were different more than I do right now. But short of starting an actual war or abandoning my clan, I have little choice. Maybe you were right all along, and neither of us ever did.

I truly am sorry, for everything.

Theodore

I waited for the crushing wave of grief to come, but I seemed to be relatively numb. Perhaps it was because after everything that had happened over the past six months, this felt aligned with the rest of my life.

Or perhaps it was because in some ways, I had been expecting this since the day I was forced to walk away from Theo at the negotiations, and even more so since I got his last letter.

I pulled my bracelet out of the nightstand drawer. My wrists had been healed for a while now, but I had never put it back on. That felt significant, somehow.

Spinning the lotus flower in my fingers, I finally took a moment to acknowledge what I had known on some level for a while now.

Theo and I were no more.

He was going to marry someone else.

He was never going to hold me in his solid arms or twirl my hair around his finger or kiss me like I was the most cherished thing in the universe again.

Each thought crushed me a little more, but after everything else that had happened, I didn't feel precisely broken.

Did that mean I had never been in that kind of love with him to begin with? And if so, what did that say about me?

Maybe I just wasn't capable of that feeling. It should have been a relief, but somehow, that felt worse, like the absence of what I thought was there was causing me nearly as much grief as losing it.

The way my parents had talked about their love, it was like it was inevitable, like no force in the universe could have kept them apart.

Whereas every force seemed to be conspiring to keep Theo and me apart.

Worse still, they seemed to be succeeding.

CHAPTER 51

E vander returned to find me tracing the edges of my bracelet and staring into space. The tears never did come. In some ways, it would have been easier if they had.

But this still didn't quite feel real.

"Shall I give you and that bracelet a moment, Lemmikki?" His tone was more reserved than usual.

I sighed. "Shall I assume Kirill told you what the letter entailed?"

"Unless you would prefer to assume that I enjoy risking the safety of my entire estate by *not* monitoring the correspondence of my prisoner and my enemy."

I shook my head, squeezing the charm between my fingers. "Well, I'm surprised you aren't in a better mood then. Isn't this all you ever wanted? To eliminate the possibility of an *alliance* between Lochlann and Elk?"

Evander grimaced. "Yes, I'm just thrilled with how everything has turned out," he paused. "What does that have to do with your bracelet?"

"He gave it to me," I said quietly.

Evander looked a little surprised.

"Where else did you think I had gotten a Socairan bracelet?" I questioned.

"I just assumed you bought it with your winnings from our

little wager." He smiled, like tricking me into helping him beat Theo was a fond memory for him, and I narrowed my eyes.

"Just when I start to forget what an *aalio* you actually are."

"Well, we can't have that," he said darkly. "So why a lotus flower then?"

My eyes squeezed shut, trying to block out the wave of emotion that accompanied that particular memory. "He said it reminded him of me. Difficult to keep alive."

And *beautiful*, Theo had said at the negotiations, but I didn't want to repeat that part in front of Evander and see the mockery on his face when he disagreed.

I wasn't really beautiful. I was more cute on a good day, especially compared to Avani. But Theo had thought I was, and that had been all that mattered for a while.

And now he was going to be with Galina, who actually *was* beautiful. I wondered if she was *different,* too, then I chastised myself for being petty when she was a pawn in the games of Socairan men every bit as much as I was.

She deserved to be *different*, to someone. Special. But why did it have to be Theo?

Evander made a sound in the back of his throat, a cross between thoughtful and derisive, but didn't say anything.

"I guess you were right all along." I shrugged.

"Naturally, but what about?"

"That two weeks isn't long enough to fall in love with someone. Not really." Saying the words out loud brought them home in a tangible, undeniable way.

I loved Theo, loved how noble and upstanding and sincere he was, but I wasn't sure that I had ever been in love with him.

I probably could have been, in time, but that was a luxury we were never given. I could have blamed Evander for that, or Iiro, or myself, but it seemed there was plenty of blame to go around these days and no real point in dwelling on any of it.

Did that mean he wasn't really in love with me, either?

My thoughts must have played out on my face because Evander sighed like he was warring with himself.

"I've known Korhonan a long time," he finally gritted out. "I haven't always liked him, but he's always been easy to read. I don't know about love, but his feelings for you were genuine."

A small weight lifted off my chest. Even though I had

believed Theo, it helped to hear it confirmed by someone else. That even if it was over, it was real while it lasted.

"But he was dead wrong about that flower," Evander snorted. "If anything, Lemmikki, you're difficult to kill."

"Oh?" I cocked my head. "What would you suggest, then?"

"I don't know." He shrugged. "A cockroach or something equally annoying and resilient."

I laughed in spite of myself. "I'm sure that would make a very appealing charm. Perhaps you can procure me one as a parting gift. After all, if Theo marries, you have no need to keep me prisoner."

He stilled, his expression closing off. "This is hardly the first time they've initiated talks with Ram. We'll wait to see if he actually goes through with it, or if this is just another one of Iiro's games."

The thought filled me with a weird mixture of anxiety and hope, but neither was a road I could afford to go down.

CHAPTER 52

The next morning, I awoke to the sound of the cat's purrs right next to me. Light streamed in through the window, though the dark curtain was only cracked instead of fully pulled back like it usually was.

Evander's voice drifted in from the sitting room along with Yuriy's, discussing one of the villages on the border of Crane.

A small meow pulled my attention back to the cat on my pillow.

"Oh, you want to be my friend now, *Koshka*?" I asked, scratching the cat behind the ears.

He responded with a soft meow and a long stretch.

"Then, I suppose we need to give you a real name." I ran through a list in my head, surveying the fluffy orange cat with his delicate white paws and his overly serious face.

"Mittens?" I could swear the cat rolled its eyes.

I listed off several others, ranging from Feliks to Max to Laird Meowington, but none of them seemed to fit.

"Boris?" I half said the name as a joke, remembering Evander's casual lesson on the meanings that names here carried.

How could a name that meant *fighter* sound so stodgy? To my surprise, the cat purred and pressed his head into my hand.

"Boris? Really? All right. Boris, it is."

"Lemmikki," Evander's voice sounded closer than I expected, and he slid the curtains open. "Do you think you will leave bed today?"

The cat and I looked up at him at the same time before I narrowed my eyes.

"No. Boris and I are rather comfortable where we are, and likely to stay here for the foreseeable future."

Evander crossed his arms, looking between me and the ball of fur now needling at my pillow.

"Boris?" He raised an eyebrow. "Naming other people's cats is presumptuous, even for you."

"I thought he wasn't your cat." I smirked.

Evander just shook his head. "So you and Boris are content where you are?"

"Yes," I said cautiously, suspicious of his overtly casual tone. "Why?"

"Because I have business to attend to at the cabin. I need to leave tomorrow."

"Oh."

In spite of our constant bickering, the idea of going back to being alone in my rooms again made it feel as if the walls were closing in. I took a steadying breath, but it did little to ease the panic rising inside me.

"I thought you might want to come along, but if you're happy where you are..."

I got to my feet.

"Now that you mention it, I find lounging in bed is getting quite monotonous." As much as I had wanted to stay here for the rest of my life only a few short moments ago, the mere idea of leaving this castle and Ava was enough to make me willing to walk all the way to the cabin if I had to.

The corner of Evander's mouth twitched. Then his eyes skated from my mess of curls down the length of his shirt that I was still wearing, before he met my gaze again.

"We should have Taisiya bring you your clothes," he said, clearing his throat. "My shirts aren't exactly road-worthy this time of year."

Tension stretched between us. The subject of me wearing his shirts was skirting dangerously close to things neither of us talked about.

"Well, that's your opinion." I shrugged. "I think it would lighten the mood substantially."

He let out a dark chuckle. "Indeed. And I'm sure my men

would be very focused with you on a horse in that. Storms, we'd be lucky if the Unclanned didn't kill us all."

"Well, that's reason enough for me," I agreed pleasantly.

Evander shook his head, looking skyward. "*Der'm*o, Lemmikki. Is there anything I could say that you wouldn't argue with?"

I pretended to consider that. "It doesn't seem likely."

He sighed and returned to the sitting room to work. Meanwhile, I could hardly sit still with anticipation.

I never imagined I would be so excited to go on a journey with Evander and his soldiers, but I would give anything to get out of this estate where Ava stalked the halls like the villain from a children's tale.

Taisiya came in later that evening bearing a tall stack of folded fabrics.

"New dresses. I had been keeping them in your room for you, but since you need them now..." Her voice held a hint of disapproval which I steadfastly ignored.

Evander, however, looked up sharply from his desk and cleared his throat pointedly. Only when Taisiya's features were drawn in apology did he excuse himself to the sitting room so I could try the dresses on.

The top set was a replacement for the one that had been ruined during the flogging, a deep forest green overlayer and a cream underpiece. It was beautiful, just like the last one had been, but I wasn't sure I wanted to be reminded of that day ever again.

I asked her to put it in the pile that stayed here.

Next, I tried on a silvery piece under ice blue skirts of crushed velvet that fell in graceful folds down to the floor. I added it to the pile to take with me, along with a similar one in deep amethyst.

But it was the last one that caught my eye.

The inner layer was pure white, with long, gathered sleeves and carved silver buttons. The deep black bodice had a strapless corset that laced in the front, cinching at the waist before spilling into full, divided skirts.

Black and white.

I would match the soldiers.

"I'll wear that one tomorrow," I told her.

The thought bolstered me in an unexpected way.

The next morning, we woke early.

Well, Evander woke early, and then he forcibly tore me from the bed as well.

I braided my mass of hair back into something that would at least be functional, if not elegant, tying it off with a black velvet ribbon to match the outfit I had chosen.

"All right, ready to go," I announced, returning to the main room.

Evander's eyes widened for a fraction of a second before he shook his head. "Not quite."

He crossed the room to his armoire, pulling out a dagger. A very unique, very familiar dagger.

My dagger.

He held it out to me. "Just...try to refrain from stabbing me."

"No promises," I breathed, taking the blade.

It was silly, really, how I felt immediately calmer, more complete. I hadn't left home without this dagger since the day my mother gave it to me, the day Laird Camdyn's sons had teased me about the...changes in my shape over the summer.

A small smile played at my lips. "Well, I'm not going to thank you for giving me back what you stole."

"I wouldn't dream of it. It is an interesting design choice," Evander coughed.

"It's a family heirloom!" I said with a trace of defensiveness.

"Interesting family, then," he said drily.

You have no idea.

He handed me my thigh sheathe, which he had confiscated at some point on the road, and I disappeared to the lavatory to buckle it into place.

Soon, we were making our way through the dark halls and out into the stables. The air was frosty, and large snowflakes fell softly around us, covering the world in a blanket of sparkling white.

"Shall we expect this to continue?" he asked, glancing around us.

It still surprised me that he never prodded me more about where I got my knowledge of the weather, but he never seemed to doubt it, either.

I surveyed the clouds in the distance for show before shaking my head. "The snow should stop falling soon enough."

He studied me curiously. "All right, then."

Instead of taking me to the stall with the horse I had ridden before, Evander walked me to where his destrier was equipped with a two-person saddle.

"With your back," he began, and I nodded my consent.

It would be difficult to support myself for the lengthy journey to the cabin. Even sharing a saddle, the jostling would likely be hell, but it would be worth it to be somewhere that wasn't Ava's estate.

Without another word, Evander helped me onto the horse and climbed up behind me, then we were off.

Twelve of us were headed to the cabin, the same group as before, plus Yuriy. It was bittersweet that Theo and Davin wouldn't be waiting for me on the other side of this trip, but I couldn't deny that I was looking forward to it all the same.

CHAPTER 53

Evander's hands kept me steady while I held the reins for most of the ride, but it was still more jostling than my back had seen since the flogging. I was grateful when we stopped early for the night, and I suspected it was for my benefit.

By the time we made it to our first inn, I assumed that Evander would rush us up to the rooms as quickly as he had each time before. But instead, he sent Taras ahead to make our arrangements with an order to meet us at the tavern across the street.

Just before we walked into the building, Evander stopped me.

"A moment, Lemmikki." He cocked his head to the side, pursing his lips while studying me.

Then he took two steps forward until we were only inches apart. There was a question lingering in his tempestuous gaze, as if he were waiting for my permission.

A sharp intake of breath broke through the silence, and I wasn't sure if it was from me, or him.

It couldn't have been me. That would have meant I was breathing to begin with.

Whatever Evander saw reflected in my eyes was answer enough for him, and the next thing I knew, his hands were on either side of my head, and he slowly lowered my hood.

"Aren't you concerned with terrifying the locals?" I asked, trying to fill the silence.

"They'll get used to it eventually if you're stuck here." Evander took a step back, his voice entirely neutral. "What do you think, Dmitriy?"

The soldier stepped closer, and I rolled my eyes when he tapped a finger to his mouth as he, too, studied me. His brows furrowed in mock thoughtfulness while he looked at me from different angles.

"I think you're right, Van. Sort of like one of those monsters under your bed that you get used to after years and years and years of it tormenting you."

I laughed and pushed him away. There was that nickname again. *Van.* Briefly, I debated testing the name out, if only to taunt him, but it was too reminiscent of things I didn't want to think about right now.

"What?" Dmitriy protested, pulling me from my thoughts. "It's true."

Evander chuckled darkly, shaking his head at his friend, and we continued toward the tavern.

Two of the small children running by stopped in their tracks, terror coating their features. A few others came over, talking to the boys in front of us, before they, too, froze at the sight of Evander.

"Look," I pointed toward the children. "I'm terrifying them already."

"It's not you they're afraid of, Lemmikki." Evander put his hands in his pockets like it didn't bother him, but the tense set of his shoulders belied the gesture.

Kirill shook his head. "He has been slowly changing the laws in the people's favor, but there's a lot of history to overcome."

I studied Evander, from the arrogant lilt of his full lips to the mocking quirk of his brow.

"That might be part of it," I allowed. "But I don't think your face is helping."

The men laughed.

"Is that so?" Evander cast a sideways glance at me. "And what's wrong with my face?"

"Objectively speaking, nothing." I paused for a little too long as the honesty of that statement rang out, long enough for him to shoot me a smug grin that made me wish I had kept my observations to myself.

"But you have resting *aalio* face," I finished up.

Kirill choked on a laugh.

"She's not wrong," Dmitriy helpfully chimed in, leaning against the wooden post of the tavern's porch.

"I never noticed it before, but she has a point," Yuriy added. "Maybe we're just used to it."

The terrified children still hadn't moved, and the adults that came to fetch them cowered nearly as badly.

An idea popped into my head—likely a terrible one, knowing me—but I didn't let that stop me. Without another thought, I bent down, scooping up a handful of snow, and threw it directly in Evander's obnoxiously flawless face.

"There, that's better."

The entire street fell silent for a span of several seconds until I couldn't hold my laughter in anymore. When the men began laughing, too, the tension with the villagers began to dissipate.

The children smiled, their eyes wide, as Evander slowly wiped the snow from his face. The quirk of his brow told me I would pay for that, but I didn't wait for retaliation.

Though, I didn't have to. My back was barely turned before a giant snowball came hurling through the air, hitting me right in the middle of the head.

This means war.

Moving closer to the children, I scooped up more snowballs, handing one to each of them. Their reluctance faded once Kirill sent one hurling toward us and soon there was a snow battle between the Bear soldiers and their lord and the village children and me.

Parents came out to scold them until they saw who else was playing. Then, they hung back warily to watch, but didn't interfere.

After being cooped up so long in the castle, being somber and in pain, I had almost forgotten that life could be fun, even in circumstances like these.

When the sun left us entirely, we dusted off the snow from our cloaks and boots and went into the tavern.

There was a shift in the general mood, the air around us feeling a little lighter than it had when we rode up.

Many of the patrons at the tavern had seen the snowy battle waged just outside in the street, so several of them cheered or laughed when we entered. A few were still wary of me or Evander, of course, but the signs to ward off evil were at least subtler than usual.

I'll take it.

All except for the barmaid who kept casting irritable glances my way, while being overly kind with the men. Particularly Evander.

I had the distinct feeling that it had nothing to do with the color of my hair, or my Lochlann blood.

Our dinner largely consisted of ale and a bowl of watery soup with a few cabbage leaves floating on top, along with a piece of hard bread. None of us complained, though. The ale was more filling than the soup, and far more delicious.

When we finished dinner, we made our way to the rooms at the inn across the road. Evander and I shared a room with two small beds.

It was strange and uncomfortable to climb into the single bed by myself after being in the other for so long. Or maybe it was just that my back was sore after a day of riding and the snowball fight.

Either way, sleep that night was harder to come by than usual. When I finally found myself in its clutches, my dreams were once again haunted by memories of my flogging and the caves.

After the third time the nightmares dragged me back to consciousness, a warm, familiar weight settled in behind me. Only then was I able to find my way back to a dreamless sleep.

CHAPTER 54

The next few days of travel continued much as the first had, with an easy pace and early stopping points. Sometimes we made it to an inn, but we stayed in a couple of barns as well.

When we arrived at the villages, we didn't scramble to our rooms, but instead visited the taverns and talked with some of the villagers.

Things were getting easier with the local Socairans, too. Instead of worrying about how they would look at me or treat me when they saw my hair, I found ways to make sure they saw me as a person first. Even if that occasionally came in the form of smashing a snowball into Evander's face.

The added benefit was the fact that it seemed to help the villagers see him as more of a person as well, even if he never acknowledged it.

Still, I breathed a sigh of relief when we finally crossed the river and found ourselves on the small road that led to the cabin. Tendrils of smoke from the chimney stretched out just beyond the hill in front of us.

It was still ridiculous to me that they called the place a cabin when it was at least five times larger than the ones I knew of back home.

"How long have you been coming here?" I asked Evander.

"Most of my life," he answered.

I thought that was going to be the end of it, but he surprised me.

"It was my mother's. And since Mairi hates to leave the estate, it was a convenient place to get away from her. My father brought me when I was younger, and later, I started to come here with my men."

Something in my chest tightened at that. This was his haven. And judging by the way his trusted soldiers responded to coming here, it was theirs as well.

"And your pets," I added, mostly just to break the weight of the moment.

"Only the most annoying ones," he teased.

"Not *all* of the most annoying ones," I disputed. "Now, if I had stuffed Boris into my satchel for the journey like I wanted to, that might be true, but as it stands..."

His chest moved with his wry chuckle, and I smiled as the cabin came into view. The sun was just beginning to set behind it, casting a hazy pink glow on the mountains.

Though our last visit had ended on such a bleak note, one I refused to think about right now, the time I had spent here was still a bright spot in my months of being in Socair.

Riina and Nico met us at the stables, helping us with the horses. They were markedly less surprised to see me this time, and even greeted me by name while we talked about the journey here until we headed into the cabin.

Flames roared in the hearth in the large entry room, not only heating the entire main floor, but also infusing the room with the rich smell of cedar. I took a deep breath in and savored the comforting smell.

After dinner, we returned to the sauna. I sat on the far corner near the door. Evander sat near the stones like he always seemed to, but I wasn't quite prepared to face the intense heat on that side of the sauna this evening.

While the men were as exuberant as ever, the week-long journey here was starting to wear on me. I was as amused by their banter as ever, but spent most of the short time fending off yawns before Kirill finally took pity on me and suggested we go to the lake early.

The icy water shot straight through my scars when I jumped in, but it was more of a shock than actually painful. When I emerged, I donned my robe and headed into the main room to dry my hair by the fire.

Evander returned sooner than I expected, and we headed up to his room.

Neither Evander nor I had mentioned the availability of the room next to his, the one I had stayed in last time. He had simply carried our packs into his room as if it were the most natural thing in the world.

And I supposed it was, at this point.

I was already nestled under the thick tartan blanket on my side of the massive bed, half asleep when Evander climbed in next to me, breaking the silence.

"We'll have company in the morning." His voice was a little too casual.

"Who?" I asked through a haze of exhaustion.

"Clan Lynx."

"Is this your business here?" I turned on my other side to face him.

"It is." Two curt words.

"Why not just say that?" I questioned.

He was being oddly close-mouthed, considering he normally conducted his business in his sitting room with the door open.

"I wasn't sure they were still coming until we got here, and Nico's bird returned with a confirmation." Something was still off in his tone.

"Why is Arès coming here?"

"He isn't. Lady Mila is, and her brother Lord Luca. To discuss an alliance."

At the sound of my friend's name, a thrill of excitement went through me, nearly pushing out my suspicions around Evander's odd behavior.

Then, I considered the situation more deeply. It was unusual enough to bring a woman along for political talks in Socair, let alone an unprecedented alliance with the most neutral clan in the--

I froze, an emotion I didn't want to identify stopping me in my tracks. My voice was curiously devoid of emotion when I spoke next.

"What kind of an alliance?"

Evander hesitated only briefly before answering. "A marriage alliance."

"Oh." I found myself at a rare loss for words.

Why did it seem so unusual that Evander would think of marrying for the good of his clan? Wasn't that what Theo was doing? What Mila had talked about doing? Though she said she would rather die than marry into Bear, but perhaps her father had convinced her the rumors were just that. Arès hadn't seemed particularly afraid of Evander, or even disdainful of him.

I was suddenly very, very conscious of the fact that I was in Evander's bed. That I had been for the past several weeks. That there was no real part of me that wanted to *not* be.

Which felt like a problem, in and of itself. Worse still, if he actually was considering...*allying* with Mila, how would she feel about this? A sick feeling churned in my gut.

"Is that something you want, though? Marriage?" I couldn't seem to stop myself from asking.

He shrugged, a barely visible movement of the outline of his shoulders. "It's generally considered an inevitability."

"How very romantic." I thought about how Theo had spoken of marriage, how he said he had chosen me to spend his life with. Of course, in the end, it hadn't been his choice to make, so maybe that wasn't better.

Evander scoffed. "Not everyone has the luxury of romance, Princess. Some of us have responsibilities."

"Yes, I'm sure marrying Mila will be a real chore for you. No one wants a wife who's funny and gorgeous and smart." There was a bite to my tone, but it wasn't directed at my friend. She was all of those things, and more.

"So, am I to understand you think Mila and I would make a good match?" He turned over to face me, something in his voice sounding just a bit mocking.

Flames from the hearth danced in his silver eyes, and I let out a frustrated breath.

"I think Mila would make a good match for anyone." I said, looking away and focusing on repositioning my pillow instead.

Evander sighed like he was the exasperated one. "Well, I'm sure Taras will be thrilled to hear that."

I abruptly stopped moving. "Taras?"

"Yes, Taras. He is the third-highest-ranking person in Bear."

My lips parted. I was almost certain he had baited me on purpose. Not that there was any reason I should care, and I didn't. *Obviously.*

"Not you." It was a statement as much as a question. "Even though marriage is an inevitability?"

"Generally, it is." He let out one of his humorless laughs. "But in my case, I would be just as happy to see the line continue through Taras. There is plenty of chaos in my life without introducing a wife into the equation."

Well, at least I didn't have to worry about offending anyone in the near future with my presence. Which was a relief.

Definitely.

CHAPTER 55

T he morning brought with it a mix of emotions.

Excitement to see Mila, but also nervousness on her behalf. She had pretended to be cavalier about marriage when she spoke of it at the Summit, but she had at least expected to stay in Lynx.

She had also said that only a marriage to a clan heir was worth switching clans for.

What had changed Arès' mind?

Whatever it was, I knew what it was to be ripped away from your home and family and to face the idea of starting a life somewhere new.

It was terrifying, even when it was exhilarating.

I changed quickly, not bothering to put my dagger back on this morning. After so long without it, the sheath chafed at my thigh, and the cabin felt safe enough not to need it.

Still, it was all I could do not to sprint down the stairs when I heard the carriage roll up.

As soon as the door opened, she came bursting through it.

She looked as gorgeous as I remembered, even after days of travel. Her brown hair was partially pinned up to fall down her back in waves, her tan skin a contrast to her flowing teal gown and silver cloak.

"Scarlet Princess!" she exclaimed in her low, raspy tone, her R's rolling nearly as thickly as Kirill's did.

Even though we had only known each other a short time,

Mila felt like the other half of my offbeat soul. I laughed, running to her and throwing my arms around her neck.

"Are you all right?" she asked, squeezing me back.

I nodded, trying not to wince as her grip bit into the tender skin on my back.

"My father swore you were fine," she said. "And I know your letters said it, but...it's Bear, and Evander." She crinkled her nose.

"I really am," I said, unable to keep the smile from my lips. "And they aren't as bad as you might think."

She shot me a skeptical look. "Well, I'll believe that when I see it."

"Fair enough," I told her.

Her grin returned as she linked her arm in mine and we made our way further from the door to allow the rest of the party entrance into the house.

"Lord Evander," she said coldly as he approached.

"Lady Mila," he responded with some version of his usual casual air, except this time, I could see there was real warmth in his expression, probably because she was here to marry his cousin.

But I doubted she noticed that.

There would be time enough for her to learn the many nuanced expressions of the Bear heirs soon, though. For now, I just wanted to see my friend.

She took a deep whiff of the sweetly spiced air and her eyes fluttered. "Is that medovukha?" she asked hopefully.

"Of course." I pulled her along to the kitchen to get us both mugs.

Riina was already ladling some of the still-steaming beverage for us. She seemed even more pleased this morning than she had before, as if she was thrilled for all of the guests, or more likely, just pleased to have more women around.

"It's freezing out there," Mila said, wrapping both of her hands around her mug and leaning in closer to me.

"Does it not get this cold in Lynx?" I asked, taking another glance at her clothes.

Though she was technically dressed for the cold, the thinner material of both her cloak and her gown didn't seem to be doing a great job of actually keeping her warm.

"No," she said bitterly, as if this was something she had been dwelling on for a while. "Not like this."

Evander, Taras, and a man I assumed was Mila's brother, judging by their nearly identical features, brushed past us, heading into the living room, while the rest of the men declared they were going on a hunt.

"Lemmikki, fetch me a medovukha," Evander called, interrupting my conversation with Mila.

One of her perfectly sculpted brows rose and she blinked slowly, looking from me to Evander.

While he occasionally sent me on errands, it was usually because he was working and not actually in the capacity of his *pet*. I narrowed my eyes at him, wondering what he was playing at, or if he was planning on acting like the same royal arseling he had at the negotiations.

Whatever it was, I supposed I could play along, for now.

"Right away, most esteemed Lord Evander." I felt Mila's eyes on me as I filled up three mugs, a smirk dancing at the edge of my mouth. Slowly, I walked one over, handing it to Lord Luca.

"Thank you, Your Highness." He nodded his head, showing the same easy grace his father always did.

There was curiosity in his gaze as well, and a keen intelligence. It would be a mistake to underestimate him.

"Of course," I said amicably.

I walked back to the kitchen, slowly bringing Taras his mug next. The barest hint of an amused smile crossed his lips, but he thanked me as well, taking it from my hand.

Finally, I crept on meandering footsteps with Evander's mug and set it down on the table next to him.

"Is there anything else you need from me, or might I go visit with my friend, by your leave, oh gracious and magnanimous owner?" I widened my eyes in an exaggerated plea.

Something dark flashed in his eyes, and he pursed his lips. To anyone else, he might have looked irritated, but I knew he was biting back one of his low chuckles. "I suppose I will allow it."

"You are too kind," I said drily, heading back to Mila.

She eyed me with a little too much insight. Before she could question me, though, I turned it around on her.

"How are you feeling?" I whispered, lifting my cup to my lips and taking a long sip. "You know, about your future being deter-mined by a room full of men?" I nodded toward the living room

She laughed. "What would you know about that?"

"Not much, but hey, maybe the lord of another territory will come and claim a blood debt, just to spice things up," I said, waggling my eyebrows at her.

"I believe there is a limit as to how many times that can happen in a year, so..."

It was my turn to laugh.

She slid her gaze to unabashedly examine Taras while the men discussed terms and dowries, and Taras' future position within the clan itself.

"To answer your question, though, I can't say that I'm entirely surprised. When Father came home after your--" She looked at me pointedly. "After your negotiations with Elk, he seemed worried. He's been talking about the different clans and allies and choosing sides, how not everyone wants the Obsidian Throne resurrected."

She shook her head and took a long drink of her medovukha.

"None of that is important right now, though, I suppose." Her eyes flitted back to Taras, who was sitting exceptionally rigidly in his chair.

I sighed. "He's...not always like this."

Which was mostly true.

Mila shrugged one slim shoulder, managing to make the motion look graceful. "It hardly matters, I knew I would have to marry someone. I just hadn't expected it to be..."

"So far from home?"

She nodded. "But if it's that or war..." Her features turned resolute.

"I think I want to be you when I grow up, Mila," I said, linking our arms again.

I wasn't really joking. Mila was a force to be reckoned with. Brilliant and unapologetically herself, but also devoted to her family, her clan, and generally doing the right thing.

She laughed in response, as if I was ridiculous. Before she could say anything, I threw out another question, this one more serious.

"Do you think it will come to that, though? War?"

I wasn't entirely sure that I wanted the answer. I didn't know much about war except that I didn't want to be involved in one, ever, after the stories my family had told. War made monsters of the meekest of men. It left scars that were both seen and not, and the cost always seemed to outweigh the perceived benefit.

Mila tilted her head, her expression going contemplative.

"I don't think that war is on our doorstep, but it must be a possibility, or I wouldn't be here." Concern colored her tone. "Especially if my father is considering having me switch clans for someone who isn't an heir."

I took a long draught from my mug, my stomach hollowing at her words.

"Does--" I gathered my courage to ask her what I wanted to know. "Does that bother you?"

She nearly spit out her drink. "Does not being married to the man who basically enslaved my friend bother me? Storms, no."

Why did that sentiment make me feel so relieved and confused, all at the same time?

"In any event, nothing is written in stone yet about any alliance, but at least I got to see you." She squeezed my hand, and I returned the gesture.

She was right. Whatever else happened, I could enjoy this unexpected gift of time with my friend.

CHAPTER 56

Luca and Mila were in the study discussing nuances of the terms while Evander and I helped ourselves to more medovukha.

"Sure you don't want me to *fetch* that for you?" I asked him sarcastically.

He chuckled. "Well, if you're offering."

I glared, and he relented, speaking in a voice barely above a whisper. "Well, your delicate reputation--and mine, of course-- would be at risk if they suspected you were anything other than a prisoner at risk of escaping. Which, of course, is exactly what you are."

Because I was sleeping in his room, he meant. It was the closest either of us had ever come to calling out the fact that there was no actual reason for me to sleep in there when Ava was several days' ride away and we both knew I wasn't going anywhere.

"Well, then, it's a good thing we're both so good at pretending." The words slipped out before I could consider them.

I wasn't even sure what I was referring to. Pretending that we were captor and prisoner now, or pretending that we weren't the rest of the time.

He held my gaze for several thundering heartbeats, as if he was trying to determine the same thing. "Are we?"

Before I could respond, Mila and Luca returned, effectively cutting off our whispered conversation.

Which was just as well, because I had no idea what I would have said.

I hadn't realized there was a chance Mila would leave, depending on how that first meeting went, but was relieved when Luca announced they were ready to be shown to their rooms.

When we finally settled her in the one I had used last time, we closed the door and climbed onto the bed to catch up without the prying ears of the others.

"I heard about Elk in talks with Ram again. Everyone did. It's part of why my father is concerned."

A familiar pang went through me, but it had already dulled in the week since I read his letter.

I shrugged with more nonchalance than I felt. "It didn't really make sense to plan for a future neither of us knew if we could have. I understand why he had to do what he did."

It was true.

Though I might have been sad, I didn't blame Theo for taking care of his clan.

"Are you really all right with all of this?" I was, admittedly, changing the subject, but I also genuinely wanted to know. "I know you didn't want to marry into Bear."

She leaned back onto the pillows, looking at the ceiling. "At least if I marry Taras, we'll be close." She winced when she realized what she had indicated. "Not that I want you to be stuck here. Surely he isn't planning on *keeping* you forever. Want me to help you off him in his sleep?"

I laughed. "It's tempting, but he isn't as bad as the rumors say. And no, I don't think he'll keep me here forever." I swallowed, not wanting to continue with that line of thought. "But I like that we'll be close for a while."

"Speaking of which, are you staying in here, too?" She gestured around the room.

The smallest thrill of panic went through me when I thought about the nightmares. About where I would be sleeping instead of here, and how Mila might feel about that.

"No," I said a little too quickly. "Evander...likes to keep me close. You know, in case I need to fetch something for him in the middle of the night," I lied.

Her features didn't reflect the surprise I was expecting, and I narrowed my eyes. "Why do I feel like you already knew that?"

"There might have been rumors. But most people think they're just that!" she added, seeing my expression. "It doesn't matter, honestly. Who cares what they think? I only cared at all when I thought he was forcing you, but now..."

"But now?"

The smallest hint of a smirk teased at her lips. "That's just not the feeling I got. Now, I just feel sorry for you. It must be awful, sleeping next to someone so vile-looking every night."

So much for them thinking it was about me being a captive.

Still, I couldn't help an answering smile. "Yeah. He's disgusting."

"The whole family is, really." She shrugged, but mirth sparkled in her eyes.

"It's a shame, honestly." I nodded gravely. "Perhaps their ancestor was a troll?"

"That would make sense," she said.

"I can...barely look at any of them." I pursed my lips.

"Ah. Indeed. Me either." Her eyes caught mine, and she let out a wicked chuckle. "Let's go barely look at them in the sauna."

I let out a startled laugh. "Why, Mila! I thought you said that was *never* sexual."

"Technically, it isn't, societally speaking." She widened her eyes. "But that doesn't mean I can't check out the potential future goods."

"Well, I can't offer much information on that front, but I do happen to know that Taras has a superior arse-to-snow imprint."

This time she laughed louder, a sound that warmed the entire room more than the fire in the hearth. "Well, that is certainly comforting. Do I even want to guess?"

I raised my eyebrows. "I have a feeling you might get to see for yourself, and I wouldn't want to ruin the surprise."

CHAPTER 57

We hurriedly found two robes for the sauna and changed out of our dresses.

First, I helped Mila go through the extensive process of unlacing hers and taking each layer off. It made me appreciate my dresses all the more, how easily I could change without the help of someone else.

I wasn't sure I would ever go back to any other style again.

Mila remarked on it as well, but when I slipped my dress over my head, she gasped as if she was in pain.

"Who did this to you?" Her voice was rough with emotion as she reached out to study my back.

The more it healed, the less I thought of the whipping. It wasn't like I ever looked at my own back. Besides, seeing the delicate crisscrossing of scars on Evander's back so often had made it normal, somehow, to think of my own.

Until I needed to explain it, of course.

I squeezed my eyes shut, trying to think of anything to say that wouldn't reveal too much of the truth.

"I will murder him myself," she growled.

"No!" I spun around, my words cutting her off mid-sentence. "No. It wasn't Evander." I tried for a more natural tone. This was common in Socair, right?

"It was punishment for an escape attempt." I added after a second. "Ordered by the duke."

Mila's wide brown eyes bore into mine, searching for something before she seemed to accept what I had told her.

And then, because all of the rumors pointed in that direction anyway, I gave her a little more honesty. Something she deserved if she would be marrying into Bear.

"The duke and his wife have some old-fashioned ideals. But Evander and his cousins—Taras—would *never* do something like this."

"Old-fashioned ideals?" she spat out. "Rowan, women wearing ruffled dresses is an old-fashioned ideal. Flogging is nothing short of barbaric." Mila shook her head bitterly. "And perhaps Evander and his cousins didn't do this, but where the storms were they when it happened?"

"Gone." I said simply. "But they came as soon as they could, and they made sure it never happened again. That's why..." I trailed off, but Mila filled in the blank.

"That's why you sleep in his rooms. Not for fun." Remorse crossed her features, probably because she had teased me about it earlier.

I let out a sigh, not liking the darker turn this conversation was taking. "No, not for fun. But honestly, it is fine. It only happened once, and it was only because of who I am."

The men had made it clear that I was the only woman flogged, publicly or otherwise, in several decades. It was a distinguishment I could have done without, but at least it meant Mila would be safe.

She let out a slow, furious breath, but reluctantly helped me slip into my robe. Then, her arms were around me, gently pulling me into a hug. She didn't say anything, or linger for too long. Just one simple gesture that said a million words.

As if she sensed how desperately I needed it, she forced a lighter tone when she spoke next.

"All right, Scarlet Princess. Let's go see my potential future husband's butt."

I had been right before. Getting into the sauna was markedly less awkward with Mila by my side.

It wasn't long before we were all talking and laughing. Luca was surprisingly easygoing, for a Socairan Lord. The fact that he was relaxing in the sauna only two spaces away from his sister told me that despite Mila's joking, they obviously did not think of this as remotely inappropriate.

Which was more than I could say for sleeping in Evander's bed.

I rubbed a hand over my face, trying to hide my expression as I came to terms with that unfortunate truth.

How had I avoided it for so long? It had been easy, I supposed, tucked away in his estate. Even on the road, his men had been so used to it that it hadn't really occurred to me until he mentioned the marriage alliance last night.

More than that, I hadn't wanted to think about it, not when that might mean I had to go back to being alone in my rooms, trapped with my nightmares and the looming threat of Ava.

Even then, I knew that wasn't the whole story.

But that was the last thing I wanted to be thinking about when the man in question was sitting diagonally across from me, and there was not nearly enough steam in here yet. He was unusually carefree tonight as well, leaning his head against the back wall while he rested his mug of ale casually on his muscled thigh.

I looked away quickly, focusing on Mila and Luca and the story they were telling about one of their guards drunkenly mistaking his horse for a woman he met at the tavern on the way here.

Tears stung my eyes, and I shook with laughter when he recounted how the guard leaned in for a kiss only to have the horse bite his hair instead.

The way Mila and Luca told stories, giggling at one another or themselves before they could even finish a sentence, reminded me of home. Even Taras couldn't help a reluctant smile.

Dmitriy ladled more water onto the stones, sending a fresh wave of steam through the room concealing us all a little more.

My gaze drifted to Evander, who was watching me through the dark, hazy room. His gray eyes locked onto mine, a grin still on his full lips from the last story Mila and Luca told.

Something crackled in the air between us. The lighter atmosphere became far heavier with the weight of his stare, the same way an unexpected storm shifted the pressure in the air on a summer's day.

I took a long sip of my ale, and in spite of every better sense I possessed, I couldn't look away. *Or wouldn't.*

One of those things was infinitely worse than the other...but which?

CHAPTER 58

The next few days passed in much the same manner. The negotiations seemed to be leaning more in favor of Mila marrying Taras than against it.

Without fail, we spent our evenings in the sauna.

It was our final night at the cabin, and we were on our fourth round of the sauna/lake cycle when Dmitriy's voice beckoned a few of the others outside. I had a sneaking suspicion I knew what was coming, so I grabbed Mila's hand and sprinted out, too.

We paused long enough to grab our robes, then followed Dmitriy.

"Wait!" I whisper-shouted. "We want in this time!"

Dmitriy let out a booming laugh, gesturing gallantly to a fresh pile of snow before he and the others turned around.

Giggling like I was closer to the twins' age, I placed my robe in the snow then held my hands out to Mila. "Brace me."

To her credit, she didn't ask why, just gave me her hands. I eased myself down into the snow until I had what I was certain was a perfect butt-print. Perhaps I was turning into a true Socairan, because I didn't even flinch when the freezing ice made contact with my skin.

I stood up to examine my work, declaring it passable, or at least, a very obvious outline of a rather round arse.

"Your turn," I told her when I was finished.

Letting out a rich, throaty laugh, she changed places with me, doing the same until she had a slightly narrower imprint right next to mine.

"Okay, we're finished!" she called, merrily dancing toward the lake without bothering to put her robe back on.

Maybe I would work my way up to that level of boldness one day. We took our turns jumping in the frigid lake, and by the time we were finished, there were eleven imprints in all.

"Oh, no," I said with mock dismay. "But who will judge if we all participated?" I scanned the group to see who probably hadn't contributed. "Evander!"

He snorted. "I'm afraid I can't help you this time, Lemmikki. Mine's the fourth one in, and it's clearly the superior arse."

"You're clearly a superior arse," I murmured back at him.

He threw his head back and laughed, maybe louder than I'd ever heard him before, and for once, didn't bother to shoot something back.

It was Lord Luca who valiantly stepped in to assist, eventually naming Kirill's sizable buttock print the actual superior arse.

Though I definitely caught Mila stealing glances of the real thing on Taras to compare it to the imprint more than once.

After alternating between the sauna and the frozen lake one more time, we eventually decided to go inside for the remainder of the evening. We sipped medovukha and the refined vodka that Luca had brought from Lynx.

Tonight, we seemed to exist in a bubble of our own making, laughing and drinking like there wasn't a war on the horizon, like none of us were prisoners in some fashion or another.

I took another long drink of my vodka, content with the way it warmed me nearly as well as the flames from the hearth. For a rare change, there wasn't anywhere I would rather be.

I didn't allow the thought to sober me. Rather, I leaned into it, embracing it for as long as it would last.

"Princess!" Kirill called from the dining table, and I walked over on slightly unsteady legs.

He had a deck of cards in his hands, shuffling them while wiggling his eyebrows suggestively.

"Shall we, Your Royal Highness?" he asked, dipping his head in a bow.

I laughed and made a show of debating it, before finally caving.

"I decree that we play Kings and Arselings! As long as the Lord of this Castle agrees, of course." I spun around to search for Evander, but he was right behind me.

"As you wish," he said, a wry grin tempting the corner of his mouth.

He pulled two chairs out from the table, gesturing for me to take one of them. A warm shiver ran down my spine. *We must be getting more snow.*

"So, the rules," I began as Evander sat down.

"I didn't think you knew how to follow rules," he commented drily.

"I didn't say I'd be following them." I raised my glass at him. "This is the one time in life where you're rewarded for shirking the rules."

He chuckled. "No wonder it's your favorite."

Ignoring him, I went on to explain the game. Mila started play, picking up a four.

"Automatic drink!" I yelled.

She happily obliged, taking a hearty swig of her vodka. Yuriy went next, pulling an eight.

"That means...you have to sing everything you say for the next three rounds," I decreed.

"I feel like you're making that up," he said suspiciously.

I was definitely making it up.

"Nope," I lied. "Rules are rules. And you already broke that one, so drink."

Henrik pulled a nine. I opened my mouth to say something, but Kirill cut in.

"That card decrees that you have to...play bar maiden until someone else draws a nine. And I'll take another medovukha. Thank you."

Henrik looked to me, and I shrugged. "The man knows his rules, Henrik."

Kirill and I exchanged a look as soon as Henrik turned his back, both of us trying to hold in our laughter.

Evander chuckled under his breath as he took his turn,

drawing the Arseling card, naturally. He surprised me by holding it up next to his face.

"Look, Lemmikki, it's my effigy."

A startled laugh bubbled out of me. I had seen Evander angry and serious and cocky, but I wasn't sure if I had ever seen him...*fun*.

Why did this feel like the most dangerous version of all?

CHAPTER 59

It was hours before Evander and I finally made our way up to our room, and we weren't even the last ones to bed.

Thankfully, we had put Kings and Arselings away a while ago, and I had managed to pace myself enough for the effects of the vodka to largely subside.

If I felt untethered and off-kilter, I wasn't sure the alcohol had anything to do with it.

"How did negotiations go?" I asked, setting my glass of water down on the low table and grabbing one of Evander's shirts on my way into the adjoining room.

A whisper of fabric told me he was changing as well. Though this is what we did every single night, though I had spent half the evening with both of us in far less clothing than this, I suddenly found it impossible to breathe.

He took longer than usual to respond, giving me entirely too much time to focus on the way he was probably tugging his shirt down over his solidly muscled chest.

"They went well," he finally answered.

Was I imagining the strain in his voice?

I was distracted enough wondering about it that I darted too quickly from the small closet and managed to plow directly into him.

He reached out his hands to brace me, one on each side of my ribcage, effectively steadying my trajectory.

Then why did it still feel like I was falling?

I looked up to meet the storm clouds churning in his eyes. His full, perfectly shaped lips parted at whatever he saw in my expression. His hands didn't move from where they were grazing the sides of my waist, separated from my bare skin by only his thin shirt that I had grown far too used to wearing.

Heat spread through my body, slowly at first, then catching on like wildfire. Before I could help myself, before I could tell myself that of every stars-blasted stupid thing I had ever done in my life, this was sure to be the worst, I leaned forward.

And I'm certain I stopped breathing.

Indecision warred on his face. His grip tightened around me, his thumbs digging into my hip bones. For a perilously long, stilted moment, I wasn't sure if he was going to push me away or pull me closer.

Then he did both.

Or neither.

I wasn't sure which, only that my back was against the wall and his body was crushed against mine. My breath came out a strangled gasp, and there was no part of me that could pry my gaze from his.

So, I saw the exact moment he gave in.

"*Der'mo*, Lemmikki." He was already leaning toward me when he muttered the words, and still, an eternity passed in the split second before he claimed my mouth with his.

Time stopped moving, stopped existing. The world itself fell away, like we were standing in the eye of a raging storm but not a single gale could reach us. Lightning crackled from his lips, his hands, from every point that his body touched mine.

He didn't kiss me like he was exploring or questioning or hesitating. He kissed me like he owned me in truth, and for once, I had no desire to argue with that.

I fused myself against him, parting my lips to deepen the kiss and running my fingers up his biceps to his muscular shoulders. His tongue darted out to tease me. There was something so *Evander* about it that I smirked, biting down on his bottom lip.

He groaned. "Two can play at that game, Lemmikki," he murmured, sliding his mouth over to my ear and gently tugging on it with his teeth.

Of course he would taunt me, even now.

And of course, I would live for every last entangled moment of it.

I tilted my head back, moving my hands up to his glorious hair while he buried his face in my neck. Evander had one hand on the wall behind us, the other sliding along the back of my thigh, igniting every inch of me as he tugged my leg upward and--

The sound of a glass shattering pulled me out of my stupor. Evander froze, and we both looked to the source of the noise.

Somewhere between his hand and my knee, we must have knocked over the glass of water I had left on the end table. Silence descended in the wake of the crash, broken only by our ragged breaths.

He gently lowered my leg to the ground and straightened to his full height, which finally gave me the courage to slide my gaze back to his.

"Apologies, I--"

"Think nothing of it," he said quickly, his voice frustratingly neutral. "I know you like to kiss all of your captors."

My lips parted, and he tracked the motion, the intensity in his gaze belying his casual insult.

"Shall I assume you like to kiss all of your pets, then?" I shot back. "I'll be sure to warn Boris when we return."

His eyes widened with shock, then squeezed shut in what might have been exasperation.

"*You* leaned in first," he said with a trace of accusation.

"And then you *threw me against a wall*." Just saying the words out loud sent another wave of heat crashing over me.

I tried to ignore it, though my heartbeat thundered in my chest. Evander went still, but the energy thrumming off of him matched mine.

"Regardless," he forced out each syllable. "All that matters is that it can't happen again."

I agreed. Of course I did.

Everything about our situation was impossible, from the many wars surrounding us to the fact that when push came to shove, I was his prisoner, and he was my captor, however reluctantly these days.

But hearing him say it still twisted my insides like a serrated knife directly to my gut.

325

Not that I would let him know that.

"I couldn't agree more," I said amicably.

"Wonderful." His tone, too, was casual--bland, even. "I'll just get something to clean up this glass."

"Perfect. And I'll just," I cleared my throat, looking anywhere but Evander's swollen lips. "Be asleep by the time you return."

"Great. Then tomorrow we can just, continue as normal."

"Yes. I wouldn't want things to be *awkward* or anything." Like this conversation.

"Indeed," he responded drily.

Then he left, saving both of us from another convoluted moment of the mess we had landed ourselves in.

CHAPTER 60

I had not been asleep by the time Evander returned, but neither of us acknowledged that fact.

He was, however, gone before I woke up.

Or at least, before I got out of bed. There was no real sleep to be had, not when every limb I shifted put me far too close to Evander, who, for all his purported nonchalance, was clearly not sleeping either.

Aalio.

Or maybe I was the *aalio*.

After last night, I wasn't actually sure.

The night had given me long, unwelcome hours to think about the fire that burned between us, the storm that had threatened to drag me under—to a place I had never wanted to go.

In the light of day, I knew he was right. Kissing Evander had been a mistake, one that I was both terrified of making and of never making again.

Hadn't I told myself that I didn't want that? That I didn't want something or someone that could break me?

I ran my fingertips across my lips and shivered, thinking about how easily Evander could break me. And how easy it would be to let him. And that was probably the most terrifying part of it all.

Forcibly pushing the thoughts away, I changed into my navy-blue dress and braided a portion of my hair away from my face before heading downstairs to tell Mila goodbye before she left.

It was a bittersweet feeling. My inclination was to be relieved that she was probably marrying Taras so I would see her more often. But then I remembered that my time here was limited either by the speed at which Theo married or how quickly my father burnt half of Socair to the ground in his quest to retrieve me.

Besides, hadn't Evander said more than once he was eager to be rid of me? *Even if that didn't feel entirely true anymore.*

Not that I could gauge anything of the sort from his expression this morning. He hadn't so much as glanced in my direction, speaking only to Luca and Taras and even telling Mila goodbye before I got to her.

Which was for the best, of course.

In the light of day, it was easy for me to see how grateful I was for that water glass. How far might things have gone without it? And would I have been able to recover from that?

Mila's warm embrace wrenched me from my thoughts. Concern was etched across her features, but I just shook my head at her questioning look.

"Have a safe trip, and I'll write to you as soon as I'm ho--back at Bear Estate."

"Of course. And maybe I'll see you soon." An uncharacteristically nervous smile played at her lips as she shot Taras a glance, and I backed away to let them have their goodbye.

Now I just had to prepare myself for an entire journey seated on Evander's horse after last night's...complication.

CHAPTER 61

I had been right to be concerned about the horse, but had somehow neglected to think about the tiny beds at the inns, which were even worse.

The first night we stopped, I was forced to wonder how sustainable any of this was. The bed was barely big enough for both of us, and whether Evander and I consciously thought or talked about what had happened between us, the lightning crackling between our bodies was evidence enough.

"I've been thinking." My voice was somehow louder in the near darkness of the room, the small flickering fire barely providing enough light for shadows. "I'm mostly healed now, and armed. There's no reason I can't return to my room at the estate."

Why were those words so hard to say?

"No." Evander's reply was immediate. "Mairi comes bearing orders from my father, feigned or otherwise. I might be limited in how I can intervene, but I am still the only one who can so much as question those without consequence."

I heard what he wasn't saying, that to put the men between myself and Ava would only lead to one of them getting hurt. It almost had already, with Yuriy.

Not for the first time, I contemplated telling him the truth. But could I trust him not to act on that truth, and inadvertently put Davin in danger? I considered what I knew about Evander, coming to a decision.

"I don't know that she will come after me again. That was--that was more of a warning."

The bed shifted as he rolled on his side to face me.

"A warning for what?" His voice was dangerously quiet.

"Because I know who she is." I told him the truth, about Mairi, about her threat to Davin, all of it.

He didn't respond. Was he angry? Shocked? His expression was completely obscured by the shadows. When the intensity of the silence was too much for me, I finally spoke again.

"You didn't notice the lips?" I asked, trying to sound casual.

"No." He shook his head, huffing out an irritable breath. "I only noticed because you and Davin have the exact same smirk. Mairi—Ava—never smiles. But if anything, that makes it twice as likely that she will try something else. You did a mediocre job, at best, of pretending to be beaten by her."

"I *was* beaten by her," I said bitterly.

"No. You weren't." He said the words without a trace of doubt. "Truth be told, Lemmikki, you held up better than most of the soldiers do."

Somewhere inside me, a small weight lifted. "And you?" I asked. "Are you ever going to tell me what you did?"

I said the words teasingly, expecting a story about a rebellious young version of Evander, so I was utterly unprepared for his response.

"Mairi--*Ava,* has always had her preferred methods of punishment."

My blood froze in my veins. The scars that looked older, *smaller* than the others. How long had she been doing this to him?

"How many times?" I had never heard this kind of quiet lethality in my own tone before.

"I stopped counting." He said it casually, like it didn't matter.

But something vicious and ugly formed inside me, expanding until it felt like it was trying to claw its way out through my chest. Pure and simple and deeper than anything I had ever felt before.

"I hate her." The words flew from my lips unbidden, but they were no less true for it.

Was this profound animosity welcome? Comforting? Or just another way to lose myself?

"So do I," he muttered darkly.

"Then why not..." I trailed off, not sure how to ask what I wanted to know.

"Dispose of her?" he supplied.

I nodded. He hesitated, like he was weighing how truthful to be. Finally, he blew out a breath through his teeth.

"I tried, once. But I trusted the wrong person. They told someone who then informed Mairi. And she made sure I wasn't able to attempt anything like that for a long time."

My lips parted in horror as I remembered Theo's accounting of what had happened between him and Evander. Theo had said he couldn't keep a secret from Iiro. Had he understood what was at stake?

Or had he just been a boy, showing that damnably persistent loyalty to a brother I was increasingly sure didn't deserve it.

Another thought, even worse, edged in. If Ava had done this to Evander, what had my Aunt Isla endured at her hands?

The ugly thing inside of me reared its head as an animosity more intense than anything I had ever felt seeped into my bones, every shred of it directed at the horrible woman.

"And now?" I asked.

"And now." He sighed. "She can't do much to a fully grown heir, so it's easier to play her games. I can't fight a war on two fronts. Ultimately, it's more important to prevent my father from ordering...the things he orders sometimes."

Some part of me broke apart with the offhanded way he outlined this reality of his life. Every time he had thrown in my face that I didn't understand difficult decisions, I had taken it as an insult.

But this, he was right. I had no real comprehension of it. All I knew is that it wasn't a position I would wish on anyone.

I cast about for solutions. "If my father knew..."

He shook his head. "There is no clan in Socair that would tolerate an outsider harming a Clan Wife, no matter the circumstances. It wouldn't have mattered, even if I had known who she was. War would be an inevitability if that happened."

"Well, there go my plans to eviscerate her with my booby dagger." I apparently spoke the thought aloud because Evander's answering chuckle sounded through the darkness.

In the light of everything we were up against, my concerns

about sharing a room felt immensely petty, so I dropped them, telling myself I would suffer through a few more months in Evander's bed.

It was better than admitting that I would be suffering when I left it, too.

CHAPTER 62

The next day of travelling was no less tense. If anything, the things we shared the night before made things more confusing.

Because we were trying so hard not to have any contact, sharing a saddle became twice as taxing on my back as having my own would have been, but I didn't know how to broach that subject without creating even more awkwardness.

I spent the ride practically laying on the horse's neck to avoid accidentally bumping against Evander.

When we finally stopped for the evening, we were surprised to find a line of villagers waiting for us. In the dusk it was difficult to determine their ages, or to see their features clearly.

Evander's arms closed protectively around me as the men came to a full stop on the road, though he managed to refrain from actually touching me.

The eleven men with us all looked around at one another, confused and on high alert. Had the Unclanned been here? Were we welcome to stay? Was this a trap?

Before any of us could ask, a large ball of snow came sailing toward us, hitting Kirill square in the chest.

The attacking boy in a blue knit hat stood frozen and waiting, with a look of pure terror on his face.

Kirill barked out a laugh, and the child's shoulders seemed to relax. The next thing we knew, a few of the men were leaping from their horses and firing snowballs back at him.

Laughter rang out among all of the children and even the few adults who had joined them this time.

Suddenly, everywhere we looked, a snow war was being waged, with Kirill, Igor, Taras, and Yuriy taking the front lines.

Evander silently directed our horse around the fray and toward the stables.

"You have only been here a few short months and already you have my people rebelling against me," he said dryly. "This is a crime punishable by death, Lemmikki."

"Of course it is. That's my specialty, after all."

Evander slid off the horse in one fluid movement, before reaching up reflexively to help me down as well. It would have been more uncomfortable to refuse him, or, at least, that's what I told myself as I put my hands on his shoulders and allowed him to assist me.

Even if my chest felt too tight and my heartbeat drummed far too loudly.

I was painfully conscious of the lack of space between his chest and mine. My mind raced back to his room at the cabin. His hands on my waist, on my thigh. The feel of his lips on mine. I took a stuttering breath in and held it, waiting.

But nothing happened.

Evander glanced back at his men, effectively breaking the tension, like a thundercloud that had finally burst open. The pressure was gone, but the danger remained.

CHAPTER 63

The fourth day brought gusts of wind and drifting snow.

Even though I had donned my warmest clothes and let Evander know to do the same, the air still managed to creep its way beneath my cloak, freezing me from the inside out.

When I shivered yet again, Evander wrapped his arms more tightly around me. It was becoming increasingly difficult to remember all of the reasons why this was a terrible idea.

Even if I could have gotten past my own unwillingness to go down this road, Evander had made it clear he wouldn't.

And even if neither of those things were true, we would have had a million obstacles standing between us, starting with Ava and spiraling in a maze of Socairan politics before lurching to a halt somewhere around my father, who would never let me stay here.

I only wished my traitorous body understood those things as well as my mind did.

It was almost a relief when the wind howled loud enough to drown out my thoughts, until it made Evander hold me tighter. I was about to suggest that we stop sooner if there was a farmhouse nearby when a rock came whizzing down off the hilltop above us.

Time slowed to a crawl as my eyes tried to track too many things at once.

The rock sailing through the air.

The horrified look on Dmitriy's face.

The blood pooling from Igor's temple as he slowly slid from his saddle to the ground.

"No!" The scream bubbled up from my throat just as Dmitriy leapt down to help him.

Evander's grip around me tightened even more, and he growled for me to keep my head down, leaning protectively over me like a shield.

More rocks came flying down from the hilltop. Our horses reared back and whinnied in pain as several of the stones hit them instead of us.

Kirill lost his seat when his horse bucked, sailing to the ground as the beast fled.

"Over there!" It was Taras' voice that called out over the whistling of the wind.

Evander spurred his horse forward, and we took off at a blinding speed to get away. We just weren't nearly fast enough. A line of men with spears blocked our path ahead. Spinning around, we tried to flee in the opposite direction, but more waited for us there, too.

Evander cursed under his breath.

We were surrounded on all sides, by hills or by the Unclanned.

Another group had found us, and this time, they were well-armed.

Evander's words about everyone having been trained in the military came back. Each of them was a skilled soldier. Had we only won before because they hadn't had the right weapons?

Even as I thought it, I caught sight of Henrick and Dmitriy off of their horses, fighting back-to-back, trying to shield Igor's unmoving body by their feet.

Several of the Unclanned hurled themselves at the two men. Each of their attackers had a sword and shield, making the battle much better matched than before.

If not turning the tides completely.

Evander cursed behind me, thrusting his rapier into my hand while he leapt from the horse with his broadsword. He looked back, capturing my gaze for a frenzied moment.

There were no admonishments to stay safe or be careful. Just a look that said far too much before he turned and charged into the fray. I was still atop the horse, sandwiched between the hillside and the protection provided by him, Dmitriy, and Henrick.

All around me were the cries of battle and blood-stained snow. I was frozen, watching Evander fly around Dmitriy and Henrick, taking down man after man that came after them.

Always, even with his back to me, he seemed to sense exactly where I was, keeping any of the Unclanned from reaching me.

The piercing sound of a painful cry echoed through the valley, and I spun around to find its source.

Kirill had fallen, a lance protruding from his calf. The man he had been fighting only moments ago was unmoving on the ground, but two others were running toward him at a breakneck speed.

I didn't even think before spurring the horse toward him. Panic surged through my chest as I raised my rapier high in the air. Kirill stood, a sword in each hand, as they reached him. He shouted through the pain but somehow held them off.

He was flagging though, and blood was pouring from his wound. He wasn't going to last.

Evander's horse seemed to understand exactly what was at stake, not letting up until we reached Kirill. I tightened the grip on my pommel and sliced the blade through the air, coming down cleanly through the neck of one of the men.

The muscles in my back cried out at the movement, but I wasn't about to give up. Circling back, I was ready to charge at the next man, but the distraction had been enough for Kirill to finish him off.

I leapt down from the horse and helped Kirill remove the lance from his leg. Tearing the bottom of my dress, I used it to act as a makeshift bandage to stop the bleeding.

Kirill removed the belt that held his dagger. Without needing him to explain, I tied it off above the injury. Gallagher's voice was in my head the entire time, as if he were here explaining exactly what to do in a situation like this.

I checked our surroundings every few seconds, just to make sure we weren't sitting ducks. Once we stopped most of the blood flow to Kirill's injury, he was back up, climbing onto Evander's horse.

He reached down for me, but I shook my head. It would be impossible for him to fight off an attacker with me impeding his movements. And there was no way he could keep weight on his leg and last for much longer in this fight.

I was looking around for another horse when I caught a glimpse of flashing steel reflecting the sunlight like a lightning storm. Evander's blade moved quickly and relentlessly, coming down on man after man.

There were now two bodies on the ground by his feet, but he and Henrick were outnumbered.

I didn't allow my mind to register that Dmitriy was no longer fighting with them. There wasn't time for that.

Instead, my feet moved of their own accord, flying through the snow toward Evander. He was fighting off two men with one sword, while his other hand grasped his ribcage. Red coated his fingers, and my heart stuttered within my chest.

I hurled myself at the man to his left. Holding the sword in both hands, I used all of my strength to slice it across the middle of his back.

He fell to his knees, a surprised look on his face before I plunged it into his stomach.

My arms shook, and my back twitched, but I fought through it, relying on adrenaline to keep moving. I hadn't so much as sparred since the whipping, and I felt the lack of it now.

When the other attacker caught sight of me, he bounded away from Evander to charge at me instead.

Evander darted a glance between us. Then, he took the hilt of his sword and slammed it into the man's temple, knocking him out cold.

I tried not to look at the bodies on the ground or the wounds that told me they weren't merely unconscious like the man Evander had knocked out.

I tried not to think about the blood seeping between Evander's fingers, wondering how much of it belonged to him, how badly he was injured.

Instead, I took all of that anger, uncertainty, and rage, and channeled it into each arc of my blade as we fought off more and more of the Unclanned until there were none left standing.

CHAPTER 64

"**A**nswer. Me." Evander's voice was colder than the ice surrounding us. Lethal, and dripping with the promise of pain, though his face was a mask of deadly calm.

He pressed the tip of his blade into the neck of the man in front of him, the man he had let live for this very purpose.

Taras was standing next to him with the same dangerous expression, his arms crossed over his chest, as if he was physically holding himself back, waiting for permission to finish the Unclanned off.

The man on the ground took a stuttering breath, his eyes wild with panic. He tried to scramble backwards, but only slipped in the melting snow.

"Please," he spoke the common tongue in an accent similar to Kirill's. "They'll die if I don't--"

His eyes darted over to me and back to Evander again.

Understanding washed over me. The men had been right before. It *was* about me. Evander's impassive face faltered for just a moment, just long enough to show the Unclanned man the full might of his fury.

"If you don't what?" Taras cut in and asked, his voice almost an exact replica of his cousin's.

"We were paid to kill the princess," he stammered. "Some woman paid us--she said there would be more for the man that succeeded."

My gut churned, and I felt hollow.

"What is her name?" Evander's voice was even colder now.

"I don't know. I was—" He raised his arms protectively as if he had sensed what was coming next. "I was just trying to feed my family."

In spite of everything, something inside me broke at his admission.

"I understand." Evander's expression remained unreadable as he arched his sword and brought it down again.

Even though I didn't blame Evander, I had to look away. I still heard the moment the man died. Still saw more red coating the snow.

My face suddenly felt too hot, my stomach twisted in knots, and my vision swam. Squeezing my eyes shut, I tried to block out the images of death. Of the Unclanned that attacked us on the way to the Summit. The group that came after them, on the way to Bear Estate.

The poor souls dead on the ground all around us.

Ava. Ava hated me so much that she allowed countless men to die in an effort to kill just one person?

My parents had told us about the war before, how hunger and poverty can make people do terrible things, but I had never seen it up close. I had never been the catalyst for it.

Someone stood next to me, nearly touching my shoulder. I didn't need to open my eyes to know it was Evander. His presence was nearly as familiar to me as my own. Peering up at him now, I saw the pain that hid behind his mask of anger.

The edges of defeat that were creeping in on him.

He looked away, and that mask slipped back into place like the armor it was.

CHAPTER 65

I t was hours before we made it to the next town with our somber procession.

We pulled the bodies of Igor and Dmitriy behind the horses on makeshift litters. The howling wind fought us each step of the way, sending snow drifts flying toward us and making the journey infinitely more difficult than it already was.

The cold had seeped well into my bones, long since numbing my extremities. The men curled in on themselves inside of their cloaks, but whether it was from the cold or from the impenetrable fog of loss and grief that had settled over us, I couldn't be certain.

Maybe it was both.

By the time we made it to the inn, we were frozen and weary. Broken. Taras volunteered to lead the men to the inn and fetch a medic for them.

Evander refused to be seen yet, insisting on escorting the fallen men to the local funeral undertaker himself, and I, of course, accompanied him.

After he made the necessary arrangements, we went back to the inn. Neither of us had spoken a word to each other since the battle. Even here, Evander went straight upstairs, mutely leading the way.

I hung back long enough to ask for food and a few other things to be sent up, then followed Evander to our room.

He sat on the bed, digging into a pack of what looked like

medical supplies, while I hovered uncertainly by the door. He winced when he took his shirt off, but didn't make a sound. Underneath was a cloth he had tied haphazardly, already soaked through with blood.

When he went to untie it, I crossed the distance between us, placing my hand over his. "Let me."

He met my eyes, hesitation plain in his own. I thought about how many times he had taken care of me, even when I didn't realize he was doing it.

Did anyone ever take care of him?

The thought bolstered me to stare back at him resolutely until he relented, lying back on the bed. I untied the cloth and made quick work of cleaning the wound with the solution in his bag, stopping only long enough to answer a knock at the door.

It was our soup and the warm water I had requested. I set the soup on the table but grabbed the water and rags to finish cleaning Evander's torso.

He hissed a breath through his teeth, but made no other sound, no expression. I thought about the wounds on his back, about the small scars that were evidence of injuries he likely got from encounters just like these.

He was clearly no stranger to pain, and that thought broke something inside of me. I despised everything that had happened in his life to make him not even flinch when I had to pour a thick, bubbling liquid over a six-inch-long gash in his side.

"I'm sorry," I said quietly as I was winding a bandage around his torso.

"It's nothing," he grunted out.

"Not about this," I clarified. "About Igor and Dmitriy. I know what they meant to you."

He nodded. "Igor was my youngest recruit, but no less loyal for it. And Dmitriy was...He was my friend."

It was an effort to swallow the emotion rising in my throat. Dmitriy had been my friend as well. Not for as long, and not as close, but one of the few I had in this place.

He had been one of the first men to accept me, to play cards with me, to tease me, even to check on me in the weeks after the negotiations when I was sinking in on myself.

And Igor, the shy young soldier who had blushed at having to handle my underthings. He had barely gotten to live before death stole him.

Before Ava did.

"They died because of me, and I wouldn't blame you if you hated me for that."

His startled eyes flitted up to meet mine. "That wasn't your fault, Lemmikki. If anything, it was mine. I wasn't paying the attention I should have."

Because of me.

Tying his bandage off quickly, I turned away so he couldn't see whatever was on my face, using the excuse of grabbing his bowl of soup.

"You ordered that?" he asked, an odd note to his tone.

"Yes. You should eat," I said.

He took the bowl without complaint, eating it slowly, and I forced myself to do the same. We didn't say anything else until I climbed into the small bed.

The threadbare blanket and the small fire in the corner of the room did nothing to quell the ice that had rooted itself in my soul. Frigid hours ticked by in silence, but I knew Evander wasn't sleeping any more than I was.

There were too many thoughts churning in my head. About Igor and Dmitriy, about Ava, and about Evander.

I thought about what he said earlier, about it being his fault.

"You know that this wasn't your fault either, right?" I said abruptly. "You have protected far more people than were lost. I've watched you do it."

Like Henrik, during the battle today.

Like me, the entire time he had known me.

He huffed out a bitter breath. "You don't know the half of the things I have done and the people I have failed to protect."

No, but I had some idea, from the rumors and his own comments. And it didn't matter.

"I don't need to know those things," I responded quietly. "I know *you*. I've seen what you do when you think no one is watching, and don't think I haven't realized that I would be dead several times over if it weren't for you."

Evander huffed. "I saw you with that sword today. I don't think I get the credit for that."

"The sword that you gave me when you didn't have to," I countered.

"After I *took* you," he fired back quickly.

"After you *saved* me from being Iiro's puppet."

Even if that wasn't his intention, he had kept me from being manipulated. Perhaps I would have even married Theo anyway, one day, but I would never have wanted it to be like that, away from my family and home and when so many things surrounding it didn't make sense.

"Don't kid yourself, Lemmikki," he argued. "We both know I would have taken you anyway. If I thought Theodore was the other half of your soul, and you were going to fling yourself from the nearest balcony as soon as you got back to the estate, I *still* would have taken you to keep that alliance from harming my clan." He let out a slow breath. "And it still wouldn't have been close to the worst thing I have ever done to keep them safe."

The veracity of his words settled over me, but they didn't sting like I expected them to. I had known all of that on some level for a while now.

It was true that Evander could be ruthless and calculating, but I couldn't honestly say that either of my parents would have done anything differently in Evander's situation.

Or that I would have, for that matter.

"I think you sometimes forget that I'm a princess," I said.

He snorted softly. "I think *you* sometimes forget that you're a princess."

Ignoring him, I went on. "I mean that I come from a family of rulers. I've never had to make the decisions you have, but I know that weighing the greater good comes with the territory."

He shifted to look at me, his features barely visible in the flickering firelight, but said nothing. Another shiver went through me, and I tried to hide it, but as usual, Evander missed nothing.

With a sigh, he stretched his arm out toward me in an invitation.

I could have said no, *should* have said no, but something in the set of his shoulders made me wonder if this was about more than my warmth. If after everything, he needed the comfort of this as much as I did.

I slid next to him on the straw mattress, laying my head

against his solid chest. Almost immediately, I began to thaw. He pulled me against himself, wrapping his muscled arm firmly around me, and I greedily inhaled his familiar scent.

He smelled like his bed, smoky, earthy, edged with something sweet, but also somehow like the air just before it rained. Powerful and unexpected and just the slightest bit dangerous.

When Theo's arms were around me, I had felt safe. Contained. Like something fragile to be protected. But being here with Evander was none of those things. I felt wild and unrestrained and *terrified*, like a part of me that had been missing my entire life was whole now.

But what did that mean for when it was gone again?

It was an unwelcome reminder of why this was everything I never wanted to feel.

A hitching breath sounded in the silence, and it took me a moment to realize it was coming from me. Evander's arm tightened around me. I wanted to be embarrassed he had heard, but instead, the unexpected comfort opened the floodgates for the tears I so often refused to shed.

I cried for everyone who had been a victim of Ava's games. Dmitriy and Igor, who had died because of them, Evander, who had suffered a childhood of abuse at her despicable hands.

But I was ashamed to admit that I also cried for myself, for this gut-wrenching feeling of losing something I never even wanted to begin with.

Evander held me quietly through it all, even as my tears soaked through his shirt. He pressed his lips into my hair, which only made me cry harder.

We stayed that way the rest of the night, and I knew he was grieving, too.

Maybe for all the same reasons that I was.

CHAPTER 66

I t was hard to believe our party had been whole and happy just a few days ago. There wasn't a trace of that happiness now, not for them, and certainly not for Evander or me.

I used the excuse of aggravating his wound to ride the horse that had belonged to Dmitriy instead of sharing Evander's, and he didn't question me. We had hardly looked at each other this morning--or rather, I had hardly been able to look at him after my embarrassing display last night.

Hollow. I was hollow, as if someone had carved out my insides with a dull, rusty spoon. It was the same emptiness that had threatened to devour me when Mac died, almost as if he were next to me, reminding me that he was still gone.

That he was never coming back.

That our family would never be happy and whole again either.

I closed my eyes against the thought. There was already too much grief going around. I wasn't sure I could handle letting him add to it.

So, on we rode, none of us talking more than necessity called for. Taras and Kirill volunteered to deliver the news of Dmitriy and Igor to their families.

The weight of their deaths only felt heavier in that light. Someone would be grieving them the way my family did Mac.

All I wanted was to sink into Evander's covers and never emerge.

But it was not to be.

We had no sooner shut the front door behind us than a shape emerged from the shadows, like a spider creeping down from its web.

Ava.

"Where have you been with our prisoner, dear Stepson?"

"*My* prisoner, you mean, unless you're contradicting my father's edict?" he continued without giving her a chance to respond. "I see you've recovered from your...illness."

I had never been more envious of his gift for appearing to be so unaffected on the outside. My eyes certainly reflected the fury I felt at this woman.

If I disposed of her while I was still Evander's *pet*, would he be held accountable? Probably, given the backward Socairan ways of thinking. Or, as he had pointed out before, it would start a war. That was the only thing that kept me from going for my dagger right then and there.

That, and the realization that if I failed, I knew now that she hadn't been bluffing about having the capability to hurt Davin. I forced my gaze to the ground, forced myself to look cowed before she turned her stare on me.

"Indeed." The word was coated in disdain. "I am feeling much improved, which appears to be more than I can say for a few of the men who were under *your* care, Evander. I understand there was trouble on the road?"

A muscle in his jaw ticked, the only sign that her words got to him. He made some kind of response that I couldn't hear over the blood roaring in my ears.

To calm myself down, I pictured bringing Ava's body to the funeral undertaker. Or perhaps we would just leave it for the wolves.

Someday, I vowed. *Someday, I will watch the life bleed from this woman until I am satisfied she can never hurt another soul.*

But until that day, I would keep my head down, literally.

At last, a gentle pressure on my arm encouraged me to walk away, to go up the stairs and into Evander's room.

Taisiya came up only moments later. "You've returned, Highness." She sounded oddly relieved, and I was a little surprised she cared so much. I nodded, too tired to say much more, and she left to order a bath drawn.

"You can take one first," I told Evander.

"I wouldn't dream of interrupting your busy schedule," he said. "Don't you have a nap in a strict half hour?"

He was giving me an out to pretend nothing had changed, and normally that's a game I would have been happy to play, but I just didn't have that kind of pretense in me today.

Not after everything.

"Indeed, I do." I walked into the adjoining bathing room before Taisiya even returned, shutting the door behind me.

Maybe tomorrow I could be that person again. But not today.

The day bled into night with only the crackling fire in the hearth and the familiar scratching of Evander's quill to break up the silence. Taisiya came in later than usual with our evening tea, as if she already knew it was going to be another long, sleepless night.

She kept darting worried glances at me that made me wonder if I looked as terrible as I felt. But fortunately, she said nothing about it as she went about tidying up the room before insisting on taking my pack with her to clean my dresses from the road.

Boris and I sank into the bed while I drank my tea, and it was only another few minutes before Evander exchanged his letters and quill for the plush pillows and blankets next to us.

He had a fresh bandage, courtesy of the castle medic, a single white swath around his muscled torso. I looked away, and he let out a slow breath, climbing into his side of the bed.

Twice, I heard a sharp intake of breath like he was about to speak.

And twice, he decided against it.

Just as I was about to open my mouth and prod him into talking, I heard the unexpected, rhythmic sound of his breathing. Sure enough, his chest was rising and falling deeply.

Had he ever fallen asleep before me? The weight of everything had to be wearing on him.

I was settling in to try to get some sleep as well when the creaking of the balcony door made me freeze. A shadowy form materialized in the space, and I reached slowly for my dagger, sure that Ava had come to finish what she started with the Unclanned.

But it wasn't her.

Taisiya gently opened the door and stepped into the firelight, one hand on her lips and the other outstretched as if to show she was unarmed.

I clutched my dagger anyway. My eyes darted back and forth between her and Evander, and I debated on whether or not to wake him before hearing her out.

The panic in her gaze gave me pause, though.

She crept closer, until she was near enough to whisper. Or at least I thought she was, but the words I heard couldn't possibly have been the ones she meant to utter.

They couldn't possibly be true.

"Your father has come for you."

CHAPTER 67

Emotions flew through my head too quickly for me to interpret or hold onto. My mind was a maelstrom, my heart even more so.

"We need to hurry," Taisiya added as she looked at Evander. "Your pack is ready to go."

She held out one of my dresses and a cloak, motioning for me to leave the bed. I shook my head, numb with disbelief and she sighed.

"Your father said to tell you, *whirlwind.*"

My lips parted. We had always known, growing up, that we might be targets, so my parents had given us each a unique word, one that meant whoever came for us was sent by them.

No one knew outside my family, but that was mine.

I wasn't sure why I was so surprised. Hadn't I always known my father would come for me? If he was here already, he had moved literal mountains to do it, or at least a hell of a lot of rubble.

If he's here.

Taisiya motioned again for me to follow. I took a look at Evander's sleeping form. Should I wake him? What would he do if I did? Theo wasn't married yet. Would he even want me to leave?

Then again, hadn't Evander said he wanted me gone as soon as I could reasonably go?

Besides, if my father really was there, he would probably kill

Evander on sight. And if he wasn't, there was no need to drag Evander into whatever trap I was walking into.

Either way, I couldn't risk leaving my father waiting. I at least needed to go see him. To talk to him and know that he was real, that he was truly here. Then I could explain things to Evander.

If I woke Evander now, he would never let me go alone.

Decision made, I followed Taisiya out onto the balcony, though I didn't drop my weapon. She shut the door behind us gently and handed me the dress. Evander still didn't stir, and a suspicion entered my mind.

"Did you drug him?"

"It was only a root to help him fall asleep faster, but it won't keep him that way. We don't have much time." The slight accent she had been using slipped, pure Lochlannian common tongue shining through.

"How?" I asked.

"You didn't think Socair was the only one with informants on the other side, did you?" she chided in a low tone. "I am loyal to Lochlann, Your Highness."

I hadn't thought about that, but it made sense. A lot of her actions made sense, actually, and her disapproval.

Besides, women made the perfect spies in a land that largely refused to see them.

Quickly, I slipped into the dress, wiping the frozen snow from the balcony off on Evander's shirt before sliding into the fur-lined boots. She wrapped my cloak around my shoulders, and I slipped Evander's black shirt into the deep pockets, unable to bring myself to leave it behind.

We climbed onto the roof, over to a small, secluded balcony, and back through the house and down into the kitchens without incident. She navigated our way through, pausing me a few times if a guard was making rounds.

We didn't stop, though, until we had passed the stables, finally tucking into a shadow behind them.

There was no one here.

I turned to her, ready to accuse her of making the entire thing up, but she had disappeared. Then, I heard a voice that nearly brought me to my knees.

"Rowan." Even in that single broken, whispered word, my father's brogue was evident.

I spun slowly, hardly daring to hope. "Da'?"

He was wearing a hat over his hair and a fur cloak that covered his towering, broad form, but I would recognize him anywhere.

I froze, blurting out the first thing that came to mind. "As it turns out, I could not go five minutes without doing something stupid."

I had only seen my father cry twice, once when the babe died and once when Mac did. But he barked out something that felt like a mix between a laugh and a sob, closing the distance between us and cocooning his arms around me. He was gentle enough that I suspected he knew about the flogging.

I didn't move, just soaked in his familiar forest scent and the safety of arms that had held me so many times before for such smaller reasons. Tears spilled down my cheeks, soaking his cloak, but still, neither of us moved.

"Da'. You came for me." I tried to stifle my sobs.

"Nothin' in this world could have stopped me from coming for ye, Rowan." His voice held nothing but resolution now, underlined with pure steel. "Y'er my daughter."

"I'm sorry. I'm so sorry I left."

He ran a hand over my hair, meeting my eyes with his.

"It doesna matter now. Y'er here, and y'er alive, and now we can go home and put this all be--" My father cut off abruptly, his attention abruptly fixed on something over my head.

I stiffened, twisting around to see what had startled him, and my heart dropped into the pit of my stomach.

Evander.

CHAPTER 68

"Lemmikki, when I said you were an escape risk, I'll admit, I didn't actually think it was true." His voice was cold, but there was an undertone there. Hurt? Betrayal?

"Evander, I was going to come back to tell--"

"It doesn't matter." He cut me off.

There was just enough moonlight to see that his features were carved into neutrality, and a sword was in his hands. My father moved me sideways in a single, lightning-fast motion, already going for his own belted sword.

"No." It took all I had not to yell the word and draw attention to us.

I lunged for my father's arm, and he looked back at me in surprise.

"Rowan?" He glanced down at me from the corner of his eyes.

"Don't." My tone was pleading, but firm. "He kept me safe."

Da's expression twisted into a deeper fury than I had ever before witnessed.

"He kept ye in his bed." He bit out each word, and something between shame and defiance rose up in me.

"Not...like that." I stepped in front of him, putting my hands on his chest. "Just, give me one minute, please, Da'."

My father still looked murderous, but he gave a single dip of his chin.

I turned toward Evander, and for the first time, I realized that even though I was desperate to see my family again, I wasn't sure I wanted to go home.

To leave him.

He stood half in the shadow of the stables, half under the moonlight. There was just enough of the silvery glow on his features for me to make out the circles under his eyes, and the way his hair was still tousled from the little sleep he had managed to eke out.

He was wearing his tartan pajama bottoms with no shoes and a simple tunic that he must have thrown on in a hurry.

Had he run from the room? Had he been worried?

I swallowed hard, taking several more steps toward him. I hadn't expected to have to make this decision so soon, or that there would ever really be a decision to make. Perhaps there wasn't, for that matter.

Evander's stoic expression wavered, like he was watching the thoughts play out in my head.

"This is for the best, Rowan," he said softly. "We both knew this was only temporary."

My heart seized in my chest.

Did we? Technically speaking, I supposed he was right, but it still chipped away at something inside me, hearing the words from his lips.

That, more than anything, gave me the strength I needed to nod, to turn around. As I walked back toward my father, a feeling came over me, a weight so heavy I could barely breathe through it.

It struck me that I hadn't spent more than a few moments away from Evander in weeks. That I had seen him daily, slept at his side, fought at his side, seen his scars and let him see mine.

He had saved me, but more than that, he had *seen* me, when few people did.

I spun back around to say something, though I wasn't sure what, but he was already walking away, leaving me feeling curiously empty in his wake.

Leaving me. Period.

Letting me go.

CHAPTER 69

My father ushered me to an area outside the estate grounds where three horses were waiting, along with my Uncle Oli.

He, too, crushed me into a hug.

"Where's Davin?" I asked when we separated.

"He's meeting us at the tunnel," Oli said, his gaze searching my face with concern.

"How did you get word to him?" I asked, trying to focus on anything other than the gaping hole inside of me.

"He got word to us." There was a rueful sort of pride in my uncle's voice. "He figured out who his informant was, apparently, and they met us in the tunnel to explain everything."

Well, that made my lack of awareness distinctly embarrassing by contrast.

I nodded, though all of this felt like a lot to process. "So it's open? But wait. How did you find us? How are you even in Socair?"

Da' helped me on to my horse, and he and Oli mounted their own horses before my father answered.

"When we found out ye' were gone..." He trailed off for a second, and guilt crashed over me.

"We went to Hagail," Uncle Oli jumped in. "We...questioned the innkeep who arranged for the smuggling, and we saw the cave-in."

"It took us months to get through the rubble," Da' said. "And then Fia came to help us find our way here."

"Fia's here?" I asked.

"No," Oli drew out the word. "After she got us where we needed to go, she returned. She said, and quote, 'Unless you want me to go shanking my way across the countryside, I'm going to get out of this Kingdom.' Apparently, she hates it here."

A ghost of a smile passed my lips. "In fairness, there are several people in Socair who could use a good shanking. Perhaps we can fetch her back."

My father shook his head, chuckling under his breath. "I've missed ye, ma bhobain."

My darling rascal.

"I've missed you too, Da'. How did you know we had gotten out on the other side?" I asked, largely to distract myself.

"We didn't," he said quietly. "But I wasna going home without ye, one way or another."

Without my body, he meant. The tears I thought had dried up stung the back of my eyes now.

I couldn't bring myself to ask about my family, and Da' didn't volunteer the information. He always seemed to be keenly aware of what I could and couldn't handle at any given moment, and a few months away hadn't changed that.

All of it felt surreal. My father coming. Finally going home after five months away. Seeing my family again.

Leaving Evander.

The reality that I might *never* see him again.

The further away from the estate we rode, the more thoughts of him came flooding in. He had let me go without a single guarantee that we wouldn't go to war. He hadn't even made me promise not to marry Theo.

Hadn't he said he would make whatever choice he needed to in order to protect his clan, that he would do it without reservation, without remorse?

But he had let me go.

That sinking feeling inside of me grew. I couldn't think about any of that right now. At least now Davin and I would be safe from--

"Ava!" I practically yelled.

Both men turned to look at me.

"She's alive. She's here, using a false name..." I trailed off at the utter lack of surprise on their faces.

My father looked furious and even guilty, but not remotely shocked.

"Aye. We ken. We've been keeping an eye on her, but we didna think anything of it. We left her alone, both for yer Aunt Isla's sake and that of peace."

"Your father wanted to go after her," Oli interjected. "But in the end, the Council deemed it too much of an unnecessary risk, knowing how the Socairans feel about Clan Wives."

So in the end, Evander had suffered because of my family's mercy? Their commitment to keeping the people of Lochlann safe?

Something about that felt so unbelievably wrong.

I was grateful when we spurred the horses onward, if only to have a break from the thoughts threatening to pull me under.

Uncle Oli checked us into an inn since he was the closest to looking Socairan. With our cloaks up, Da' and I made our way up to the room while Oli had food sent up.

We ate quickly and in silence. Perhaps it was because our Lochlannian accents would have given us away, but it seemed more likely that both men knew how little I had left to give tonight.

There was one huge bed, so I was sandwiched in the middle while each of them slept with their sword within arm's reach.

It struck me that all this time I had told myself I couldn't bear to sleep away from Evander because I wouldn't feel safe, but there were few places in the world safer than I was right now.

Still, panic set in.

More than that, a bone deep emptiness, the kind that felt like it had no beginning and no end.

So as it turned out, that was just one of the many, many things I had lied to myself about.

CHAPTER 70

After days of hard riding, we made it back to the familiar craggy landscape where this all started. My chest tightened with each mile we drew nearer the tunnels, panic seeping into my every pore.

I wasn't sure if it was the thought of going back in to face the cold, dark, and seemingly endless tunnels all over again, or if, more likely, it was that a part of me broke the further away we went from Bear.

From Evander.

Fortunately, there were no more attacks from the Unclanned or surprises from any patrolling soldiers at the narrow border between Bear, Bison, and Elk.

There was also nothing that offered a single distraction.

At least, not until I saw Davin's face in the distance, his form outlined by the setting of the sun. A small cry of relief clambered out of me, and tears pricked at the back of my eyes.

I hadn't realized how much I had needed to see him until now, how much I needed to assure myself that he was still alive and well. As we neared, he jogged over to meet me at my horse, holding his arms out. I practically flung myself into them, squeezing my eyes shut.

"How do we keep bumping into each other like this?" He was striving for a neutral tone, but a little emotion slipped in at the end, and he cleared his throat.

I laughed, wrapping my arms more tightly around him.

When I opened my eyes, it was to a wholly unexpected sight.

There, at the entrance to the tunnel, was a tall, broad form with tan skin and white-blond hair that I would recognize anywhere. His face was downcast as he studied me through those earnest green-and-gold eyes of his.

Theo didn't make any sudden moves; he didn't try to approach me. He only stood there, waiting.

Davin sighed, nudging me with his arm. "I suppose he wasn't so bad, in the end. Though, I'll be just as happy to never see anyone from Clan Elk as long as I live."

Shaking my head, I took a few steps forward and Theo did the same, meeting me in the middle.

An awkward silence lingered between us. Da' reluctantly gave me a little privacy while he and a couple of Elk soldiers loaded a small supply wagon hitched to a donkey, leading into the tunnel entrance.

At least this time, we would be more prepared.

Following my gaze, he cleared his throat. "Your sword is in the trunks, along with a bottle of vodka. For your sister, of course."

Something that might have been a smile tugged at his lips, though it was weaker than his used to be. I tried to match it, but mine felt even frailer than his.

"Thank you," I said sincerely. After everything, it meant more than I could say. "For that, and for taking care of Davin."

Theo nodded and cleared his throat. "Of course. It was the least I could do. I really am so s--"

"You don't need to apologize for what someone else did, Theo."

Perhaps it was easier for me to be forgiving when, all things considered, Iiro trapping me in a tunnel and trying to trick me into marriage was fairly mild compared to the treatment I got from Ava.

Or perhaps it was the sincerity shining from Theo's gaze.

We may not have had the kind of visceral, unstoppable love I thought we did, but Theo had fought for me when no one else would. He had protected me at risk to himself.

He had wrapped his arms around me and shielded me, even from the messes I made myself, and now he was here, making sure Davin and I got home safely, just like he promised.

And for all of that, he had never asked for anything in return.

"You're a good person, Theo," I told him.

"I'm not so sure about that." He studied my features. "I never should have given up. I said that I would fight for you, but then, I found out what my brother did, and I couldn't bear the thought that I had inadvertently *tricked* you into a betrothal. And then time went by, and I realized that no matter how we got where we were, the feelings were real."

"It doesn't matter anymore," I reminded him quietly. "You have Galina, and—"

"No, I don't." He interrupted me. "We stopped the talks with Ram before they even really began."

"What?" I blinked, confused. Or overwhelmed. Or both. "Why?"

"Because my brother has a great many enemies, but he found he did not like me being one of them." His features were harder than I had ever seen them.

"You told him no?" I couldn't keep the shock from my tone.

"Not in as many words, but I made my displeasure clear," he said, taking a small step closer.

My brow furrowed. "I thought you needed to marry quickly, for your clan."

"I convinced him that it's more important to marry right than to marry quickly. That some things are worth waiting for." The way he looked at me then said more than he ever could. "Worth fighting for, even when things are stacked against them."

I blinked rapidly up at him, barely able to process what he was getting at. "I don't know if I have any fight left in me."

Theo's steady gaze latched on mine. "Then I'll fight for both of us."

While I cast around for a response to that, an arm came around my shoulders. "Time to go, Row," Davin said.

Everyone was still loading up last-minute supplies, but Davin must have seen that I needed an out. I nodded, turning back to Theo. Closing the distance between us, I wrapped my arms around him and gave him a chaste kiss on the cheek.

"Goodbye, Theo."

With that, I turned to join my family.

To finally go home.

EPILOGUE

I had planned for this moment, but I wasn't sure that anything could have ever truly prepared me to face it.

To face *him*.

It felt like a lifetime ago that I was in Socair.

Nothing had felt right since I came back, despite my family's assurances. Something was still missing or wrong. Or maybe it was just me.

Either way, when the sound of the carriage wheels rolled up on the loose stones of the courtyard, I held my breath, bracing myself. The slow clacking of a pair of boots made their way across the main hall, echoing into the drawing room where I was waiting.

With each step, I wondered exactly what I would say, what he would say. Somehow in all of my imaginings for the future, I had never quite pictured him here, in Lochlann.

The footsteps halted, and the whispering of voices sounded just behind the door as the handle turned ever so slowly.

When the maid appeared, her face was a careful mask of neutrality, but her eyes told a different story.

"Your Highness." She curtseyed, meeting my gaze with apprehension. "The Socairan Lord is here to see you."

Pronunciation Guide

Rowan	ROE-an (long O)
Evander	ee-VAN-der
Theo	THEE-oe
Davin	DAV-in (short A)
Iiro	EER-oe
Avani	ah-VAHN-ee
Mila	MEE-lah
Taras	TAH-ras
Kirill	kee-REEL
Yuriy	YOO-ree
Socair	soe-CARE
Lochlann	LOCK-lan
Lemmikki	lem-EEK-ee
Der'mo	DER-mo
Aalio	AH-leo

Clan Elk
Duke: Iiro
Colors: Navy & Tan

Clan Bison
Duke: Ivan
Colors: Orange & Gray

Clan Ram
Duke: Mikhail
Colors: White & Red

Clan Viper
Duke: Andreyev
Colors: Green & Gold

Clan Wolf
Duke: Nils
Colors: Gray & White

Clan Lynx
Duke: Arès
Colors: Teal & Gold

Clan Crane
Duke: Danil
Colors: Yellow & Black

Clan Eagle
Duke: Timofey
Colors: White & Brown

Clan Bear
Duke: Aleksander
Colors: Black & White

A MESSAGE FROM US

We need your help!

Did you know that authors, in particular indie authors like us, make their living on reviews? If you liked this book, or even if you didn't, please take a moment to let people know on Amazon, Bookbub and/or Goodreads!

Remember, reviews don't have to be long. It can be as simple as a star rating and an: 'I loved it!' or: 'Not my cup of tea...'

So please, take a moment to let us know what you think. We depend on your feedback!

Now that that's out of the way, if you want to come shenani-gate with us, rant and rave about these books and others, get access to awesome giveaways, exclusive content and some pretty ridiculous live videos, come join us on Facebook here: Drifters and Wanderers

For even more freebies and some behind-the-scenes content, you can also sign up for our newsletter by visiting our website here: www.mahleandmadison.com

ROBIN'S ACKNOWLEDGMENTS

This deadline was insaaaane, so my first infinite thank you goes out to my husband for being so patient with my ridiculous never-ending work schedule for the past few weeks. I promise lots of vacations and breaks in our near future!

To our amazing Alpha/Beta team, we can't even imagine doing this without you guys. You give us life and hilarity and the pick me ups we need when editing is a beast. You also provide us with super helpful, if occasionally hateful feedback. (You know who you are.) But for real, I love you guys, and I would never want to go another project without your hilarious group chat!

To Amanda. No boobies in this one, but no less love. Thank you for not just spreading the word this time, but for all the career and human and friend advice you've given over the years. I wish you were here so I could rub your mermaid hair on my face, but I have to content myself with being faraway and sad. Seriously, we would still be somewhere stuck in our careers if you hadn't taken us under your ample bosom wing. Thank you!

Jamie, You never cease to amaze us with the way that you haven't actually murdered us yet for all the pain-in-the-assery we bestow upon you. Thank you for editing our books beautifully and being so flexible when we're such disasters!

Kate, do you ever get tired of my late night did something stupid messages? I know I never do. Thank you so much for going out of your way when a need arose and helping us out time after time. <3

A huuuuge, giant thank you to our NEW AMAZING PA, Emily. Seriously, we've never had a release go so smoothly or be able to promo so much at the same time because we are usually, badly, balancing both. You have made our lives immensely easier and we've all had so much fun along the way!

We really do have the best, most supportive author friends anyone could hope for. You guys know who you are and there are too many to name, but late night messaging and release day support and blurb help and general commiseration has been the only thing that got us through this deadline!

And finally, to Elle-bear, the co-creator of the world's sexiest man with me. Does anything else need to be said? Seriously, though, thank you for running with me when I called you up about this crazy Lochlann princess, and thank you for making her story so much more than I could have imagined. I can't wait to finish out this crazy ride with you!

ELLE'S ACKNOWLEDGMENTS

First and foremost; Robin, this is our tenth published book together and twelfth project! Right? I think I'm starting to lose count!

I can't believe how much we have written together and all of the projects we still have planned!

These books just happen to be my favorite because they feel the most like us. Our friendship and general shenanigans are showcased in Rowan and her friendship with Davin, her banter with Evander, the inappropriate comments she makes to Theo and her sardonic way of looking at life's problems.

This story has been the breath of fresh air that we needed. (Well, in general... not at all in the case of Tarnished Crown... this bastard was a pain in our arses...but you know what I mean.)

I can't wait to see what Obsidian Throne brings!

There are always so many people to thank when we release a book. So many people who help us craft our stories and patiently read every iteration we write until we settle on the final result.

So that being said, we owe a massive thank you to our phenomenal **PA Emily.**

We would have crashed and burned hard if it hadn't been for you. You seriously came into our lives at the most perfect time and helped us organize and manage this deadline like a boss. It's insane how quickly you became an invaluable and irreplaceable part of our team. Never leave us!!!

Another huge thank you goes to our **Beta team** for being instrumental in us getting this story out on time, and for being so biased that we realized exactly where we went wrong in our story.

You ladies are the best ever and we adore each of you!!

I will never not thank **Amanda Steele.** You have no idea

how important you are to us, and how instrumental you have been to helping us stay on track, refine our branding, and your amazing business **Book of Matches Media** has been responsible for helping us spread the word about this story and reaching so so many new readers. Thank you for your support and your ample bosoms.

Jamie, you are the best editor two ridiculous messes could ask for. Thank you for putting up with us, we really do know how difficult we make things for you. I would swear that we were going to change, but I feel like three years of working together has proven that probably won't happen. Thank you for sticking with us and loving us and our stories in spite of that. <3

Kate, where would we actually be without you??? Blessed be the fruit.

Thank you to our **friends and family** who have put up with us and our ridiculous deadlines this year. For being patient and understanding when problems came up within the book and it took more time and energy from us than we accounted for.

We love you all and your endless well of support keeps us going <3

And finally... **to my hubby.**

Thank you for your love and your patience. Thank you for taking such great care of our family and always making sure there is coffee or wine at the ready when I came up for air during this project. Thank you for loving me even when I, once again, put you through three weeks of hell while I was in my writing cave.

I love you and our beautiful boys more than all the brownie batter in the world.

ABOUT THE AUTHORS

Elle and Robin can usually be found on road trips around the US haunting taco-festivals and taking selfies with unsuspecting Spice Girls impersonators.

They have a combined PH.D in Faery Folklore and keep a romance advice column under a British pen-name for raccoons.

They have a rare blood type made up solely of red wine and can only write books while under the influence of the full moon.

Perhaps mildly obsessed, they continue to write stories with enemies to lover tension, forced bed sharing, arranged marriages and far too relatable characters that are possible manifestations of their actual flaws.

Between the two of them they've created a small army of insatiable humans and when not wrangling them into their cages, they can be seen dancing jigs and sacrificing brownie batter to the pits of their stomachs.

And somewhere between their busy schedules, they still find time to create worlds and put them into books.

ALSO BY ELLE & ROBIN

Made in United States
Troutdale, OR
04/02/2024